BRASH
BOSS

A.S. ROBERTS

I am an English author and I write in British English. Except if a character is American, then I may use American slang.

Editor: Karen J
Proofreading: Freda Smith
Beta Readers: Fireball Fillies
Photo Credit: Eric Battershell photography.
Model: Zeke Samples.
Cover Design: JM Walker @justwritecreations

Brash Boss is a standalone story inspired by Vi Keeland and Penelope Ward's Playboy Pilot. It's published as part of the Cocky Hero Club world, a series of original works, written by various authors, and inspired by Keeland and Ward's *New York Times* bestselling series.

Baby, Let's play house-

Elvis Presley.

CHAPTER ONE

Nico

Last summer

'I LOVE IT ALL, NICO. It complements the surroundings, which is something a villa this size wouldn't normally do. The traditional flooring, the colours you've chosen, everything about it is beautiful. But you need to understand that I shouldn't be the one moving in here.'

'Have you seen the infinity pool?' I added, knowing how much she loved to swim and realising she was going to take some persuading by the tone of her voice.

'You know I have. The colour of the water is the exact same colour of the water in the bay, it's all very clever,' she sighed.

I watched her as she moved away from the floor to ceiling window that looked out over her beloved Mirabello Bay. It had been deliberate that I'd chosen to build the home I'd designed with my brother Cade's help here, near her place of birth. I knew what made her happy in life. This place was one of those things and us, her only grandsons, were the other. Crete was the place she had been born and had lived until she'd met my Italian grandfather. They had then left for a new life in America, leaving behind everything she had once known.

So, with her in mind, and because of the fact that I too had fallen in love with Crete, I'd had the new villa built deep into the hills above Agios Nikolaos, in the rust and grey coloured local stones that the builders had used around here for centuries. The large building sat nestled into the hillside and if it wasn't for the way the sunlight occasionally hit the large panes of glass, you could have been excused for not even realising it was there at all. Honestly, that was just the way I liked it. I appreciated the way it looked so much that I'd shipped over the same stone for my home in Vegas and I'd used much of the same footprint for the two builds. Call me an arrogant bastard, but always having what I wanted and what I knew worked for me was how I lived my life.

I crossed my arms over my shirt-covered chest and leant against the wall, waiting for the next argument to leave her mouth.

'You need a *wife*. *You* need children, Nico.'

I didn't need to bother working out a response to her argument, it was the same conversation we'd been rehashing ever since I'd told her of my plans to build a home on her native island of Crete.

I let out what I hoped was a quiet sigh. If she'd have been anyone else, I'd have let my feelings be audibly heard, but out of the few things my father had taught me of any use in this life, respect towards my elders was one.

'You need a family.' She spun back around to face me to add emphasis to what she'd just voiced.

I looked at her petite frame just in time to see her wave her right hand high in the air with all her fingers pinched together. It was a typical hot-blooded, Mediterranean way of making sure the words were emphasised enough to make you actually feel them.

I stopped a smile from breaking out on my face and looked at her as seriously as I could.

'Nonna, we've spoken about this over and over… I don't need a wife and I definitely don't want the responsibility of children, I'm happy with my life just the way it is.'

'You don't know what's good for you… you're a man, you need looking after.'

'I have staff to do that.' A smile was twitching at the corners of my mouth.

The argument I knew we were on the cusp of falling back into, for at least the hundredth time, was so pointless it was comical.

'Staff? Staff don't anchor you to this life and give you something to look forward to coming home to.'

'I don't need anyone to anchor me,' I tried to reason with her, even though I knew any argument I put up would be futile.

'Men like you need reminding to come home.'

'Men like me, hmmm… I'm sure my secretary would remind me.' I stifled a laugh.

'There you go again!' The volume of her voice rose. 'They are just people paid to like you. They share your home or your life because you pay them, not because they want to be with you.'

'But I have you, and you want to be with me… Nonna, I'd like you to share my home.'

'Ahhh, Nico this house is *so* very beautiful…' I could see I was starting to appeal to the side of my grandmother that loved a little flattery, when her cheeks pinked in colour. Then she added a little, 'But…'

'But, what?' Again, I stopped myself from sighing out loud.

Why I couldn't deal with family like I dealt with business I'd never know. I was able to read anyone in business, because I cared nothing about them whatsoever, but family, I struggled to comprehend at all.

Perhaps I've made it that way? I pondered this for a few seconds, knowing it was probably true. It had definitely been an easier way to live, not allowing myself to be close to the only two members of my family that I had left, until a couple of years ago when I decided the time was right to re-enter their lives.

I'd inherited a nightmare, and the man I'd had to become to allow me to sort out everything my father had destroyed, in his depraved need to obliterate everyone and everything he'd come into contact with, had extinguished the good inside of me. I'd had to embrace the parts of me that I hated and that I knew came directly from him. I'd had to give life to the diablo that I knew would always reside inside in me, meaning I not only looked like my bastard of a father, but I'd had to become him. But there was no way in hell I would have ever unleashed that on my family. They'd already suffered at his hands, there was no way they were going to suffer at mine.

Building this house and the one in Vegas had heralded the start of something different for me.

A new beginning maybe?

In my head I'd already gone over all the objections I thought my grandmother would possibly use a thousand times. I wanted her safe, I wanted her comfortable, I wanted her looked after and I was prepared for anything.

'I cannot be the mistress of this house.'

Okay, I wasn't prepared for that.

'All you have to do is to live here, Nonna, that's all.'

'I will not be mistress of your house.'

'Nonna, over half the year I'll still be in Vegas… I'm not old enough to retire just yet. You can be the mistress of my house, because it will be your own home for most of the year.' I offered her a small smile, hoping she would just give in and accept what I wanted.

'Nico you could retire, and you could walk away, just as easily as…' She snapped her fingers together.

'Does anyone in our *family* business just retire?' My eyes flicked back to hers as I asked the question.

'No, they don't. But that doesn't make it right.'

I saw the pain flicker across her face. She was a stunning lady even now. Having seen photographs of her as a sixteen-year-old bride, I could see what my twenty-year-old, Sicilian grandfather, who was out to make his way in the world, had seen in her. He had wanted a strong, resilient woman and he had found it in her. He'd struck gold, because she was all of that and so very much more. She was beautiful inside and out and they had remained happily married until my grandfather had been struck down with a fatal heart attack.

'I want you to change the fortunes of this family, Nico.'

I looked at her quizzically and moved myself away from the wall as I straightened up, mentally preparing myself for what she was going to say next. This wasn't the way this argument normally went.

'I want you to take a wife.'

'I'm not getting married.' I said the words gently, but shook my head at her hoping she'd get the message.

'Your mamma always used to say that you were going to be a man who needed a wife.'

'So you've said before.' I tried not to show how her words were stirring up the hurt inside me.

'Help me keep my promise to her, Nico. Find a wife and make your home here, away from Vegas, and raise a family with her. Money and business are one thing, family and blood ties are another.'

'I don't need a woman in my life, Nonna.'

'How can you say that?' She opened hers arms wide as she pleaded with me.

I crossed the floor in between us and taking hold of her elbow, I gently steered her towards the large couch that was positioned near to the window and guided her to sit down next to me. Then I turned my body to face hers.

'This branch of our family, Nonna… It needs to end with me. I'm too much like him to dare to breed another generation.'

'Don't you dare say that, you're nothing like him.'

She may have been petite, but the anger that ran through her hot-blooded veins took hold of her temper. The slap I felt to my left cheek stung, even though her hand was only half the size of my cheek and the power behind it let me know how much she hated my statement.

'You forget, I knew him even better than you did.' Tears filled her eyes and the sudden pain I'd subjected her to was evident on her face. I felt myself grimace at once again causing her so much agony. 'You and Cade are not your father; you are both nothing like the only child that God allowed me to keep.'

'I wasn't talking about Cade… only me.'

'You're wrong, Nico…So, so wrong about what you see in yourself.'

I could see the pain in her eyes, and still hear the disbelief in her voice that her only surviving child could grow up to be such a heartless, depraved bastard.

I had heard her tell the stories time after time of how she and my grandfather had struggled at first, in the country they had chosen to make their new home. The new country they had chosen in which to raise a large family. But God had never seen fit to let them have that large family, so instead they'd worked hard to make a better life for themselves and my father. My grandfather had worked so hard he'd risen in stature in the local area, making a name for himself, until eventually he'd been so prominent in New York that he'd decided to move the family business out to Vegas. The family had become mafia royalty in one of the main gambling cities of the U.S. and, until my father's time, had held the respect of everyone around us.

My father had ruined every single belief I had about family life.

'You deserve more, Nico. Promise me you'll allow yourself to have more.'

'I'll think on it.' I wasn't going to do anything of the kind. But I wanted her to move in here and I also wanted the direction of the conversation changed, fast.

'No, Nico… I want your promise here and now that you will find a wife who can love and care for you. Your mamma was right, God rest her soul. Do it for her, do it for me, but most of all do it for yourself and allow yourself to live.' The hand that she'd only minutes before slapped me with, started to gently stroke my cheek that was still burning.

'I…I don't know.'

'I cannot and will not rest until you swear on your mamma's grave that you will look for a wife.'

My spine stiffened at what she was demanding.

'Using her is uncalled for.' I stood up quickly and moved to stand in front of the windows. I pushed my hands deep into the pockets of my pants and exhaled loudly. Using the calm of the sea in my vision, as it gently swayed backwards and forwards, I cleared the picture of my beautiful mamma hanging dead from the mezzanine level of her bedroom. Then imagining the noise of the waves crashing against the rocks below us, I tried to erase the screams of my younger brother as we'd tried to save her.

She'd taken her life to escape our father and all the depravity he had forced onto her and us. I sure as hell wouldn't ever bring another woman or child into my life, not one I cared for or could love. I'd steered clear of those. I'd had many relationships with women, but the minute they'd declared they needed more from me than to accompany me out to functions or to spend the night in my bed, I'd deposited an amount of money into their bank account and sent them something diamond encrusted from Cartier's and cast them aside.

'I use whatever's necessary, Nico. You need a wife. Your mamma wanted you and Cade to marry and to experience what life has to offer with a family around you. I'm here to look after you, now she can no longer do so. I'm here to do her bidding for her. Take a year, Nico, but find yourself a wife by the end of it… Now, I want you to swear to me on her grave, Nico.'

I wasn't shocked at what she was asking. It was fairly common for a passionate, God-fearing Catholic woman, to ask you to swear on the grave of someone you loved, to get their way. But I could manipulate with the best of them and that included my grandmother. I wanted her agreement to move into the villa, so I agreed to her demands, knowing I would do her bidding on my terms only.

'You're a formidable adversary… I swear, on mamma's grave, Nonna.' I placed my hand on top of hers and smiled at her.

CHAPTER TWO

Barbara

Present day

THE PORCH DOOR FLEXED on its spring, and banged itself shut behind me.

'Pearl,' I shouted out, trying to make myself loud enough to be heard above the radio that was constantly on twenty-four hours a day, seven days a week in her small condo.

I got it, seriously I did.

She was in her early seventies and retired. Having spent her whole life as a croupier in some of Las Vegas's top casinos, fitting in falling in love and having a family just hadn't happened. Looking after me and the sounds from her radio filled a void in her life. At thirty-three and with the way my life was going, I wondered if I would be in the exact same situation or even worse when I was her age.

'I'm in here, Bee,' she called out from the small second bedroom, which she had recently turned into her sewing room.

I walked through the kitchen, into the square hallway and peered around the door frame to find her. With her soft pink hair, which needed retouching at the roots, long false eyelashes and a garishly bright green, crushed velvet tracksuit, she would attract more than a passing glance from a stranger. But I was used to her strange dress sense and I could see past it all, to the warm-hearted woman inside.

'What are you making?' I smiled my question at her, taking in the small, floral patterned fabric she was measuring.

Her eyes found mine and then a guilty look shot over her features.

'Now, don't call me overbearing, but I just figured that it's been a long time since the drapes in your home had been changed.'

I looked down at my hands, they were holding the glass dish that I'd come around to return. She had once again provided tonight's dinner and tears pricked the back of my eyes.

'You do know how much I appreciate everything you do for me, don't you?'

'Mmmmhmmm.'

When she didn't reply with actual words, I looked at her again. With some expert planning on her part, her mouth was now full of pins and she had effectively found her way out of the conversation.

'But it's not necessary, I'm not your problem.'

Her kind eyes, framed by her ridiculously long lashes, found mine and she hurriedly took out all the pins from her mouth.

'You're right, you aren't my problem, you're my family. I promised your aunt when she popped her clogs that I'd always look out for you, you know that. You help me and I help you, that's how we work.'

'I know.' I sniffed, trying to dislodge the feeling of helplessness that engulfed me.

I had been her neighbour ever since my mom had taken too many pills and checked out of her life, and I'd moved in with my aunty. But given our ages I knew I was the one that should be providing for her. I did at times, but right now I was going through another bad patch and without anything being spoken between us, she instinctively seemed to recognise it. For the past couple of months, she had been providing most of my meals, saying they were new recipes she was trying out and she'd cooked too much, or that the flavour wasn't to her liking. I knew better, but indebted to her I hadn't questioned her lies. Because ever since my aunty had died ten years ago leaving me her condo, this is what we did for each other. Our relationship was like a seesaw, when she struggled with her depression I was there for her, when I struggled with my gambling addiction she supported me.

'Have you spoken to Brody?'

'No, I can't. This time I need to sort it out myself. I know you think I should call him, but I can't.'

'He'd want to help, Bee.'

'He's far too busy with his own life.' I didn't mean to sound so accusing, but even I heard the bitterness in my voice. Our lives couldn't have been more different now, yet once all we had was each other. We'd been two American kids growing up in England on a USAF base and our family had been falling apart, making us cling to each other. But he had moved on, leaving me behind him and floundering in his wake. He was the lead singer with one of the U.S.'s top rock bands, Default Distraction, and was travelling the world. Whereas I was struggling to hold down a croupier's job in Vegas with no disposable income, and an addiction to gambling that was threatening to engulf me. Sure, he'd thrown money at me before, paid for rehab and got me out of debt. Then once I was dealt with, he'd pulled himself away from having any real regular contact. Right now, we were back to Christmas cards and the money he would put into my bank account on my birthday. Somehow, I always managed to find myself back in trouble and this time I wasn't going to be asking him to bail me out.

Shaking my head, I dislodged my melancholy thoughts.

I walked the few steps over to where she sat, placed a quick kiss to the top of her soft hair and moved away quickly. I knew that no matter how much she liked the affection she would chastise me afterwards, as her life hadn't taught her how to willingly accept human contact.

'Get off, you dafty, you need to get to work, your shift is eight p.m. until three a.m. isn't it?'

'You been checking my diary, Pearl?'

'I just like to know when you'll be home, that's all.'

She stopped pinning the material for a second and looked up at me. At the same time my phone pinged with an incoming text message. Pulling my phone from my pocket, I glanced quickly at the words on my screen.

Your time is up. I want my money by tomorrow.

I read the words hurriedly and tried not to show Pearl my reaction to them.

'Yes, that's my shift. I'll come straight home, I promise,' I answered Pearl.

Then I looked down and typed quickly into my phone.

I'll get it.

I pressed send and hastily dropped the phone back into my pocket as if holding on to it any longer might cause it to brand its cautionary threat into my palm.

'Never make a promise you can't keep, Barbara. I'll see you tomorrow,' Pearl called out as I left her condo quickly, fighting the rising panic inside me.

CHAPTER THREE

Nico

Present day

I CLOSED THE ZIP on my brown leather holdall and knowing I was still expected to have dinner with my grandmother before I left to fly home, I left it on the bed. I hated to admit it, but I was enjoying my bi-monthly visits to see her more and more. My property on this beautiful island was nearly ten months old now and I felt more comfortable here every time I came to visit. Crossing the room, I went to look out of the window at the views I knew I'd miss the moment I touched back down into the dry heat of Vegas.

A tap on my bedroom door caught my attention and I turned around to answer it.

'Yes.'

'Mr. Morello, Mrs. Morello wanted me to let you know your friend Carter has arrived.'

I felt my forehead crease into a frown as I puzzled on the maid's words.

Trip was early?

'Thanks,' I replied and hearing him laugh with my grandmother, I took the stairs two at a time to find out what was going on. I reached the bottom of the stairs, crossed the large tiled hallway and found them both in the kitchen.

Sure enough, I found Trip resting his long, lean frame over the huge island in the centre of the room, wearing his navy Pilot's uniform and twirling his white cap over and over on one of his fingers. I could see by the way my grandmother was fawning over him and the phone he was holding out in his other hand for her to look at, that he was showing her updated photos of his four-year-old son, Bruce, and his beautiful wife Kendall.

'There you are, Nico. Come and see the new photos of Carter's family.'

Trip looked sideways up at me and grinned. Out of my grandmother's view, I shook my head and mouthed, *'Asswipe'* at him.

'Sure.' I reluctantly walked nearer to them and held out my hand for his phone. I moved the phone to get a better look at the two people I knew I'd find there. The image on the screen that met my eyes showed his beautiful wife, Kendall, holding Bruce, sat on the beach near to where they lived. She was a beautiful woman and their son was apparently as good looking as his dad, or so Trip said. But, it did nothing for me. Maybe I hadn't been made in the same way everyone else seemed to have been, but I really couldn't see the attraction of linking up into a monogamous relationship and producing small replicas of yourself.

Because, even with all the best care in the world, they could end up inheriting our defective DNA and become yet another bastard in the Morello family lineage.

It all ends here, because it has to. I shook my head to dislodge my thoughts.

'They're very nice,' I offered, trying to make my voice lighten up.

'Honestly, Nico, look at them harder, see the joy there, feel their love for each other,' my grandmother encouraged. 'You do see it, don't you?' she questioned with a pain threading through her tone which let me know that even at thirty-five years old I still concerned her. She worried that perhaps her grandson was so broken he actually couldn't feel or see exactly what love was. She was right to worry, because I was convinced it was the one hundred percent truth, although I'd never admit it to her.

'Yes,' I answered flatly, understanding quickly that my time was now running out. She wasn't going to let up. I had to find myself a wife for her sake, to take away the pain I knew I was causing her. But also, for me, I had to make good on what I'd sworn on my mamma's grave.

She tutted, as though I hadn't quite managed to convince her and moved back to the oven to check on the lasagne and cannoli that she was making for our last dinner together, and it now appeared one we would be sharing with my traitor of a friend.

'Evening, boss.' Trip laughed after he spoke.

'Evening,' I replied. 'You're here early.'

'Ahhh, well you see Nonna invited me for dinner with you both. I changed the flight plans and came in early.'

'I bet she did.' I cast a quick eye over at my grandmother who was busying herself about twenty feet away. I knew exactly why; she saw him as a great example of what she wanted me to be. He'd once been a playboy pilot who travelled the world bedding any woman who fell at his feet. Then he'd met Kendall and fallen in love. The fact they also had a child together was, as far as my grandmother could see, the icing on the cake. He was everything she wanted to turn me into.

'And don't tell me... She made it a stipulation in the invite that in order for you to eat dinner with us you had to turn up wearing your full pilot's uniform?' I knew Trip had lived in a retirement community for a few years after being left a condo in Boca Raton, Florida and he had learnt from that experience just how to woo a more mature lady.

'I like to give pleasure wherever I go, you know that.'

'You're an asswipe, I do know that,' I stated with a smile.

'It's been said before.' He grinned back at me.

I stepped closer to him and we man hugged it out for a few seconds. As I slapped him wholeheartedly on the back I thought, not for the first time, how much I appreciated having him as a friend.

We'd met a couple of years ago. Captain Carter Clynes, triple C or Trip to his friends, had been an airline pilot for one of the large carriers. But after being left several million dollars from an old guy he'd looked after like a dad in the retirement community, he'd semi-retired and now only picked up the jobs he wanted to do.

Luckily for me, I was one of those jobs.

We'd first met when I'd employed him to pilot my plane, after my usual pilot had called in sick. I liked him as soon as we'd met. He'd taken absolutely no notice of the fact that we'd security vetted him down to what make of boxers he wore. He didn't blink twice at the expensive Italian suit I was wearing, the fact that heavily armed security travelled with me, nor my obvious mafia lineage. The fact that all of that hadn't seemed to affect him at all, made me respect the man. I hadn't known it at the time we'd first met, but the detritus I'd been wading through for years was finally beginning to clear and my life was at last going to be able to take a different turn. From then on, he'd become my pilot of choice and surprisingly he took on nearly every job I offered him. I admired him, when normally I admired no one. We'd quickly found out that we both came from catholic backgrounds and apart from that, and the deep clefts on our chins, that was where our similarities ended.

It was refreshing to spend time with him.

I'd wanted to learn to fly and he offered to show me how. After many hours sitting together up front as we flew my Gulfstream, he'd encouraged me to talk. He had started to tell me about his life and had urged me to do the same. He had a few strange theories in life and one of them was that you could tell anyone you met everything they really needed to know about you in one minute flat. I remembered laughing at the crazy, carefree guy and in my reluctance to talk about me he'd told me all about himself. I'd held my phone in my hand to use it as a stopwatch and had laughed out loud when I'd seen that surprisingly he was right. Initially, I'd held back, knowing that my background wasn't something to share, but he'd called me out on my crap. He told me that he knew exactly who I was, and that he took me for the friend he spent time with, nothing more and nothing less.

Every flight I took, I got to know him a bit better. I'd soon found out that he was astute, upfront and accepted no bullshit from anyone. After a few flights, with him sharing so much of his life willingly with me, I began to tell him about who I was, some of the bullshit my family had been involved in, and how I was trying hard to legalise as much of our business as I could. Once again, he accepted me for myself, and he took his place as the only real friend I'd ever had.

Trip, I'd quickly found out, was a happy optimist who made every effort to convince me that my life was only going to get better from now onwards. I think he thought of me as a project and like my grandmother I let him believe he could change me for the better, when I knew that down deep inside I was far too damaged and set in my ways to change for anyone and that included him.

'Come and get it while it's hot,' my grandmother called out from the other side of the vast kitchen.

Trip spun around and started towards her. I watched, as wearing her well-worn, stained oven gloves to protect her hands from the searing heat, she placed a large, rectangular dish onto the huge, well-worn table she'd insisted on moving into the otherwise bespoke kitchen. She'd finally succumbed a few months back and moved into my home on Crete, but one of the things she'd insisted on bringing with her was the old table we were about to sit down at. It looked completely out of place, but she'd claimed that the large piece of damaged, disfigured oak was necessary to family life and slowly I'd begun to understand why. The table was as wounded and scarred by life as we all were. The old piece of furniture offered us a place where we could sit and talk. It was a place where absolutely no pretences were suffered and also where no topic was off the table, so to speak. Nonna said the table was so old it had seen and heard it all before and nothing we had to say would shock it, nor the family and friends sat around it.

'Help yourself, Carter. There's plenty of lasagne. I know it's not your favourite pizza, but I promise I'll make that for you next time you come to dinner.' She encouraged him by handing him the ladle as soon as we both reached the table. 'There's also plenty of salad in the glass dish.'

'There won't be a next time,' I pushed in quickly, only to be ignored by them both.

'Thank you, Mrs. Morello,' he replied.

'I've told you before, please call me Nonna. It's lovely to have you here to share a meal with us, Carter. You're a welcome breath of fresh air, unlike my grandson who doesn't know how to relax and enjoy himself.'

I watched as Trip made himself comfortable by removing his tie and rolling up the sleeves on his crisp, white shirt as he relaxed, and I looked down at myself. Even having had a few days break, I still couldn't unwind enough to lose the smart dress pants and fitted, long sleeved shirt I always wore.

'Don't mind me.' I picked up the ladle next, to dish up a large portion of my grandmother's famous lasagne and dropped it unceremoniously onto my plate.

'Now tell me more about what Brucey is up to at the moment.' She used Trip's nickname for his son, and I knew she was fully focussed on him and her dreams of having her own great grandchildren.

She didn't even turn her head at my retort as he started to tell her for the millionth time about his son and how well he was doing, having recently started Kindergarten.

I reacted by burying myself in her glorious food and remembered occasionally to make an odd comment or listening noise. I forked in my lasagne at a rate that would have scared someone in a pie eating competition. She might give me grief about my lifestyle choices, but her homemade food outweighed everything I had to put up with.

'That's wonderful. I know you and Kendall are so very proud of him.' I could tell by the smile that she was now aiming in Trip's direction, that her plot to invite him here to share our last dinner together was going exactly how she'd planned it all out in her mind. Before she lost me again to Vegas, she wanted to remind me of the promise I'd sworn to her last year. 'Perhaps you could do me a favour, Carter?' she asked sweetly as she ladled another helping of lasagne onto his plate.

'Anything, although my washing-up skills are pretty poor.' He smiled back at her and dug his fork back into the meat layer of his lasagne.

It was like watching a slow car crash of my own life as between them they went through the well-rehearsed dialogue that we all knew was coming.

'Can you please explain to my grandson that the life you have with Kendall and Bruce far overshadows his way of life?'

Trip grinned across the table at me when he saw my shoulders slump down, in resignation at the fact she wasn't going to let me forget my promise to her. I hadn't realised that the conversation had stuttered for a few seconds until I heard Trip answer her, but direct his reply to me.

'I have tried, Mrs. Morello.'

'Carter. Once again call me Nonna… I insist,' she reprimanded him lightly.

'Well played… well played both of you.' I picked up my glass of wine and lifted it up high and toasted them both.

'**The fool on the hill,** by **The Beatles** would suit this life changing moment,' Trip offered, before he burst out laughing.

I knew he was referring to me as the fool in the song title. It was another one of Trip's crazy theories, that all life changing moments had a Beatles song already written for them. I hadn't a clue why a patriotic, Michigan born American, would choose a British group's music over an American one, but this was one of his crazy theories I'd embraced wholeheartedly and loving Elvis Presley's music and his connection to the city I'd lived the majority of my life in, I'd decided that his songs suited my life better.

'No… the song would be, **Don't** by **Elvis Presley**.'

I over emphasised the *Don't* and laughter broke free from Trip's mouth.

'I'm working on it, Nonna.' I looked back at her and offered her my half-hearted words.

'Then work harder, Nico. Your year is nearly up.'

She smiled sweetly at me, looking over the table laden with her home-cooked food, giving off her "butter wouldn't melt in my mouth" look that she did so damn well, but I knew better. I'd sworn to her to find a wife and she wasn't about to let me shirk on my promise.

CHAPTER FOUR

NICO

'HEY, BOSS.'

I lifted up my head to look at Franco who had, without knocking, poked his head around the door to my office at our main casino. Only Franco, my head of security, would take such a liberty, and only because of the amount of years we'd been working together.

'This better be good, Fran,' I admonished him.

'Well, you did say to let you know if she came in again.'

I lifted my head up from the keyboard and turning my head sideways, I looked questioningly at Fran who was now stood fully in my office with the door closed firmly behind him.

'She?' I questioned.

I had no idea why I'd asked him who he was talking about and from the slight uplift in the corners of his mouth I knew I hadn't fooled him either with my nonchalant question.

'Barbara Daniels, Boss.'

Picking up a pen off my desk, I leant back into my chair, twisted my left wrist over to take a look at my Patek Phillippe watch and took note of the hour. It was just after five a.m. Then pinching each end of the pen between the thumb and forefinger of each hand, I began to roll it around in between them.

'How long has she been in here?' I asked, while still rolling the pen as I thought.

'About an hour,' he replied.

For some reason unknown to me, a whooshing sound started behind my eardrums as my blood pressure rose. I was often to be found in the office above one of my casinos in the early hours of the morning, so it wasn't that I was tired. I didn't have high blood pressure and I kept myself fit by working out at least five days a week. I was cool under pressure, in business and in my very controlled social life. But today, knowing she was back in here and sat at one of my tables, irritated the hell out of me.

'Exactly how long has she been in my casino, Franco?' I enunciated each word slowly and waited for his reaction.

His eyes jumped up from watching me look at my watch and found the cold, hard stare that had replaced the earlier look of welcome on my face.

'Forty-seven… no that would be forty-nine minutes now,' he replied, shifting his weight and standing just a bit taller as though he was now on parade.

'Where?'

'Blackjack, always…'

'I know, always at the blackjack tables.'

What the hell are you up to, Barbara? And why the hell does it bother me so much that you're in here doing it?

I moved my chair and repositioned myself to quickly type what I needed to into my keyboard and then sat up straight to watch as the wooden panelling that covered the TV monitors in my office began to open up. I stood up in response, suddenly feeling too uneasy to sit still, and crossed my arms over my chest. Then with my eyes transfixed on the blank screens, I parked my ass on the side of my overly large desk and gave the voice-controlled software my next instructions.

'All screens, blackjack tables.'

No sooner had I given the state-of-the-art technology my instructions than it sprang to life. I ran my eyes quickly over the twenty flat screens that all showed a different table or angle, desperately trying to find the one I needed so I could see her.

'Franco.'

I didn't have to go on any further, the demanding tone of my voice told him what I wanted.

'B18,' he replied.

'All screens, convert to one screen, area B18.'

And there she was suddenly filling the whole of one wall of my office. I took in everything about her with one quick sweep of my eyes. I hadn't seen her in a few months, but I could see she'd lost weight and that her eyes looked tired. Everything about her body language and subsequent fidgeting, screamed anxiety. I took notice of people's body language to give myself the upper hand in business, and it was obvious that she had arrived here straight after work, such was her desperation to be back at the blackjack tables. The striped silver and black waistcoat she normally wore as a croupier in a nearby casino had been discarded, and I could have placed a bet on it, if I was a gambling man, that it was probably shoved in a bag somewhere at her feet. She was wearing her simple white uniform shirt and I knew that had I been able to see under the table, I would have found her in the black fitted skirt and fine black tights that were also part of her uniform. She was trying so hard to blend into the background, when to me she stood out like the light shining from a lighthouse.

My eyes watched transfixed as a piece of her long blonde hair, which had obviously been piled neatly on top of her head when she'd started work, fell out haphazardly and brushed across her prominent cheek bone. My fingers twitched on top of my bicep with something that I didn't quite recognise, as she lifted a shaking hand and tucked the piece of hair behind her ear. To me she was showing how she was beginning to literally fall apart, she was vulnerable, and a vulnerable woman was my kryptonite.

I watched her expertly, with one flick of her wrist, turn over the new card she'd been dealt, then her face subsequently crumble and fall. I'd seen it so many times before as it was how I made my living, but the look on her face devastated me.

Barbara Daniels was the sister of Brody, who sang lead in Default Distraction, the same band my little brother Cade had found fame and fortune with. The guys in his band were also where Cade had found the solace and escape he had needed, away from our family at a time when I needed him well out of the way of the war that had engulfed us. As the years had gone on, while I was busy sorting out the consequences of the damage our father had done, they'd taken care of my little brother. In doing so, they had become like distant family to me, so I helped them out whenever a situation arose where I could. Within a large Sicilian family doing favours for each other, if that's what you want to call them, is what kept us close, they tied us together to form strong family bonds. It made us indebted to each other, although generally as our family's "Godfather" useful people were nearly always indebted to me. It was how our family had worked for centuries. I knew that the other guys in the band had helped Cade to deal with his past, and his demons. This had left me indebted to them whether they understood that or not.

We'd been here before, Barbara and me.

I'd notified Brody when she'd needed help before. Hell, I'd hoped that the rehab he'd placed her into had sorted her out once and for all, but I could see by looking at her body language on the screen in front of me that she'd fallen back down into the hole again. The way her face was now flushed in panic and carried a light sheen of sweat, showed me that things weren't working out in her favour.

I need to help her. But even more disturbing was the fact I wanted to help her.

I was still busy staring at her, because even under pressure and wearing her cheap uniform, Barbara Daniels was one amazing looking woman.

'Yeah?' Franco's voice interrupted my train of thought.

I turned my head away from observing her on the screens to look at him, he had his first two fingers pressed tightly into his right ear as he listened to the voice coming from his earpiece. I twisted my head at him in question.

'Raul has just informed me that Miss Daniels has eyes on her... some of Barzini's men are in the casino, Boss.'

'Get her up here *now* and get Raul to escort them from my building.'

Without saying another word to me, he started to relay to Raul my exact instructions and turned to leave the room at the same time to retrieve Barbara. This instantaneous reaction to my instructions was why I paid Franco the obscene amount of money I did.

As my door shut behind him, I inhaled a calming breath. My whole body had jumped up quickly onto high alert as yet again my blood pressure rose higher, making every part of me twitch with the adrenalin that my sudden anger had released around my system.

What the hell was Barzini playing at?

'Call Antonio Barzini,' I shouted out loud into my office.

CHAPTER FIVE

Barbara

'MISS DANIELS.' I HEARD a deep voice behind me, closed my eyes briefly and let out a soft sigh. When I opened them again, I found the others sitting at the same table staring at me in question. 'Would you come with me please?'

'Shit,' I mumbled under my breath. Without turning around, I knew who I was going to find behind me. I couldn't remember his name, but I knew the voice and it belonged to Nico Morello's head of security.

You stupid woman, you shouldn't have come in here. But I had, because so many other doors were now closed to me.

Brody will find out.

I was so fed up with my pathetic life, I could cry. I had just wanted one last attempt at getting my money back and then I could have paid everyone off. The cards had been going well up to about thirty minutes ago, when once again lady luck had turned against me and I'd begun to lose hand after hand.

You should have stopped when it was going well. I heard the voice in my head and let a small laugh leave my mouth at my own stupidity. Because even I recognised that I had a problem, but the fact was I didn't know how to stop. I'd spent time in rehab courtesy of my brother, who'd employed countless therapists for me to talk to and had bailed me out time after time. After everything he'd paid out for, I was ashamed to be in the same position again, but the roll of the dice and the flip of the cards gave me a buzz I couldn't find anywhere else in my life, because my life was an empty void of nothing.

Resigned to whatever my fate was, I started to pick up the small stack of chips in front of me and like the pretend high roller I was, I tipped the croupier with a few of them.

'It's okay,' I offered the enquiring eyes taking in everything they could about my interaction with the suit behind me, 'we're old friends, aren't we?' I tried so hard to sound confident, but knew I'd failed spectacularly.

I turned around on my seat slowly and stepped down gingerly. I hadn't eaten in nearly twelve hours and I couldn't trust myself not to make an even bigger fool of myself than I already had. Grabbing hold of the walnut-edged, green baize table I started to bend down low to pick up my bag from the floor.

'Allow me.' I could hear the pity in his voice as the guy whose face was familiar, but whose name I couldn't have remembered even if my life depended on it, bent down to sweep up my bag with one arm.

'Thank you,' I whispered back to him, as the situation I was in and its probable ensuing magnitude started to play on my mind.

Once he was back upright, still holding onto my bag, he used his other hand to take a gentle but secure hold on my arm. With apprehension building up inside of me I let him begin to guide me to wherever his boss had demanded he should take me. I walked along beside him, taking two steps to each one of his enormous great strides with my head cast down in shame. My eyes followed the brightly coloured carpet as it twirled and danced ahead of me in its bright reds and golds. The casinos were all the same in Vegas, brightly coloured with flashing lights to tempt you in. They promised you everything and once they'd taken all you had to give, they spat you out like the trash you were.

And here I was, the trash.

Suddenly, the toes of my worn-out black shoes hit the gold coloured metal edging strip of the carpet. We had reached the hard wood of one of the many walkways that threaded themselves through the casino and had strangely come to a complete standstill. I lifted my head to try to work out why and heard a gasp leave my mouth as I saw two of Barzini's henchmen being walked out of the casino by several of Morello's security.

What had I been thinking?

It was an unwritten rule, or perhaps it was written down somewhere in the "mafia handbook," that other families didn't enter the property of their rivals. Even a nobody like me understood that. I grasped what had very nearly just happened and knew that it would all have been down to me and my stupidity. I owed Barzini so much money that his men had taken the decision to follow me in here. God knows what would have become of me if they'd managed to lay their hands on me before the huge man stood next to me had. Luckily for me it seemed, I'd been seen by the security and rescued.

I knew my time to pay up had run out two days ago and Barzini wanted what he was owed. An involuntary shiver ran down my back at just what my fate could have been at their hands, or worse still the blackmail they could have demanded from my brother Brody. Although, I still couldn't believe Barzini had allowed his men to enter one of Morello's casinos, because Nico's reputation preceded him, and he must have taken into account the sort of trouble that could erupt between him and a Morello.

As soon as the security guy holding on to me was certain that Barzini's men had seen us together as they passed us on their way out of the building, he started to move again and walked us towards a bank of elevators. As we walked, in my shame I faced the truth. The problem was I hadn't been thinking properly again for the last few months. My stomach turned over in terror at the realisation I hadn't a clue how to conduct myself anymore in real life. My gambling was so far out of control, I was now a liability to anyone who knew me.

The elevator doors opened on a whoosh and we stepped inside. The doors closed and only then did the large man with me press his thumb onto the security panel. The elevator ascended quickly.

'Is Mr. Morello aware that I'm here?' My voice was hesitant as I asked the question that I already knew the answer to. But the compulsion to break the silence between the two of us was strong. I felt uncomfortable that he knew just what a sorry excuse for a human being I was, and I needed the conversation between me and the nameless stranger to try to bridge the gap between us.

'Yes,' he replied, offering me only the one word.

The doors of the elevator opened and instinctively I wrapped my arms around myself, before stepping out to follow him.

'This way,' he politely offered, holding out his hand as he directed me off to the left. He needn't have bothered, as I'm sure he remembered that I'd already done the walk of shame before.

'Go in, Mr. Morello is expecting you.'

I put my hand out towards the door handle, but before I could open the door to whatever my fate was, I turned back to him, feeling the need to at least thank him for making sure I had been kept safe this evening.

'Thank you… Hmmm…'

'It's Franco.'

'Thank you, Franco.'

'It was the Boss's orders, nothing to do with me, Ma'am,' he replied brusquely as he turned to walk away, back to the elevator that had delivered us.

I turned back towards the closed black door and placed a shaking hand onto the brushed silver handle. Taking in a deep breath, I began to hesitantly place downward pressure onto it.

'Come in, Barbara,' came a deep, demanding voice reverberating through a tiny speaker set above the door.

Of course, he would know I was standing here.

I looked up at where his voice had come from and noticed a camera at the same time. I tentatively offered the camera a small smile and pushed the door open wide enough for me to walk through. In my peripheral view, to the left I could see the large frame of Nico Morello sat behind his enormous desk. Unable, in my shame, to make eye contact with him yet, I turned around quickly to push the door closed behind me. The door was heavy and I knew instantly that it would have closed by itself, but I needed those few seconds to compose myself.

The catch clicking into place made every nerve in my body jump.

'Take a seat, Barbara.' The deep, brash voice that only minutes ago was demanding I enter his lair, had taken on a slightly gentler tone.

'Thank you, Mr. Morello.' Still without looking at him, I moved myself into position and sat down gratefully onto the chair in front of his desk.

'So, let's get straight down to it, shall we? What does Barzini want from you?'

The question he had just projected into the room was now hanging between us. I swallowed deeply, hoping to clear the sudden constriction that the interrogative and fear-provoking question had caused.

With no words seemingly available to me at the moment, I continued to look down at my hands. I could only guess what a complete mess I looked to him. My body was in an utter state of panic and had been for at least the last few days, if not weeks. I hadn't slept properly in forever and the dark lines under my eyes could no longer be effectively covered up with make-up. My cheap uniform clothes were beginning to hang off me and it was only because Pearl was feeding me once a day that I was actually eating anything at all.

'I…I.' I tried to answer him, but no words were coming out of my mouth. I lifted one of my clammy hands up from my lap and placed it to my throat. Over the top of his desk my eyes finally found his dark brown orbs and I watched as alarm spread over his face. He stood up suddenly, sending his chair crashing into the wall behind him.

My vision went blurry and my view changed as I fell.

I felt a pain in my shoulder as the world went black around me.

CHAPTER SIX

Barbara

'She's awake, Boss.' I heard a male voice speaking over the top of me and then the same voice spoke again. 'Hello, Miss Daniels.'

Slowly, the world came back into view. I swept my eyes down myself and noticed I was lying down on a dark coloured, uncomfortable couch. Moving my eyes, but not my head, I took in the room with its light grey walls and solid, heavy-looking black furniture.

Morello's office.

An older man, who was smartly dressed in a dark grey suit. was stood next to where I was lying, holding my wrist in one hand and looking at his watch.

'You're safe… you don't need to panic… you fainted.'

'I've never fainted before,' I voiced to myself and to anyone else who was listening.

'Well you're either not very well or have just had a shock,' he replied.

'Luca you can leave us now.' A deep booming voice filled the room.

A smile spread over the older man's face and he placed my arm back down onto my white shirt and released my wrist. I instinctively placed my hands together and started rubbing my thumb over the hand that the stranger had been holding, trying to offer myself a modicum of comfort. Staring up at the ceiling I sighed out loud, unable to hold in my disappointment in myself, then slowly I started to move my head as I tried to search out my dark-eyed interrogator. The door clicking shut behind Luca as he left on his boss's orders ramped up my heart rate as I waited for Nico to speak again.

'Barbara, you need to start having more respect for yourself.'

Even in my fragile state my anger ignited at his words and I turned my head to look at the man properly for the first time since I'd arrived in his office. I found him leaning against the wall opposite the black Chesterfield couch I'd been picked up and placed onto, as if he was trying to keep as far away from me as possible.

I swept my eyes up and down him quickly as I rolled my eyes at him trying to show my disgust at his erroneous words. But, all the action did for me, was to take all of him in. He was dark, brooding and so powerful looking he made my heart rate stutter.

What the hell is wrong with me?

I must be delusional.

His presence was even more commanding than I remembered from our one and only previous meeting, which had been a very short encounter. The bits and pieces of gossip that I heard from other women that had come into contact with him more recently, certainly didn't do the man justice. His dark hair was short, well-kept and held in place with some sort of product. He had a square, masculine jaw and his face was clean shaven, which showed off his cleft chin. His dark eyes which were firmly fixed onto mine were becoming more penetrating with every second that passed. They were framed by long, thick eyelashes that were as black as pitch and framed his orbs perfectly. Even in my weakened state I had to reluctantly admit that the man did things to me. He was power, sin, sex and lust all wrapped up in a beautifully presented package. He was dressed with impeccable taste, a three-piece, black suit, pale blue shirt which stretched over his well-defined chest, with a striped blue and black Windsor knotted tie. It had to be recognised, even by me, that the man carried a suit damn well, so well in fact, I believed he was a serious risk to all ovulating females. His arms were crossed over his chest as he waited for me to answer him, leaving me in no doubt of the anger he was concealing behind his eyes.

'How dare you, I have respect for myself… you know nothing about my life.'

'And that's your first mistake… a lie… I know everything about you.' The disappointment in his voice left me stunned.

'Why? How do you know anything about me? Why would you want to?' I was shaking my head from side to side as I reeled out question after question in disbelief at what he'd just said.

Does Brody know that I'm back in this position?

The humiliation I felt at his statement and my subsequent worry, caused an almost instantaneous reaction inside me. The pressure behind my eyes began to build until all my previously held in pain, terror and disgrace, began to run down my face in rapid, thick rivulets. I tore my eyes away from his and placed my hands over my face as I tried, to no avail to hide my feelings from him. A few minutes passed without anything more being said between us. Eventually, my tears subsided and comprehending that he hadn't moved from his earlier position, I slowly rolled my head to look at him again.

My tear-filled eyes met his and the air in the room changed suddenly.

'Why are you that interested in me? No one is that interested in me, other than my feral cat and my neighbour…'

'Pearl and you've called the cat Tiger; I presume because of his colouring.'

The view that met my eyes was completely different to what I was expecting. The previous air of arrogant indifference that I knew Nico Morello was renowned for showing to the world, had been replaced with a look of concern. He pushed himself off the wall behind him and shrugged his broad shoulders out of his suit jacket, throwing it over his desk as he walked past. My eyes immediately jumped to the brown leather shoulder holster that had been exposed by his action.

What the hell?

Nico continued to cross the large room and finally, when he'd nearly reached me, he took hold of a nearby chair, twisted it around on one leg and straddled it. Folding his arms, he rested them on the seat back and looked down at me.

'You don't take care of yourself, Barbara. You've lost weight since I saw you last and judging by the way you passed out in here tonight, I would say you're also dehydrated.'

'You've been spying on me, why would you do that?'

'Call it keeping an eye on you.'

'I prefer spying,' I retorted.

'Call it what you want, I obviously haven't done a good enough job, have I?'

'I'm nothing to you, it's not your responsibility to look out for me. So, I appreciate your weird concern, but I need to go home.'

'Home to what? A cat and an older lady with a brightly coloured clothing obsession?'

'You really have been spying on me,' I spat out in disgust.

'No.' He shook his head, 'Call it due concern.'

I sat bolt upright and as my head protested, I quickly comprehended that I'd moved too quickly. Slowly, and reluctantly, I lowered myself backwards to the prone position I'd previously been in and started to take some deep breaths to calm my erratic heart rate. The deep breaths I was attempting to inhale were my second big mistake, the smell of the man permeated my nostrils. He smelt fresh and clean, like the ocean after a storm and the aroma of the man rapidly became something I needed more of. Fear of looking like even more of a loser in his eyes, I stopped myself inhaling through my nostrils and started to take in air through my mouth.

'Is this the position you sit in when you interrogate people, Mr. Morello?'

I wasn't quite sure where my sassiness was coming from tonight, but maybe it was a primal instinct. I knew his reputation and felt I needed to fight fire with fire.

'I want to help you, Barbara.' I couldn't believe what I thought my ears had actually heard.

'I'm sorry…I… What did you just say?'

A sigh left him and then he cleared his throat loudly, his previous look of concern was gone and replaced by his mask of arrogant indifference. 'I have a proposition for you.'

'Well as you've brought a gun to a tiddly wink competition, I can hardly not hear you out, can I?'

He twisted his head slightly and his left eye narrowed on me as he took in what I'd said. I could have sworn that the corners of his mouth twitched with a grin he managed to supress.

'Twenty minutes ago, I paid Antonio Barzini the money you owed him.'

'WHAT?... Why on earth would you have done that?' I sat up quickly in response to his words, ignoring the pain in my head. It was difficult to blink as my eyes felt dry after crying so much, but I forced my eyelids together in order to sever our connection.

'Because now I own you, Barbara.'

The chair creaked as he shifted his weight around while he waited for his statement to filter through to me.

An incoherent noise left my lips, followed by a whispered, 'I don't understand.'

'It's straightforward. Your life was in danger, and now it's not.'

'You could have fooled me... I'm here with you, and your reputation is far worse than Barzini's.' I emitted the words rapidly.

Terror and a feeling of downright stupidity unravelled inside of me at the situation I had willingly placed myself into.

Again, his head twisted to the side as he mulled over what I had just said. 'That's true, but I want to marry you, which is definitely not what Barzini and his men had in mind for you.'

CHAPTER SEVEN

Nico

'I CAN'T MARRY YOU!'

I could see she was still struggling. I could see the flight response captured in her bluey green iridescent eyes. The same eyes that had captivated me the moment she'd finally looked at me properly. The woman wanted to sit up, she wanted to stand and to run away. She wanted to escape the large room we were in and I knew why. I too could feel how the walls felt like they were closing in on us. The temperature in the room felt like it was increasing rapidly when it was normally controlled to the absolute degree, even I was beginning to feel uncomfortable. And, in probably what was the most important business meeting I had ever conducted, I appreciated that I was staring at her breasts as her chest rose with each and every unpredictable breath she inhaled. The briefest glimpse of her white, lace bra showed each and every time she drew in a breath as her buttons strained and a small gap appeared between two of them. She'd lost weight everywhere else, but the man in me had already noted that her breasts were still beautifully round.

'You don't know what you're asking,' she stated after I made no reply.

'That's where you're wrong, Barbara. I plan everything down to the last detail.' I forced my eyes back up to hers once again, to make sure she understood the power behind my last sentence. She didn't need to know that this plan of mine had only come into fruition less than an hour ago.

'We can't get married, we're not in love,' she uttered, shaking her head ever so slightly at me as she contemplated just what I was demanding of her.

'That's what makes this proposition that I'm offering you perfect.'

'I don't understand...'

I sat up straighter and pushing my arms straight on the back of the chair, I leant backwards, pulling myself away from the woman who was drawing me in closer with each breath she took.

'This is the deal.' I started speaking, but when she jumped I realised that it was in a harsher tone than I would have chosen, as I attempted to widen the imaginary gap between us. 'I've paid off all your debts.'

'All of my debts?'

'All of them... even the electric company.' I watched her nod as she tried to take in what I was saying. 'And I need to take a wife.'

'Why?' she shot back at me.

'You understand what it's like to be beholden to family members don't you, Barbara?'

She nodded just a fraction.

'Well,' I continued. 'My grandmother, Nonna, wants me to marry to carry on our wonderful family.' A loud laugh left my mouth at the ridiculousness of it all. 'I will fulfil my promise to her, to make her happy, but I will never "marry" in the true sense of the word… and without a doubt I will never embrace a family that has my father's faulty DNA in it.'

'So, let me get this straight… you want us to marry to placate her?' I could see the questioning look in her eyes.

'Yes, it's that simple.'

'Marriage isn't simple, I watched my parents' marriage come crashing down around their ears.' Pain overtook her features and I gripped my fingers into the back of the chair to stop reaching forward to touch her face.

What the actual hell?

'This marriage would be.'

'I don't think so,' she answered and began to sit up again.

I watched as she swung her legs off the couch, showing me her shapely legs, and placed her scruffy looking shoes onto the floor.

She was making to leave.

What felt like panic reared up inside of me. 'Barbara… You have two choices.' I deliberately spoke harshly this time, I needed her to understand that what I wanted was going to happen.

'What?' Her brow furrowed and her eyes found mine and stayed there for longer than she'd allowed before.

I straightened my back and sat up taller, to emphasise what I was about to land on her.

'Two choices. Marry me and be my pretend wife for one year or… well the phones on the desk, do you want to call Brody or shall I?'

I let my words rest for a few seconds and then to add my pretend indifference to them, I swung my leg back over the chair I'd been sitting on and moved to stand in front of her, deliberately placing my feet either side of hers and effectively trapping her in. I wanted to make sure she could feel my towering presence while she thought over her choices.

'I don't want Brody involved,' she whispered, and my heart rate accelerated in what felt like excitement.

Again, what the actual hell?

Knowing her eyes weren't on me I shook my head at myself.

'One year?' she questioned and I looked down at her and took in how beautiful her naturally blonde hair was.

'Yes,' I replied. *Look up at me.*

'Then we divorce and go our separate ways?'

'Our marriage will be fake, but for all intents and purposes will look from the outside like a real marriage, my nonna won't be fooled by anything else… But, yes, at the end of the year we will divorce and go our separate ways… I'll make sure you're well provided for.'

'I want… well, I want more.'

'More?' I unwittingly reached out and placed two fingers under her chin to lift her eyes up to mine.

The simple touch of my fingers on her soft skin set all the nerves in my hand and up my arm on edge, which took me by complete surprise, when nothing ever really surprised me. Then compliantly she allowed me to gently lift her head until she was looking demurely up at me with her expressive eyes.

'More?' My head was screaming at me to break the connection between the two of us, but it was as though my fingers were magnetized to her. I couldn't release the tiny hold I had on her and even worse the pad of my thumb was caressing her chin gently as I held her.

'I need help, Nico.' Her eyes began to fill with tears once again and I exhaled. A woman crying was my kryptonite, it reminded me of my mamma.

'What do you need?'

'I need help to beat this addiction. I'll marry you; I'll pretend with you for one year, but I need help… please.'

Relief swept through me. Then it was quickly and fleetingly replaced with an edge of disappointment when I reflected that was all she wanted from me.

'That's a given; I was always going to get you the help you needed. I'll employ the best doctor to help you.' I smiled at her in reassurance. 'My wife can't have a gambling addiction; she needs to be above all of that.'

'But I won't let you send me away… I can't be sent away again.' She started to shake her head vehemently. One solitary tear left her and started to run down her cheek.

I felt my left eye narrow as I studied her. I knew her history, her parents splitting and her family being torn into two, perhaps this was why all the money Brody had thrown at her before to help with her addiction had never actually helped her?

I lifted my other hand and gently brushed the tear away from her cheek with my fingertips.

'I'll be with you every step of the way.'

'Then you have yourself a deal.'

I smiled at her and then placed a kiss gently to the top of her head and allowed myself to inhale her vanilla shampoo.

Standing still and caressing the woman who had agreed to be my wife set off a chain reaction inside me. Something clicked inside my head, my hand dropped away from her chin and I stepped away from her quickly, before thoughts of owning her in every way possible consumed me. That was something that I knew needed to be kept well out of this arrangement. Once my back was turned to her, I strode purposefully over to pick up my jacket from my desk, inhaling deeply as I tried to rid her perfume from my nostrils.

'Come on, let's get you home.'

'My condo?'

'Yes, at first... as you will have to pick up what you need and I'm sure you'll want to tell Pearl the good news.' I shot a questioning look back over my shoulder at her and took in the fear on her face. 'Then to my home out at Red Rock Canyon.'

'You know she'll never believe me and what will I do about Tiger?' I could hear the sudden panic in her voice and knew it didn't all stem from the fact she was going to have to lie to Pearl and leave her beloved moggy behind. The realisation of what she'd agreed to do had hit her like a ten-ton truck.

'I'm sure you can convince her, after all you've been lying to her about how bad your addiction was for some time haven't you?'

'She didn't believe that either.'

'Then we'll have to try really hard to convince her, won't we?' I couldn't help but smile at the thought of what we might have to do to convince her good friend.

'You're prepared to playact tonight?'

'Technically the sun is rising and it's a brand new day here in the city, and yes, I'm prepared to kiss you senseless, so you'll be more than convincing as the blushing bride.'

With her ass still planted on my couch, I watched as she swallowed deeply and felt my hand twitch at the thought of holding onto her neck as my mouth consumed hers.

It was going to be a good day; I could feel it.

CHAPTER EIGHT

Barbara

Driving out to my condo, which was situated in the cheap area of Sunrise, so early in the morning, was something I hadn't appreciated in a very long time. It meant that Vegas was bathed in the red and gold light from the beautiful colouring in the sky. Various hotels shimmered under their metallic coverings and their colours bled into my soul, making me feel warm inside. This morning my heart felt just that little bit lighter as for the first time in what seemed like forever, I contemplated that I might have a chance at a future.

Out of the corner of my eye, I took a look at the devastatingly handsome man sat beside me and then moved my eyes quickly back to the front. His reputation preceded him, but I couldn't believe that the man who'd shown me so much compassion earlier could be all bad. Although, I was nervous at just what game he was going to play once we got back to my home. I continued to look over at Nico sporadically, and I tried to comprehend what I'd agreed to and just what it would involve.

The man himself was quiet on our journey, occasionally singing the odd few words to an Elvis soundtrack he had playing quietly in the car. I felt he was probably contemplating the exact same questions as me, but I felt sure, having witnessed the corners of his mouth twitch on more than one occasion, that he was much happier or at least more comfortable than I was about the deal we had made.

In fact, it appeared that he was almost enjoying our charade.

'It's beautiful, don't you think?' I asked trying to break through the silence.

'The sunrise?' he questioned.

'Yes, I've always thought it would make a stunning photo.'

'Are you into photography, Barbara?'

'No, I don't even own a camera.' I laughed at the question. 'Maybe in a different life I could have been.' I trailed my finger on the crystal-clear glass of the passenger window. 'I used to think how stunning the colours would look against the backdrop of the hills around us.' Not wanting to mark his pristine car I pulled my finger back in quickly and clasped my hands together on my lap as I tried hard to relax.

'Well, maybe this might be the start of your different life.'

'You think?' I turned to focus on Nico, while his eyes remained fixed on the road ahead.

The fact he was driving the two of us had come as a complete surprise. I'd seen his limo with its blacked-out windows and personalised number plate sweep up and down The Boulevard on numerous occasions before and expected to travel in that. He'd informed me in his

A.S. ROBERTS

large private garage underneath the casino, that whenever he could he liked to be in charge of his own fate, and he was also studying to become a pilot. As his words sunk home, I understood just how much I could get used to someone helping me steer my own fate and the thought was sobering.

'Our marriage, this year together, well… it's to help us both out. There is no reason why you can't do something for you as well, while you concentrate on getting better.'

I was momentarily stunned at his thoughtfulness.

'It's the next right,' I offered, breaking through the companionable yet contemplative quiet.

For the first time, he turned his head towards me and without answering me he nodded.

'You knew that already, didn't you?'

'Yes,' he answered truthfully.

'Why that doesn't freak me out… I have no idea.'

He competently turned the steering wheel of the navy Lamborghini Veneno with absolute precision and the engine roared its disgust at having to slow down.

'The reason it doesn't freak you out, as you put it, is because the longer you think on this, the more you're coming to terms with the best decision you ever made.'

'Mmmm.' I wasn't convinced I could carry this off in front of Pearl, let alone his overbearing grandmother. 'Have you ever actually been here yourself before now?' I asked, suddenly feeling the answer was important.

'What would you prefer me to say?'

'I don't know.'

'Second lie,' he challenged with a smile spreading over his gorgeous features.

'Okay, okay. In truth, I'd prefer that you'd only ever had your security here. Them making sure I was alright and reporting back to you somehow sits better with me.'

'Then, that's the answer.' He turned his head to look at me and with a broad smile over his face, showing me a dimple I hadn't seen before in person or in the media, he offered me a quick conspirator's wink. His usual composed persona had dissolved a little around the edges. Standing next to anyone else in a suit, Nico would have still looked the better dressed and the more perfectly put together. But against his own crazily high standards, little things were beginning to look less than perfect, and God did it suit him.

I felt my mouth fall open agog. He looked relaxed and could it be said, almost playful. It was as though I'd been allowed to catch a glimpse of the boy beneath the man his well-publicised life had turned him into.

Close your mouth and stop looking at him.

As we pulled up outside my scruffy looking condo, I closed my eyes quickly to compose myself. It was one thing having people know just how desperate your life had become, but it was completely different having them see it with their own eyes. The two small windows at the front at least looked a little more decent than they had yesterday. Pearl had hung my new drapes and although they weren't in a fabric I'd have chosen by choice, I was more grateful than she would ever know.

Nico pushed a button on his console and spoke loudly. 'We're here, area clean?'

'Yes, Boss.'

'Good. Leave a couple of teams local, Fran.'

'Already done, Boss,' came the very direct reply from a microphone hidden somewhere in the state-of-the-art car.

He's staying here with me. I could almost see myself with wide open eyes, like a rabbit caught in the headlights. *Don't be stupid, what did you expect?*

'Stay there,' he demanded without turning his head to look at me.

I watched him get out of the car. He buttoned up his suit jacket, took a good look around the area, then walked around the front of his prized vehicle and opened up my door. I looked up nervously from the passenger seat as he offered his hand for me to take hold of.

As his hand hovered there in mid-air, and as I stared at his well-manicured fingernails and the Morello family signet ring on his finger, I knew that by taking hold of his hand I was truly accepting everything he was coercing me into. For a split second, I contemplated my next move, but understanding that he really did seem to have thought of everything, and that we truly could help each other out of the difficult situations we were in, I lifted up my hand and took hold of his fingers.

Jesus.

It took all I had not to pull my hand away, as what felt like a jolt of static electricity travelled up my arm and into my very obviously extremely tired body. Instead, I took in a deep breath and offered him a small smile as he closed the door to his Lamborghini behind me. After threading his large fingers in between my smaller ones, he pulled me in closely to his side, so close that his cologne engulfed me. Then he walked us up to the metal fence that surrounded my tiny property.

Once we reached the gate, he pushed it open and stood back for me to walk in front of him. By the time I reached the peeling paint on what should have been a bright red door, my hand was shaking as I attempted to put my key into the lock. Finally, I managed to drive it home and hoped he hadn't noticed my mini breakdown due to nerves and the anxiety that seemed ever present.

I pushed open the door as quietly as I could, knowing that Pearl would sometimes hear me come home and would pop around to see if I was okay, and it was far too soon for me to face her. As the door closed behind the two of us, I dropped my keys onto the small, fake antique corner table that my aunty had loved so much and strode purposefully into the kitchen.

'Coffee?' I tried to casually push into the suddenly tense atmosphere.

'Black please,' I heard him say, as his voice disappeared into the living area.

'That's lucky,' I said under my breath as I filled the kettle with water and placed it onto the stove in front of me. I knew there was no milk in the fridge and couldn't have offered anything other than black anyway.

Silence engulfed my tiny condo.

I tried to imagine just what he was seeing as he looked around my sparse living area. Anything that had held any value, I had already pawned in the local shop in Sunrise, the cheap area of Vegas that I resided in. I knew all that would meet his probably disapproving eyes were an almost antiquated reclining chair, a couple of upright chairs against one wall and a low table. Even the walls had rectangular dirty marks on them, left behind from when I had taken down and sold a couple of prints that I'd treated myself to when things were a little better for me.

The kettle, starting to produce its low whistle to let me know it was nearly ready, made me jump. I grabbed a glass from the cupboard and filled it up with water. As soon I felt the cool glass on my lips my body went into overdrive, my mouth was suddenly more parched than it had ever felt before and I drank it all down, relishing the way the liquid quelled the burning in my throat. The whistle became high-pitched, bringing me to. I hastily refilled my glass and then grabbed an oven glove to lift the kettle off the stove.

'Thank you, Pearl,' I whispered as I placed a spoon full of coffee into an "I love Vegas" mug. I knew that behind the scenes she was making sure I had the bare minimum in my condo to get by and that she had recently topped up my coffee. 'What would I do without you?'

Tears pricked the back of my eyes as I thought about leaving her behind here for a year. She had become like a mom to me over the years and I knew we relied on each other.

What will she do without me to look after?

Trying to lose my melancholy thoughts I concentrated on stirring the coffee, watching as the boiling water whooshed around in its confines. Then, letting out a soft sigh, I picked up the mug and my glass of water and tried hard to walk confidently into the living area.

'Here you…' I stopped speaking immediately as I took in the sight that met my eyes.

There resting asleep on the dilapidated recliner chair was the man I had only two hours ago agreed to marry. Even asleep his presence filled the whole of my living space.

His suit jacket had been discarded, his tie had been loosened and his gun, still in its shoulder holster, was laid out in his lap. I cast my eyes down to see that his shoes were in a heap on the floor beneath him. The man who had most of Vegas at his beck and call, the man who I was sure owned every luxury known to the rich, and who I doubt ever relaxed, looked totally at ease in my tiny, rundown home, in a comfortable but broken armchair. I couldn't help the smile that stretched my mouth from cheek to cheek.

But the best of it was his face. I leant myself against my doorframe and studied him a little harder, not knowing when I'd ever get another chance. Still holding the hot drink in my hands, I started to sip at the coffee that I'd originally made for him.

Nico Morello was attractive in a way you normally only read about in romance books. He was the epitome of tall, dark and handsome, with risk thrown in for good measure. He was over six foot, probably by about a couple of inches. His shoulders were broad, and it was fairly obvious that he took good care of himself by the way his shirt stretched across his firm chest. His face had lost the look of total indifference he normally showed to the world, it was instead peaceful and dare I say it relaxed? His short dark brown hair was messed up and a five o'clock shadow had covered his jaw, which suited him even though it concealed the cleft in his chin. There was no getting away from the danger that surrounded him, but I could also sense that there was a different man residing under the mantle he had created to exist in his world, and the two sides of him totally captivated me.

I closed my eyes momentarily as I recognised the long forgotten feeling of butterflies in my stomach and my heart was skipping happily, from just being able to look at him. My fingers longed to touch him, so I made myself stand stock still and hoped that the feeling would ebb away soon.

I took another sip of the strong coffee, knowing that it would most definitely keep me awake today.

I shook my head laughing silently at the excuse.

I had been lying to myself for years about my addiction to gambling, so I recognised another lie as soon as the thought swept through my head.

Be truthful.

I probably wasn't going to be able to sleep this morning anyway, knowing he was in here, because I already knew that spending a year with this man would most definitely prove to be an even greater challenge than giving up gambling.

I knew without a doubt, even after only spending a few hours in his company, that if the man continued to surprise me with his kindness and concern for my well-being, Nico Morello could prove to be my greatest ever addiction.

CHAPTER NINE

NICO

I CRACKED OPEN ONE eye and took in my surroundings.

The tiny room, which was badly in need of decorating, met my eye and feeling a crick in my neck I immediately remembered where I must have fallen asleep.

How the hell had I even slept?

I moved one hand from behind my head feeling the inflexibility that a night in the chair had given it and placed it over the top of the gun on my lap. Pausing to listen to anything I could make out in the small space around me, I pressed the hard comfort of my gun and the leather that housed it into my morning wood, just trying to get a moment of reprieve before I saw Barbara again.

I listened for a few seconds, to find to my relief that the condo was completely silent.

Time to make a couple of calls.

I knew I needed to put a few plans together before she woke up and panicked at our impending marriage. I moved to the side to reach for my jacket and cursed under my breath at the state of it as I picked it up to retrieve my cell. Hearing the chair underneath me groan and reverberate its protest into the silence of her small living space put me on edge, worried that I just might have disturbed her too. The screen flashed on and I saw it was a little before one in the afternoon, which surprised the hell out of me. I couldn't remember the last time I'd slept for over four hours straight and I'd never passed out in an old reclining chair.

Not wanting to disturb Barbara before I'd put some of the plans I knew we needed into place, I eased myself off the chair, not bothering to close it up in case it made even more noise. I wrapped my gun up inside my jacket and left them on top of my shoes and then made my way out to what I thought must be the kitchen.

The door I pushed open revealed I was right. I flicked my eyes around rapidly to find the coffee machine, desperate for some caffeine. It became obvious that the kitchen was not very well equipped and the realisation that this was how she'd been living was painful. The few tatty bits of furniture in her living area had seemed bad enough, but right now the kitchen seemed even worse. I'd been keeping tabs on her from afar, making sure she had a job and still had a place to live, but I realised, as my eyes found the bare worktops, that "living" was hardly the word to describe what she'd obviously been experiencing for a while. This, her life, was an existence and nothing more.

You've done a crap job, Morello.

I should have stepped in sooner, but in truth when I searched deep inside myself for any ounce of feelings I might still have, up until last night I had believed she was truly better off without my input. Because, if I was being honest, I had always thought she was one of the most naturally beautiful women I had ever laid eyes on. She didn't need a bastard like me in her life, controlling it and taking it over with my demands and offering her nothing in return.

But now she did need me, and I needed her, so we had come to a crossroads.

Not finding a coffee machine, I unlocked the back door and stepped out into her yard. It was the hottest time of the day and the heat was already intense. After pressing a few buttons and with my cell to my ear as it dialled the call, I unbuttoned my shirt and pulled it free from the waistband of my pants. Then without thinking it through, I pulled off one sock at a time, dropped them down beside me and gripped the long grass with my toes, relishing in something I hadn't done in a long time.

'Hey, Trip.'

'Well, if it's not the Italian stud.' His words teased and I laughed. At the same time, I heard Kendall talking to their son Bruce in the background.

'I have some news that I think will surprise you.'

'Interesting, get on with it then.' Then his voice changed as he informed Kendall that he couldn't hear what I was saying so he was stepping outside for a few minutes. I could imagine him stood by the ocean outside their home in Florida, with a fresh breeze blowing off the sea and in my head I cursed the hot as hell, dry heat I was standing in and flexed my toes again onto the grass underfoot. A feeling not unlike homesickness rushed through me and I knew without a doubt that Crete was where we needed to take our vows.

'First of all, what are you doing with your sad little semi-retired life in about, well say ten days' time?'

'As little as possible... how about you, workaholic?'

'Well, I need some asshat to fly me and the future Mrs. Morello over to Crete. I also need a best man and Barbara will need a witness.' My statement was met with complete silence for a few seconds and I let a grin spread over my face when it appeared I had rendered him speechless.

'Barbara? Well *fuck* me sideways.'

'No thanks, I prefer blonde beauties with perky tits.' Trip's wife was a pretty blonde and I knew he occasionally called her perky, due to his love of her breasts, and I loved being able to wind him up just a bit about his perfect life.

'Shut it!... Seriously, I don't know what to say.'

'Don't say I've rendered you speechless, Trip?'

I laughed out loud and then reined myself in, as I reminded myself I was supposed to be trying not to disturb Barbara or her neighbour.

'Yes, Boss... I hate to say it, but you have... Although I have some questions... How and when did all of this happen and does this poor woman actually know she's marrying you or will Franco have to kidnap her just before the plane takes off?'

'Ha-ha. We've known of each other for a few years and no she'll get on the plane willingly.'

The conversation went on, with him mainly taking the rise out of me and finally, after we'd discussed the arrangements he needed to make with flight plans, I hung up and dialled the other number I needed. It took about a minute for the international call to go through and while I was waiting, I walked around in a circle on the small patch of grass I was stood on.

'Nipote.' I could hear the glee in her voice as she answered. 'How lovely of you to call.'

'Nonna, I have some news.'

'Good news?'

'Yes, extremely good… in fact it's the best.' I tried hard to take the business-like tone out of my voice and let the warmth of being able to help Barbara fill me up with happiness. I knew if I conducted this phone call in any other way my grandmother would see right through my carefully made up ruse.

'Well, then let me sit down, hold on a minute.' I could hear her heels clicking on the marble flooring underneath her feet.

I can't wait to show Barbara my home.

I looked up at the clear blue sky and closed my eyes as the heat of the sun found my face. I was seriously messed up; it had been a strange night/early morning after all.

'I'm sitting, what do you have to tell me, Nico?'

'I'm getting married.'

'YOU ARE?' Her voice lifted as she almost screamed back her excitement to me. 'When?'

'Do you think you could organise it for two weeks' time?'

'You want me to organise it all?'

'I do.' I smiled at the happiness in her voice.

'But what about your bride-to-be, surely she'll want some input into her own wedding? What's her name?'

Shit.

'Barbara, her name's Barbara and she wants to get married in Crete,' I lied and hoped at the same time. 'And she's happy to have a traditional wedding and... well, we both thought it was something you'd enjoy organising.'

I hoped what I was saying wasn't far from the truth and regressed to a childish habit of crossing my fingers as I wished.

'Barbara would?' I could hear Nonna crying what I was sure were tears of happiness and my cold, hard heart felt a little warmer.

'Yes. So, is it possible? It's Saturday today, could it happen two weeks from today?'

'I'm sure I can arrange all of that, what about a dress?' she questioned. 'And how many guests will be coming?' A long list of questions fell from her mouth, one after the other.

'She'll find a dress here and we'll bring it with us,' I answered.

Then I explained to her that all Barbara had was Brody, and as Default Distraction were on tour in Asia that neither him nor my brother Cade would be there. So, it would be us, Barbara, and Trip and his family. I also told her that I wanted the flowers to be blue with as much green foliage in them as possible to pick out Barbara's eye colour and at that I'd heard a sob fall from Nonna's mouth, and I knew I'd managed to convince her.

Then we said our goodbyes. She was happy I was keeping my promise to her and I was happy because of... well something that I couldn't quite put my finger on.

'Good morning.'

I heard a voice call over the fence behind me and placing my cell back into my pocket I turned around to face it.

'Morning,' I answered and offered the woman who must have been standing on something to look over the six-foot fence a quick smile. I knew who she was, the pink coloured hair with its greying roots could only belong to Pearl, Barbara's neighbour.

Shit.

Everything up until now had been going to plan and that was just how I liked my life. In order and going to plan. But with not knowing Pearl at all, this wasn't a conversation I wanted to have without Barbara present.

'Well, you're a sight I never thought I'd see standing in that girl's backyard.'

I nodded at her, grimacing at her words and the flicker of recognition she had in her eyes beneath her ridiculously long, false eyelashes.

Again, shit.

I watched her eyes narrow on me as she studied me that little bit harder.

'You're a Morello, aren't you? In fact, forgive me, you're *the* Morello, now aren't you?'

Reluctantly, I stepped closer towards her and offered her my hand, which she didn't shake but stared at suspiciously.

'I am, and you must be the Pearl that Barbara's always talking about,' I acknowledged and dropped my offered hand.

Fleetingly, the small amount of flattery, the recognition I'd just given her, appeared to work and I saw a smile begin to break out on her lips. Then, just as fast as it appeared, she shelved it as suspicion wrapped itself around her once again.

'So, will I be getting an invite to this wedding of yours?'

'You'd come out to Crete with us?' I questioned, hoping the answer would be no.

'I don't like flying, but for that girl I'd do anything to make sure she was safe, do you understand where I'm coming from, Mr. Morello?'

'Call me Nico,' I offered.

'Hmmm, I'll be right around, don't you go anywhere.'

'I wouldn't dare,' I replied under my breath as her pink hair disappeared from view.

'Trip if you were here, the song that suits this life changing moment would be **Suspicious Minds** by **Elvis.**'

CHAPTER TEN

Nico

I TURNED AROUND, WALKED the couple of steps to pull open the door to the kitchen and enjoyed the blast of cool air from the air con. The sight that met my eyes was something I didn't think I'd ever forget.

Stood in the small space with the kettle now boiling on the stove, was Barbara. I let my eyes wander down her, slowly trying to take in everything about her. I could only see her from the side view, but I could see that her face was devoid of make-up and her cheeks were pinked having just woken up. Her thick, long blonde hair was freshly brushed and hanging all the way down her back, finally curling at the ends just above the beautiful round globes of her ass. My hand ached to grab a hold, to pull her head backwards exposing her neck to my mouth. My eyes left her hair and I tried to ignore what the hell was happening in my trunks and took in the rest of her. She was wearing a tight fitting, white vest top which left nothing to the imagination and tiny cotton sleep shorts.

All semblance of my self-control snapped loudly in my ears.

What in actual hell was wrong with me?

Hearing her front door bang and knowing that now was the time for playacting, I took the couple of steps I needed and closed the gap between us until her back was in front of me. I prayed to my mamma's God that she reacted in the way we needed her to, then I wrapped one of my arms around her waist and lifting her up slightly I pulled her tightly into me. Moving her hair to one side with my other hand, I let my mouth feast on her neck as I inhaled everything about the woman in my arms.

The taste of her skin was exquisite.

At first, she let out a small squeal, but when she put up no fight against what seemed an entirely normal thing for us to be doing in her kitchen, I knew that she'd realised we had a visitor. I heard Barbara put down the spoon she'd been holding and then felt the touch of her hand on my arm as she clasped onto my forearm and leant herself back into me allowing herself to feel me, to feel us.

The moan she emitted from her lips travelled straight to my groin and I knew she understood just what she'd done to me when she wiggled instinctively against my cock.

'Don't,' I whispered in her ear and then I bit down softly onto her lobe.

Immediately, she ceased wriggling at my reprimand, and I smiled into her neck.

'I'm sorry, Barbara… I didn't mean to intrude.' I heard Pearl speak and forced my mouth reluctantly away from Barbara's neck.

'You're fine, Pearl,' I answered. 'It was my fault anyhow… I just couldn't resist her.' Reluctantly, I released my arm from around Barbara and let her feet find the ground again. Then I stepped back, twisted around and held out my hand to Pearl again.

'Nico Morello.'

This time she gave me a reprieve and shook it.

'Pearl Marie Paltrow… and no, I know we look similar, but I'm no relation of Gwyneth.'

For a second, I was rendered dumbstruck as I fought with everything inside me to stop my eyebrow raising at her and laughing. Luckily, I quickly understood that she really thought she looked like the actress. I reached to the side of me, grateful to have Barbara by my side and placing an arm around her waist I pulled her into me. I looked down as she wrapped her arms around me with no hesitation.

'I'm pleased to meet you.'

'Are you?' she questioned, as she took in the two of us together. 'I've met you before, many years ago when you were a little boy, you see I used to work for your father.'

It happened occasionally that I was reminded of the bastard whose blood coursed through my veins, this time I managed to not let it knock me off kilter.

'For that, Ma'am, I can only offer my deepest apologies.'

Her eyes opened wide as she absorbed my words and then she nodded as she seemed to accept my apology.

'So, can one of you two please tell me what's happening?'

'Oh, Pearl… This is Nico, Nico Morello as you've already realised… I don't know what to say, other than we're together and he makes me happy… So very happy.'

I watched the old bird nod and her mouth fall open in surprise. I had to stop my mouth from following suit, because my future wife was such a damn good liar that I was almost convinced she'd fallen for me.

'I'm sorry I didn't tell you about Nico and I running into each other a few weeks ago, but I was sure that I couldn't get that lucky and that us seeing each other would come to nothing,' Barbara continued.

'I've just heard him making arrangements for a wedding.' I watched the wily old bird cross her spindly arms over her non-existent chest as she continued to question us both, but having heard Barbara sound so convincing I left her to it.

'He asked me to marry him last night… and I know it's quick, but it's for all the right reasons, Pearl. So, I said yes.' To add more credence to what she was saying she snuggled further into me and like some crazy in love fool I pressed a quick kiss to the top of her head.

'Oh, Barbara. Are you happy with him? If you are then you won't hear another word from me, because you deserve happiness.'

I felt derelict the moment she moved away from me. She took Pearl's hands into her own before she spoke again. 'I am, Pearl. Being with Nico is offering me everything I can't be by myself.'

Well she wasn't lying. I admired her way with words.

'But, your problems, Barbara?' Pearl's eyes flicked between Barbara and me. I relaxed, Pearl truly cared about her and I knew she was deliberately not going into details in case Barbara hadn't shared her gambling addiction with me. I was suddenly pleased Barbara had her in her life, no matter how much of a problem she might pose to us now.

'I know all there is to know about her addictions, Pearl. We're going to face them together. She has no need to work anymore, which takes her away from the temptation and together we're going to talk to therapists and doctors that can help.' I finally entered the conversation.

'I can't not work.' Barbara spun around to face me again and it took all I had to keep my eyes on hers and not the shape and swell of her breasts under her ridiculously thin sleep vest.

'You can't seriously think you can still work in a casino?' I questioned, crossing my arms over my chest.

'Well, no,' she admitted, sucking her bottom lip quickly into her mouth and releasing it again when she watched my eyes follow it. 'But I need a life, Nico and something that's just for me.' I knew what she was saying, she needed something that would be there when I was gone.

'Take up photography.' Shit even I had to admit I was fast at thinking on my feet.

'Photography?'

'You said it was something you'd always wanted to do… so do it with my full support.'

'Could I?'

'Why not? I have to work. You'll have time on your hands and both of my homes are surrounded by beautiful scenery. In fact, getting married out in Crete and spending time there for our honeymoon will give you somewhere to start.'

I opened my eyes up wide as I wordlessly pleaded with her to accept my idea and to us getting married in Crete.

'Thank you.' Barbara quickly moved back to me and flung herself into my arms. Without thinking what I was doing I accepted her with equal enthusiasm and wrapping my arms around her, held her to me.

'Well then, what can I say?' Pearl questioned.

'Congratulations?' I smiled over Barbara's shoulder at her.

'Congratulations, Barbara and to you too, Nico, and welcome to our small family.'

A quick shower later and a change of clothes, which I always kept in my car in case I spent the night with a woman, I found myself freshened up and sitting having lunch in the local IHOP with my wife to be and her oddly dressed adopted mom.

I didn't think anyone was more amazed than me.

Looking around me at the family clientele, I realised I stuck out like a sore thumb. I'd forgone a jacket and tie, but my expensive, fine wool, blue suit pants and fitted white shirt screamed majorly out of place. I was sat next to Barbara in her shorts and cotton top on a bench seat in a booth opposite the pink haired Pearl.

And I couldn't have cared less.

If only Cade could see me now. I could see my brother Cade laughing his head off.

Barbara was talking to Pearl about what style she would like as a wedding dress and the joy on her face was evident. I drowned out their excited voices and placed my arm over the back of the bench seat, giving in to the need to touch her again and to obviously playact our engaged situation. Lowering my hand, I touched the bare skin of her shoulder and used my index finger to make small circles on her bare flesh.

I could get very used to touching this woman. The thought was sobering and contrary to every rule I'd ever allowed myself to live by.

The vibration of my cell in my pocket brought me to. I retrieved it and checked the screen. It was from Trip, who was confirming our flight plans and his employment of a second officer and flight crew to fly with him. He'd undoubtedly already gone through Franco due to the security he knew I always had in place around me. I read his message and was just about to place my cell back in my pocket when a second one lit up the screen.

It was from my secretary. It wasn't important, but it gave me the excuse I needed to make a move. I needed to be back with solid ground under my feet, instead of this strange virtual world I'd resided in since the small hours of this morning. I read her message and put my cell away, I'd reply to Trip later when I was back in the office and feeling more at ease with myself.

Barbara was now safe, and I'd leave a security team with her to make sure she stayed so. She was fed and well. I had my pretend bride for my grandmother, so another plan was working out just as I wanted it to. Now, I needed to make my excuses and get the hell out of Dodge.

'Ladies, that was my secretary. She was just reminding me I have work to do today. So, my suggestion is that I drop you both at a wedding boutique with my credit card and permission to use it?' I smiled the question to the both of them as the lie just dripped off my tongue.

'Do you really have to go?' Barbara turned slightly towards me and brushed her fingers down the front of my shirt. I watched them toy with a couple of the buttons as they moved.

'Yes, for a few hours, I have some work to catch up with and you need a dress to get married in, we leave in ten days. Also use my driver to take you to get yourself a camera.'

'Thank you, Nico… you're too kind.'

If only she knew. Her people radar was so far off it was alarming.

Looking into her eyes and glancing between them and her lips, all thoughts vacated my head. I felt her hand as she lifted it up from my chest to rest it on the stubble on the side of my face. Feeling the warmth of her hand on me, I finally succumbed and lowering my mouth slowly towards her I gently brushed my lips on hers. Our eyes remained open for the length of the kiss and somewhere in that brief touch of our skin on each other's, for the first time I understood that the one thing I'd never planned on happening had just spread its wings and taken flight.

CHAPTER ELEVEN

Barbara

Ten days later

I LOOKED AWAY FROM the clear blue sky outside the window, as the plane reached its cruising altitude having just left London Heathrow. Apparently, the plane we were travelling in was Nico's. I really wasn't sure I was going to be able to get used to the life I was living in at the moment.

You don't have to, Barbara… It's just a pretence for a year.

'This is your supreme commander speaking, buckle up for our final leg of the journey. Your flight today will take just under four hours and the forecast for the weather in Crete is warm and sunny.'

I smiled at hearing Trip's voice and looked across at Kendall who was also grinning and shaking her head a little, probably at all the memories hearing Trip like this conjured up. I'd spent most of the previous flight from Vegas to London chatting with her and playing with Bruce, her and Trip's young son. All the while Pearl had slept, after taking enough sleeping tablets to knock out a small army, and Nico had worked. I was eager to spend some quality time with Kendall, having not had a friend the same age to talk to in a long time, and the fact she was married to Nico's best friend was an added bonus. I hoped that eventually she could give me a better insight into the man I was going to marry. Instead, she had told me about how her and Trip had met and the obstacles they'd overcome to stay together. In turn, I'd told her how Nico and I had known about each other for years through our brothers, but had only recently reconnected and how things had blossomed from there. She had remained quiet and had listened carefully to everything I had told her and although she hadn't offered me anymore information about Nico, to my absolute relief at the end she had grabbed at my hand and told me how pleased she was for the two of us.

'Wait for it.' Kendall smiled at me as she stroked Bruce's dark hair. 'He's just thinking about what song to treat us all to.'

I felt my mouth drop open in question when, just as she'd predicted, Trip's voice came back over the intercom as he started to sing **Here Comes The Sun** by **The Beatles.**

We listened, smiling at each other as he sang his way through the entirety of the song without missing a beat, then as he spoke again.

'Come on, Boss, you workaholic, give me something to work with.' When nothing came from Nico in the office he carried on, 'I win then.'

Catching the questioning look in my eyes, Kendall filled me in on what was going on.

'What would normally happen is Nico would appear and sing something back to Trip, but it would be by Elvis instead,' she offered me. 'It's a game they play, you know boys will be boys.' I laughed with her as my stomach rolled and my heart beat faster expectantly.

Then I turned my head towards the other compartment that Nico had been holed up in for most of our previous flight and for what looked like maybe all of this one too. But sadly, he nor his voice appeared.

'Bee, do you mind if I catch some sleep?' I was pleased that Kendall having heard Pearl use my nickname earlier was also using it, it made me feel like we'd known each other for a much longer time than we had.

'Of course, I don't,' I replied.

'Now this one's asleep, I should follow and get some rest as well.' She tipped her head at her son sleeping curled up next to her.

'I understand completely.'

I watched as she snuggled further into a blanket and lowered the chair she was sitting in backwards, all the time keeping a hand on her son's head, while she coiled some of his hair around her index finger.

In no time at all she was asleep and I was left to my own thoughts.

The worries inside my head began to take hold.

I'd hardly seen Nico since our lunch at the IHOP. He'd kissed me, awakening feelings inside of me that I was still struggling to cope with and then he'd abruptly left.

He'd been as good as his word; Pearl and I had been dropped off at one of the most expensive bridal shops Vegas had to offer. Nico had left us there with Raul, while he went back to work. I remembered seeing Raul escort Barzini's henchman out of Nico's casino the night Franco had taken me to see Nico. At first, I'd been intimidated by the enormous black man, as he was as wide as he was tall. But, as I'd tried on dress after dress, he'd become important to the whole operation as he'd given a man's opinion and slowly, I'd seen the guy's softer side. Without trying to rush us, he'd helped Pearl and I as we'd narrowed down my choices, until I'd finally settled on the one. Nico's black credit card had been handed over to pay for my dress and the trousseau the wait staff had insisted I also needed. Then, under Nico's instructions, Raul had taken us both to a nearby shop, where a helpful lady had shown me exactly what I needed to get started on my new hobby of photography.

I'd been beyond happy after the retail therapy, having bought myself nothing at all in a long time and laughing at Pearl's dry sense of humour as we'd clambered back into Nico's limo. After I'd packed up what I needed from my sparse home and had given Tiger to Pearl to look after, I'd left the run-down area of Sunrise. The limo, with only me inside it, then swept across Vegas to Nico's home and my excitement had begun to ramp up. Nico's home was stunning, set high up in the hills above Summerlin, in the Red Rock Canyon, and I'd pressed my nose against the cool glass feeling a lot like Cinderella. The building, his driver informed me, had apparently been designed by him and was built using local stones from Crete. It incorporated huge picture windows situated to overlook the lights of Vegas in the distance.

As I'd been shown to my room in Nico's fortress by his housekeeper, I'd realised with a very heavy heart that Nico wasn't even in the building. I'd wanted to tease him a little about what my wedding dress looked like and I had been looking forward to showing him the camera and accessories he'd paid for.

But mostly, I'd wanted him to kiss me again.

The understanding that those things weren't going to happen, because what we had between us was a pretence and that this wasn't a real relationship, hit me hard. In truth, if I could have escaped Nico's home, gotten past his security and stolen one of his cars, I would have. I had a strong compulsion inside of me to find somewhere that could offer me a roll of the dice or the turn of the cards that I so desperately needed. They were risks I understood, unlike the risk of handing over my life to a total stranger for a year.

So instead, I'd cried myself to sleep.

The next day a red Cartier box had arrived for me. Initially I'd been thrilled as security had handed it over for me to sign for, but as I'd cracked open the box to peer inside a sense of overwhelming sadness had overcome me. I knew it was stupid. I knew what I was living was merely an arrangement to help us both, but as I pushed the platinum band with its solitaire diamond onto my ring finger, tears had once again started to flow. I was certain the ring had cost Nico an absolute fortune and that most women would have given their second kidney to own it, but it wasn't me and it showed that really, we knew nothing about each other at all.

Nico had stayed at an apartment he had at the casino for most of the past week, and when he'd come home it had been a fleeting visit. I'd told him that I was lonely and he'd apologised saying that he had a lot of work to do, so that he could take the time off for our wedding and the couple of weeks afterwards for a honeymoon. Then he'd explained to me that I could be taken anywhere I wanted to go, all I had to do was to inform Franco and he'd make sure I had a car and the security he insisted

I needed. The whole conversation had been polite, formal and held like I assumed he would a business meeting.

I longed for the man I'd seen a glimpse of, who had fallen asleep on my broken recliner. I was unequivocally certain that down deep, behind the brash, uncaring mantle he projected to the world, he really did exist.

The one light, in an otherwise long week, had been the two meetings we'd had with my new therapist, Mrs. Davison. Nico had introduced himself as my future husband and then had sat patiently beside me as she'd listened and probed into my life. As I'd opened up to her about my childhood with my now famous brother, my parents' separation and divorce and then finally, through my tears of my mom's death, he'd reached over and taken hold of my hand. Squeezing it softly, encouraging me to talk to her he had once again convinced me that despite his better judgement he cared for me.

I twisted the ring around my finger as I tried to erase the thoughts from my head.

The door to the cockpit opening caught my eye and I looked up from my hand and offered the tall figure of Trip a smile. He smiled back, closed the door behind him and walked towards where I was sitting with his family.

'Hi,' he offered, and then seeing Pearl shift in her sleep as his voice disturbed her, he lowered his voice, 'all okay, Bee?' I nodded back my answer and offered him a weak smile. Then as he came alongside where we were sitting, he bent down to place a quick kiss on top of his wife and son's heads.

'Is he still locked up in there?'

Trip used his thumb to gesticulate towards the separate compartment that held Nico.

'Yes,' I whispered back. 'He's working.'

'He's crazy and this won't be the first or last time I'm about to let him know just that.' He smiled his reassurance at me. 'Why the hell is he locked up in there and you're out here?'

I shrugged in answer, unable to say anything as emotion tightened its grip around my voice box.

'Well, no more. Leave it with me, the asshat is about to get my boot up his ass.'

CHAPTER TWELVE

NICO

THE DOOR OPENED WITHOUT even being knocked in the first place and I looked up ready to lay into whichever of my staff it was who had broken my peace and contemplation.

'Nico.' I heard Trip's voice as the door closed behind him and I slowly raised my eyes to his.

'Don't you have a plane to fly?' I asked rudely, not wanting to get into a conversation with even him.

'It's my rest period.'

'Shouldn't you be sleeping then?' I looked up at him with total disdain, hoping my friend would forgive my downright rudeness that was driven by fear.

I watched as he sat on the end of the bed in the compartment I'd been locked away in and I knew without a doubt he could see right through me.

'Shouldn't you be out there with your fiancée? Instead of locked away in here.'

'I'm working.' I stared at him again, hoping he'd leave it.

'Woah. Now this isn't a face I recognise… something is going on here that I haven't been made party to… so spill it.'

I looked at him square in the eyes with every thought and fear about my impending nuptials gathered there for him to read. Then I sighed out loud as his face showed absolutely no evidence of understanding.

After staring at me for a few seconds, he opened up his arms and showed me his upturned palms 'What?'

'My up and coming marriage to Barbara, well… It's an arrangement,' I spat out. I hoped that by voicing the truth to him I would be in a better place to deal with it.

His eyes stared just that bit harder at me as he tried to take in what I was saying.

'An arrangement?'

'Yes, you know… a deal, an agreement, a business…'

'STOP!... Stop right there. You've managed to get that gorgeous, intelligent woman out there to agree to marry you for a deal?'

'Yes,' I answered him and at the same time I pushed my back further into the seat behind me, while I watched as he jumped up and began to pace around the small room.

'You know, I gotta say I could have seen this coming after that last dinner with your grandmother, and if Barbara had been some wannabe celebrity I'd have known straight away, but…'

'But, what?' I asked, just slightly amused as I watched him still pacing around the small area in disbelief.

'Morello, you're unbelievable... She's... well, she's so normal.'

'Of course, she's normal.' I took hold of the signet ring that bore my families crest and began to turn it around my finger as I waited for him to speak again. *I may not be, but she is.* 'Do you think anything other than normal would have placated Nonna?'

'No, you're right it wouldn't have. But... If she's so *normal,* why the hell did she agree to marry you for a business deal?'

'Because she needs help with something.' I wasn't prepared to share what demons Barbara was fighting, because, well because it felt wrong. The fact I wasn't prepared to share her problems in itself was completely baffling.

Why do I care? This is a business deal and nothing more.

Needing to break eye contact with Trip, I stood up. Then I rolled my head around my shoulders as I tried to release the tension in my neck that this conversation was causing and walked around the side of the built-in desk. Picking up the bottle I had my eyes on, I unscrewed the top of the Bourbon and poured myself a large measure, then knocked it back, relishing the burn as it hit the back of my throat.

I'd been like this since I'd allowed myself to kiss the damn woman at the IHOP. I had never in my life needed anything from a woman before. I could see two or three different women a week, happily take them to bed and then walk away in the morning. But that simple brush of my mouth on hers had meant that I'd spent the last few days holed up at the casino with my head buried in work, shouting just a bit more than usual at any of my staff who even dared to look at me sideways. But it had done little to erase what was going on inside of me. The two meetings with her new therapist had proven the most difficult and had nearly been my downfall. When she'd started to open up about her life, her heartache at being left behind by everyone she had once thought loved her, it had taken every single ounce of my self-control not to wrap her up tightly into my arms.

So, I was keeping my distance, until I could get my head straightened out.

'Drinking?' he accused.

'Yes, and so?'

'So, let me get this straight, whatever is going on, it's bad enough for you to drink in the day?'

'It's just one drink… It's not…'

'Wait a minute, let me get my head around what you're saying,' he interrupted.

'You've come to an arrangement with that beautiful, normal looking woman to get you the wife you need to fool Nonna?'

'Yes.'

'And in return you'll help her with whatever she's facing?' I truly loved the pain in my ass like a brother, for not questioning me any further on just what Barbara's problem was. I had no idea how an utter bastard like myself had been lucky enough to find him, because he truly was a decent guy.

'Yes,' I replied again.

'Where did you find her?'

'I didn't really find her, so to speak. Our paths crossed again. She's Barbara Daniels, sister of Brody who's in the same band as Cade. I've known of her for years.'

'Default Distraction.' He wasn't asking a question, just stating the facts as he attempted to wrap his head around what I was saying.

'Yeah,' I replied, trying to change it up.

'So, you're marrying that woman out there, who is the sister of one of Cade's band mates to fool your grandmother?'

'Again, yes!' I put the tumbler down that I'd been clutching and pushed my hands deep down into my pockets, turned around and placed my backside on the edge of the unit behind me. Then I cast my eyes downwards as I tried to get my head around just why the hell he was asking me so many questions, when normally no one questioned what I did, ever.

'Who else knows?'

'No one, just me, Barbara and now, you.'

'Well, Jesus… you're fucked.'

My head snapped back up to face him as I got ready to shout down his words.

'Why?' I asked the question knowing the answer already.

'How long do you think you're going to be able to keep up the pretence when we're in Crete and your grandmother is watching you?'

'I can pretend… she's easy on the eye and easy to be around.'

'Yeah, you can. But, answer me this, if it's so easy, why the hell have you been avoiding her since the moment we started travelling?'

If only you knew I've been avoiding her for far longer than that.

'I've had work to do.' It wasn't a complete lie.

'Mmmm.' he replied. 'I won't lie to Perky.' Trip shook his head as he spoke about Kendall.

'I'm not asking you to,' I assured him.

He walked back towards the door.

'I think you need to know… She's feeling lonely and vulnerable out there by herself. If you don't act quickly to support her in your lie, she might well pull out before we even make Crete.'

'She wouldn't do that.' *Would she?* Fear unravelled itself in my gut, that I might just lose her before our year together had even begun.

I knew I hadn't been fair to her over the last week, by avoiding her and leaving her by herself.

'I'm not so sure, and can you afford to take that chance?'

'No,' I reluctantly admitted.

'Then I'll leave you with this. You might be able to lie and pretend enough to fool Nonna and that pink haired woman outside.' He tilted his head towards where we both knew Pearl was situated sleeping. 'You might be able to persuade them into believing that this is a real marriage… but how much longer are you going to be able to lie to yourself that she doesn't affect you?'

I shook my head at him in disgust and turned back to the Bourbon. As my hand grabbed around the neck of the bottle, I heard him speak again.

'You're avoiding her already; I can see it. How are you going to be able to touch her, to kiss her, when all eyes are looking at the happy couple? And how long will it be, Nic, before you're ready to admit that you might actually like Barbara? Oh, and just for the record, for this life changing moment I can hear, **Ticket To Ride** by, of course, **The Beatles**.'

Saying nothing in reply I shook my head at his questions and his song choice, and having nothing to say I closed my eyes, shutting him out until the door clicked shut behind him.

Without pouring a measure into a glass, I swigged a mouthful from the bottle and drank it down, hoping to repress the emotions inside me.

You can do this, I thought resolutely.

Having listened to what Trip had to say and then washing it down with the swig of Bourbon, I was even more determined. I slammed the bottle back down onto the unit.

Hell, I was even going to enjoy being married to the woman who had trusted me with her life for the year we had, and then at the end of our time together I would let her go.

It was simple, it was a deal after all and nothing more.

CHAPTER THIRTEEN

Barbara

ABOUT AN HOUR AFTER Trip had come back out into the main compartment, Nico finally appeared.

From my peripheral view, I looked on mesmerised as the captivatingly beautiful man shrugged himself out of his suit jacket then loosened and removed his tie. It was as if he was trying to convince himself, or maybe me, that he really could relax. My eyes widened in disbelief after he dismissed the cabin staff when they automatically began to circulate around him trying to predict his every need, and he set about making a coffee. I looked up at him in surprise when he also placed a coffee down in front of me, and he offered me a perceptive smile. Then he lowered his tall frame down in the seat beside me and took my hand in his.

Already stunned at his actions so far, I watched even more surprised as he pulled out some heavy framed, rectangular glasses from his shirt pocket and put them on. Right up until that minute I hadn't even realised he wore glasses. My hand was now being securely held on his lap and trying to ignore the warmth from his firm thigh seeping into my bare arm, I tried to relax enough to study him as he began to read the latest news headlines on his iPad.

A few minutes later, Trip offered me a nod and a quick smile at Nico's arrival. With his family still sleeping soundly, he stood up from our seating area and left to go back to the cockpit.

Nico lifted his head from his iPad to watch Trip depart and after he was safely out of ear shot, he lifted my hand up to his lips and kissed the back of it. I turned my head back towards him in surprise and as my eyes sought out his he offered up an apology.

'I'm sorry I've had to work so much in the last few days, Barbara.' His voice was deep and sounded like I imagined a soothing blanket would as it wound itself around me. I moved my shoulders suddenly to shake myself free of its pseudo comfort.

I took a quick look around the cabin and checked no one who was awake was near enough to listen to the conversation I wanted to have.

'You bailed on me. You came up with this stupid idea, got me to agree and then left me to it.'

'I did genuinely have work to do and I kept my promise and attended your therapy sessions.' His tone of voice was all business as he let me know he wasn't amused with my accusation.

I sighed loudly and rolled my eyes at him.

'I need to be honest with you, Nico... seeing as you're having so much difficulty in being honest with yourself.' His long eyelashes flickered beneath his glasses and he swallowed deeply waiting for me to restart. 'Spending all that time by myself in your house, without you in it, I quickly came to an understanding that I really don't know much about you at all, and to be frank what I do know isn't enough.'

'I'm sorry, you're right...I shouldn't have left you alone.' His tone changed again with acceptance.

'No, you shouldn't have. You came up with this idea in the first place... and yes, I know I was crazy enough to agree, but...'

He tightened his grip on my hand, like he was afraid I was going to pull it away.

'Look, Barbara... It's not much of an excuse, but I'm not used to having to think about anyone other than myself. It's going to take some time to get my head around that.'

'Well, news flash, we don't have much time left... and to make it worse you've been holed up in there,' I gesticulated towards the other compartment behind us with my empty hand, 'since we left Vegas...I've had to play the part of your girlfriend in front of your friends and Pearl while you've... I don't know, what have you been doing, working or just avoiding me?'

It was his turn to sigh and, give him his due, he began to look uncomfortable like I'd caught him out somehow.

'I don't know, I'm really not sure that this can work.' I shrugged my shoulders at him.

A genuine look of concern flooded his features and then his left eye narrowed on me, as concentrating hard he tried to read further into my mind, behind the words I'd given him. I warmed slightly knowing that I now had his complete attention. 'And now I'm sitting here with you, holding your hand... Now how do you feel?'

'Confused,' I answered truthfully, feeling a little calmer after releasing my frustrations from the last few days.

'About?' he questioned.

'You blow hot and cold, and truly I don't think you're a man I can keep up with.'

'I'm not an easy man, Barbara. But I never told you I'd be easy to be around, did I?'

'No, I know you're not and I know you didn't... but I don't think I can marry you if you're going to be like this.' My heart was pounding in my chest as I released out loud just what had been going over and over in my head for the past week.

I felt his thumb moving brusquely over the huge diamond on my finger, in what felt like anger, as he moved the contentious object from side to side. But when I allowed myself to delve further into his eyes, the only thing I could find there was perplexity.

'It's just that I see this side of you, Nico, when for a few hours you let me in past the façade you present to the world. Then you pull away because I think you're scared I've seen too much and I don't see you for days.'

'There is no façade, Barbara. Take every rumour you've ever heard about me and double it. I am the man you've heard all about. I'm heartless, arrogant, single-minded and controlling. I'm not a nice person. I have done and ordered things to be done that would turn your stomach...' He let out a loud sigh. 'What I'm trying to say is, please don't get some romantic idea in your head and think for one minute that you can see anything more inside of me. Because I can assure you, you'd be imagining something that categorically doesn't exist.'

I tried to shelve the hurt that had unfolded itself inside of me at my stupidity and hoped my face didn't give me away.

'You have remembered that this is only an arrangement between us, haven't you, Barbara?'

'Of course, I have. But you need to understand that for us to pull this off, we need to be in this together,' I countered quickly, pretending that I really couldn't care less.

'I agree, so let's have some fun doing it. I more than like you, Barbara, and I know that I'm not mistaken when I say that I know you feel the same.'

'Just what exactly are you asking me for?' My heart rate increased with either panic or excitement, I wasn't sure which.

'Nothing more than what we've already agreed… Let's enjoy each other's company and see where it goes…I know this is a strange situation between us, but at the end of it you'll be in a better place and I'll have given my grandmother what she requires from me… I know that we can carry this off with more commitment from me.'

'If I agree to carry on with this, you'll most definitely need to be more available to me, and also I want your oath that you will not see any other women while we remain engaged or married… I might, in your eyes, look like I have stupid romantic notions of you being something more than a merciless bastard, but I will not be made to look a fool in anyone else's… Do you understand me?'

A smile decorated his perfectly square jaw.

'I understand perfectly, and I expect the same commitment from you also. Now drink your coffee and get some sleep if you can. My grandmother is looking forward to meeting and spending some time with you.'

'What Nonna wants, Nonna gets?'

'Exactly,' he answered.

'Then that shows me that you're not heartless, Nico. Whatever you want to believe about yourself.'

With his hand refusing to let go of mine I started to recline my seat and, turning my head away from him, I closed my eyes and began to pray that sleep would carry me away.

I looked down at our conjoined hands, trying not to look surprised that even though we had left the plane and were walking over the tarmac to get to security, he still hadn't attempted to break our connection. Surprisingly, holding his hand felt like the most natural thing in the world and from the looks we'd been getting from our small entourage I could almost hear the "ahhhh's" going around their heads.

I hadn't slept as he'd demanded and was beginning to feel tired and emotional. I'd sat in the plane for an hour feigning sleep, all the while feeling the warmth of his hand on mine and the more I thought on our previous conversation, the more I understood he was trying to warn me not to get too close to him.

The man was truly a mass of contradictions and conflicting actions. I was struggling to keep up.

Suddenly, a man with what sounded like an Australian accent shouted over to us.

'G'day, mate.' I watched as the guy jogged the short distance between our two groups and he talked to Trip almost as if they'd met before. Franco and his men instinctively gathered closer, only to be ordered away by a quick shake of Nico's head.

'Hey.' Trip stopped and a smile spread over his face.

'It's you, isn't it? You're the pilot we met a few years ago in New York,' the charismatic looking Aussie questioned.

'Yeah, I remember. You were trying to check in your goat, what was its name?'

'Mutton… or Snowflake, it depends on who you ask.' The guy laughed at the memory.

Check in a goat? I was starting to think that I was so tired my mind was playing tricks on me.

'That's it.' Trip released a small laugh at the memory. I watched Kendall as she smiled too, like she'd heard the surreal story before.

'Well, some things don't change… This time though I'm trying to collect my wife's *pet,* any idea where I go?'

I could sense that Nico was as confused as I was, as we carried on walking towards the main building listening to the weird conversation.

'You'll need to go out to the cargo facility. I can't believe your "pet" is still travelling with you.'

'Oh, you'd better believe it, mate. My wife Aubrey could sell oil to a tycoon.' He waved at a beautiful red-haired lady who immediately waved back at him.

'Anyways, thanks for the info, I'll be seeing ya.'

We all watched as the man jogged back to his wife and placed his arm around her shoulders.

'You make some strange acquaintances, Trip.' Nico laughed as he provoked him.

Trip turned his head to look at Nico and with a deadpan expression on his face he answered, 'You don't say, Boss?'

CHAPTER FOURTEEN

Barbara

THE FEEL OF THE sand between my toes and listening to the waves as they lapped at the shore was grounding. I hadn't been this close to the sea since I'd lived in the U.K. as a young child and although that period of my life didn't have many happy memories, spending time at a beach near to where my dad was stationed was one of them.

It didn't matter whether it was cold and windy, or warm and sunny like I knew today would eventually be, I found the beach a refreshing and cathartic place to be. One of the only good memories I had of my mom, involved her spinning around and around with her arms open wide as the sea breeze rushed over her. I could hear her voice in my head, see the rapturous smile on her face and her blonde hair as it whipped up and away from her shoulders as she shouted over at Brody and I to join her. Soon we were spinning right beside her while she shouted over the top of the wind to "feel the freedom" while my dad sat on a nearby sandbank and laughed at the three of us.

The warm water lapping at my bare toes brought me out of my memory. I wiped away the solitary tear that was running down my face, but as I did so I acknowledged that although the memory had made me sad, I also had a smile stretched right across my face. The memory of the beach was one of the last truly happy times in my life.

I had a feeling deep down inside of me that from the brief glimpse I'd had so far of Crete that I was going to love it. It was an awe-inspiring place, with natural beauty to be found everywhere you looked. So far, I'd been able to hear the sea as it gently lapped against its shores or crashed against the rocks every place we'd been. Stupidly the thought had been going over in my head that I thought I could be really happy here.

Snap out of it, you're jet lagged. This is only for a year!

I took a quick look up behind me and saw the house Nico had brought us to. It was large but built very sympathetically from the two different coloured stones you could see almost everywhere on the island. The light had to be just right for you to detect his home was even there, nestled safely away in the hills. From here, and probably from various viewpoints around the land that contained his property, I was certain you wouldn't get any clues as to just what the well-designed construction concealed within it.

The infinity pool was one of the hidden gems and a swim in it was most definitely on my list of things to do later that day. The previous night, after the incredible dinner made by his grandmother, I had taken myself off and had sat down on a lounger that was bathed by the muted lighting at the pool side. Eventually, I hadn't been able to resist any longer and after having taken off my sandals, I'd plunged my aching feet and legs into the cool water. I'd sat there alone lost in my own thoughts for a while, before Nico had come out to find me. He'd smiled at me as he noted the obvious pleasure I was receiving from the tranquil space and had then sat down beside me. Sitting close together in a comfortable silence, we'd both watched as the most beautiful iridescent dragonflies swooped and flew around us. They'd danced just above the pool and dipped their legs momentarily into the cool water washing away the heat of the day, completely ignoring the fact that the two of us were even there. Watching them was truly one of the most magical things I'd ever witnessed, and I was even more pleased to be sharing the experience with him. I'd looked over at him once or twice as we'd watched together and delighted in the relaxed, fascinated expression on his face as I knew it matched my own.

Finally, they'd flown away and almost like Nico felt the need to mark sharing the experience with me, he had once again picked up my hand and pressed his lips to it. The touch of his lips on my skin was lingering, as was the feeling it left me with after he'd lowered our conjoined hands back to the tiles between us.

Watching the dragonflies and experiencing that moment with him, I resolved there and then that they would be one of the subjects I was going to concentrate my very limited photography skills on.

His home here, I had quickly found out yesterday evening as he'd shown me around, was to the exact same specifications as his home in Red Rock Canyon. Although I'd been given the master bedroom as my room here in Crete, I had easily managed to find my way around and out of the large building before the sun had even risen this morning, to come for a walk on the private beach.

I looked out to the horizon again, just in time to watch the warm colours of the sunrise as they began to light up the hills to the right-hand side of where I was stood, and I lifted my camera up to my face. I'd had enough time locked away in Nico's stone fortress in Vegas to study everything I needed to know to begin taking some amateur shots. Not being able to sleep in the large master bedroom all by myself with the smell of Nico's cologne permeating from the furniture, I'd decided that now was the ideal time to start my new hobby.

The click of the shutter as it drew in the beautiful sight that was appearing as if by magic, as this part of the world began its brand new day, ignited my blood. The fact that I knew it would hold this sight within its confines, until I was ready to expose it to the world, was an enlightening experience and it was hard to contain the childish excitement that was whipping around inside of me. To have felt dead for so long and to then be suddenly thrust into feeling everything was overwhelming, but so far it was overwhelming in a good way.

I flicked the switch to auto and heard as the camera began to relay shot after shot as the yellows spread to oranges and then eventually the warm reds grew ever bigger, consuming the paler colours. I was beginning to feel the warmth of the rays already on the bare skin of my chilled arms, which was a welcome relief. I hadn't thought it through properly in my bid to escape my confines, that this early hour of the morning would still contain the cold chill of night in its air, when back in Vegas no matter what the hour it was always warm. So, I had only just grabbed at one of the sundresses I had hung up yesterday and pulled it quickly off the hanger. All the while I had been trying hard not to acknowledge that Nico's clothing was hung up beside mine, and captured within the offending material was the strong fresh ocean scented cologne he always seemed to wear. The smell of the man had drifted up and into my nose as soon as I'd opened the door of the closet. With my dress clutched in one hand I had closed the door as quickly as I could.

Inhaling a deep breath, I cleared my thoughts and concentrated on the job in hand.

High above the warm glow of the impending sunrise the stars and the crescent moon were still visible and in the very bottom of my lens I saw them all reflected on the surface of the water. I knew it would make an amazing picture.

Stars were hardly ever noticeable above Vegas due to all the light polluting the sky, but here in this beautiful place, through the protection of my camera lens, I could see the start of the brand new day and the demise of the old. I hoped above all else that this was an omen for the way my life was going to progress from this day forward. What I was experiencing was truly miraculous and I wanted to do it justice by taking a decent picture.

'Good morning.' I ever so slightly started as Nico's deep, warming voice entered my bloodstream and caused an involuntary shiver to travel down my back. I was only wearing the pale blue sundress and had put my hair up into a ponytail in preparation for what I knew would be another beautifully warm day. But I instantly recognised that my choice of dress wasn't nearly enough to protect me from the sensation of having him so close to me.

'Morning,' I answered, but didn't stop the automatic function on the camera. Instead, I gratefully held it in place in front of my face, as a form of protection from the man who was stood directly behind me, so close I could feel his every exhale on the back of my exposed neck.

'It's beautiful here at this time of day.' Nico placed his hands on the top of both of my arms and began to slowly and gently rub at the bare skin in an attempt to warm me.

'It truly is, breathtaking almost.' My voice left me on a whisper and the only sound to be heard now, apart from the sea and the camera as it kept on taking picture after picture, was my own pulse as it pounded against my eardrums.

'Couldn't you sleep?' he questioned.

'No.'

As the sun finally exposed the whole of its warm globe over the hills beside us, I reluctantly flicked the auto button off and lowered the camera from my face.

'Me neither… I went down to make some coffee and saw your wrap on the chair by the door. I figured you'd taken a walk and well, the only walk that's near enough is down to the beach.'

'So, you found me.'

'Uh huh.' The vibration in his voice rippled through me.

'Thank you for bringing me here, Nico. I've only been here a few hours, but I feel at home and at peace already.'

'Thank you for agreeing to share this with me, I'm happy you're here and so is my grandmother. I could see by the look on her face last night that you surprised her in every sense of the word.'

'I did?'

'Yes… and in a good way. I think, like Trip, she expected me to marry some Botox-filled, silicon-breasted celebrity wannabe.' He laughed at his own words and his laughter helped to warm me.

The inclination to turn around in his arms as his hands continued to gently rub my skin was growing ever stronger. So, for once, I let my instinct control me. I released the camera from my hands and let it fall gently until its weight was on the strap around my neck and turned around in his hold.

I allowed my eyes to run over him. The man holding on to me seemed different to any other version I'd seen of him before. He was casually dressed, and after forgoing what I guessed was probably his morning ritual of a shave, he was sporting a thick growth of stubble. His hair wasn't being held perfectly and he was wearing a short-sleeved linen shirt which was completely unbuttoned, over the top of some smart looking Chino shorts.

'You look different somehow?'

'I am.'

I smiled up at him, knowing my face was presenting a puzzled expression.

'Why?'

'I took in everything you said yesterday and as I'm getting married tomorrow, I thought a more relaxed looking husband-to-be would be more convincing to the natives.'

'You're talking about Nonna?'

'Yes, I am… but I'm also talking about Pearl and to be honest, Bee, I thought that this version of me might be easier for you to live with.' I'd heard every word he said, but the one I was hung up on the most was the fact that for the first time he'd called me by my nickname.

'You called me Bee.'

'I did, is that okay? I want us to be friends.'

'It's fine by me… I'd like to be your friend too, Nico.'

And so very much more. I closed my eyes to erase the thought in my head.

The man that was stood on the beach with me in the glow of sunrise was like every woman's wet dream. The more time I spent with him, the more convoluted he was becoming in my eyes. Nico was so multi-faceted that I was left reeling as once again his persona changed. This, I was convinced, was the version I liked best at the moment. Sure, the suited, brash, arrogant asshole had his time and place, and he was so very easy on the eyes. But this version, the one he'd been showing me since the second he had taken my hand in the plane yesterday, was so far unsurpassed in my eyes. Right now, he was attentive, romantic and gentle and I wanted the absolute entirety of the man.

His eyes refocussed on my face and his hands stopped their gentle massage on the tops of my arms as his gaze moved down to my lips. The palpable tension that had been slowly building between us since the moment he'd said good morning ramped up ever quicker. My tongue flicked out swiftly over my suddenly very dry lips and the involuntary action from me had him releasing a groan. I watched, unable to tear my eyes away from him, as he fought within himself and his long eyelashes flicked as he slow blinked trying to clear me from his view.

'You know the longer we stand here, the more I want to kiss you?' His voice sounded the deepest I'd ever heard it.

His left arm lifted away from my arm and his thumb brushed gently over my lips as if he needed to feel them before he tasted them.

'Then…'

'Shhhh…' One of his fingers came down gently over the top of my lips. 'But how would you like me to kiss you, Bee?… Soft and gentle like our meeting here on the beach at sunrise dictates?'

He stopped speaking and I watched as in slow motion his head dipped down towards mine. I watched until the very last minute, when my eyelids closed heavily like I was drugged and the whole of my body prepared itself to receive his kiss. It was as if my body was systematically closing down all of my other senses as it prepared itself to focus on the feeling of the touch of his flesh on mine. I could feel his breath, his fresh smelling cologne as it entered my nostrils, and my feet began to feel unsteady beneath me. As if he could sense all of this, his hold on my one arm increased.

But no matter how on edge my body was, no matter how geared up I was to receive the touch of his flesh on mine, it never came.

Slowly, my body awoke from the trance he had momentarily subdued me into, and my heavy eyes burst open.

'What are you doing?'

'Research,' he answered as his left eye narrowed on me and I felt every syllable leave his mouth as it caressed the sensitive skin of my lips. 'I think, Bee, that you would prefer that I kissed you another way.'

Nico's left hand moved quickly. He placed it behind me and after putting it around my waist he pulled me quickly into him, making my feet rise up until my only connection with the sand was my toes. As our bodies collided all of the air in my lungs expelled in shock. My eyes found his and I saw a new sort of want captured behind his dark eyes. The camera was the only thing that separated us, trapped between our two bodies. His erection pushing into my stomach caught my attention first and then the movement of his right hand as he slowly and sensually brushed it down the length of my neck.

'You really are a beautiful woman.' His words set off a riot of fireflies in my stomach.

My neck reacted to his touch, wherever his fingers touched me a trail of goose bumps were left behind in their wake. When his large hand spread over the front of my throat and the whole of his grip tightened as his hand held me in place, I initially felt panic rising up inside of me. But when I looked into his eyes, I saw nothing in them to make me afraid; all that shone back was reverence.

'I can see that you'd prefer me to kiss you like this. I already know you well enough, Bee, to know that although you think you prefer the gentle side of me, this is the one that excites you more.'

'I...' I was about to protest what he'd just said, but it was too late.

With his arm behind my waist and his hand holding my bare neck as he pushed my head backwards slightly, Nico's mouth crashed down onto mine. As our mouths connected, my first instinct was to gasp. The moment my lips parted; Nico's tongue swept in. It teased and caressed every single part of me as we began our dance. I surprised myself as my need for the man took over and I met him back with equal passion. Our teeth clashed together with the sudden and urgent need that took over us both and my hands that had been hanging limp by my sides lifted to hold the sides of his head. I placed one hand either side of his face and hung on for dear life as he kissed me to just within the edge of all reason and all coherent thoughts left my head. His tongue swept over every single nerve ending that had seemingly collected together inside the small space and he teased them over and over again.

'Nico…' The sound of Nico's grandmother's shout drifting out on the breeze broke through the early morning. Having spotted us down on the beach her tone changed. 'Nico, Barbara… Breakfast is on the table.'

Then just as quickly as it had started, it was over. Nico's hold on my waist began to relax as soon as his grandmother's voice travelled down to us. My feet were slowly placed back down to the ground, his grip on my neck released and he trailed his fingertips slowly down my neck until finally his hand left my skin. My body screamed in protest as his hold over me relaxed until we were two separate beings once again.

'Well, now we've been caught at our playacting. Isn't this getting interesting,' he stated with a smile on his face.

Nico turned away from me suddenly, and immediately I felt the pain of rejection as it seeped into me. With my feet still frozen in the position he'd left me, I was too terrified to follow in case everything I was now feeling was true. He must have taken three steps towards the start of the manmade walkway that led up to his home when he realised that I wasn't right there beside him. He turned his head and offering me an almost shy smile he lifted up his hand.

'Bee.'

Without any hesitation whatsoever, I took a couple of steps towards him and reaching out with my arm, I shelved my unwanted fears and placed my hand in his.

CHAPTER FIFTEEN

Bee

'STEP BACK AWAY FROM the mirror a little, you'll be able to see all of the dress to its full effect,' Kendall instructed and like clockwork I did her bidding.

She was right, just two steps back and I could see all of my off-white gown.

'Are you pleased, Bee?' Pearl questioned me.

'I'm, well I'm…'

'She's speechless,' Kendall offered.

'I am. I honestly couldn't be happier with the way the dress, my shoes…' I turned myself to the side to take in as much as I could about my hair. 'And my hair is spectacular, I've never seen anything like it before. It's a work of art.'

In the background I heard Nico's grandmother speak in Greek to the hairdresser she had called in for the day.

'Please tell Maria how pleased I am with what she's done.' I smiled over to her and Nonna nodded at me and began talking again.

My dress which I'd chosen back in Vegas with Pearl and Raul, was absolute perfection. The gown was sleeveless, with a sheer chiffon top and a sweetheart shaped boned bodice underneath, a cinched waist and a voluminous tulle skirt that reached the middle of my calves. The skirt swished around my bare legs every time I moved in front of the mirror and the hand placed pearl beads that covered the entirety of the gown caught the light as I moved. The icing on the cake was my hair and I could not believe just what Maria the magician of a hairdresser had created. My thick hair which normally met the top of my backside, had been coiled into flowers that looked like roses and were held in place with pins that had pearl heads to match my dress. Although my hair was still loose, it now only came down to just below my shoulder blades. My make-up had been done by Kendall. It was very natural and complemented my skin which glowed with a sun kissed effect, even after only a few days by the beach. My lips looked plump and shaped by the lip gloss she had added, which was as near to my natural colour as she could find, and my eyes popped with the pearlized eyeshadow she'd chosen to go with my dress.

'Thank you, ladies. I truly couldn't be happier with how I look.' I watched my reflection as my eyes grew glassy and they filled up with tears. So, it had appeared that in creating a pretend wedding, I had stupidly chosen everything I would have ever wanted for my real one.

You stupid girl. I shook my head a little in the mirror and hoped that the movement would catch no one else's eyes.

Looking deep inside myself, I nodded with relief as an understanding washed over me.

That's it. Of course.

I hadn't done it deliberately and the thought was reassuring.

I wasn't imagining that this wedding was real, instead I realised that no one would ever go wedding dress shopping with the thought that they'd have this dress and shoes for now, and that next time for their "proper" wedding they'd choose the ones they really wanted, would they?

'Now, these are from Nico.' I was handed a bouquet of blue and cream roses with lots of green foliage. 'He told me about your extraordinarily coloured eyes, with their blue and green and told me to try to reflect them in your bouquet. And lastly, if you'll permit me, I have a gift to you from Nico's mamma.' I heard Nonna's heels click over the wooden floor to the bed behind me and I began to twist my head around to follow the sound.

I felt my eyes widen in panic at what on earth it could be.

'Turn and face the mirror a moment please, Barbara.'

I did as I was told and watched in the mirror as she placed a dainty, rose gold cross and chain around my neck. I lifted my hand on instinct and gently touched my pearlized manicured fingertips, courtesy of Kendall, to the four-way cross.

'Thank you.' I spoke to her and caught her eyes with my own in the mirror.

'And now she's here with us and that makes me very happy.'

'This is from me, Bee. I wore it when Trip and I got married in Australia.' I looked to the side of me to see Kendall twirling a white garter around her finger.

'So, lift up your dress and I'll put it up on your thigh for Nico to find later.'

Laughter filled the room as Kendall bent down in her long, sage green bridesmaid dress that surprisingly I would have chosen had I had any input in it at all, but once again Nonna had come up trumps.

'Something borrowed, tick.' Kendall stood up and spoke at the same time.

'Something blue are the roses in my bouquet,' I replied.

'Something new is your dress,' added Pearl.

'Something old.' I touched my fingers once again to Nico's mamma's necklace.

'Something new isn't your dress, but it's also from Nico,' Nonna interrupted.

'It is?' I questioned in disbelief.

'Yes, he said to tell you that it will remind you of your first night together here on Crete.' A few soft "ahhhh's" left the mouths of the others in the room.

I watched enthralled as she opened up her hand. In the middle of her palm was a small blue opal, dragonfly pin.

Tentatively I reached out my hand and took it from her, lifting it up to my face to take a better look. The pin was small, but beautifully made. The choice of opal had to be deliberate, the stone had the same iridescent quality that the real dragonflies we had watched dancing together had.

'Nico had this made for me?' I whispered into the quiet room.

'Yes, by one of the local jewellers. He visited them *personally* yesterday and it was delivered early this morning… He checked it earlier, making sure it was exactly as he had ordered. He wanted it to be just right for you.' I heard her overly pronounce the personally and I knew exactly why. I was just as stunned as she was, Nico had many minions who would jump at his every word. So, for him to take the time to do something like this was unquestionably out of the ordinary.

'That's so romantic, Bee,' Kendall gasped next to me, 'where do you want to put it?'

'Isn't it though?' Nonna added, and as I looked at the flush on her cheeks and her smile of happiness it dawned on me exactly why Nico had personally had it made.

What Nonna wants, Nonna gets. She wanted him happily married and he was "playacting" a very convincing part in the whole very elaborate charade.

'Anywhere,' I answered Kendall, in a tone that said everything I was suddenly feeling.

I saw her head snap around as she looked at me in surprise.

I bet she thinks I'm a right bitch.

'What I meant to say was,' I offered her a smile and tried to recover the situation, 'anywhere under my skirts… I think it would be better pinned inside the dress as we don't want to clash with Nico's mamma's cross and chain, do we?'

Appearing appeased, Kendall took the pin from my hand and bent down once again in front of me, I heard the tulle of the skirt sound as she flicked it up a little and pinned my new gift inside one of the layers.

'I think you should put the cross inside your dress, wear it close to your heart, so she can feel your heartbeat when you marry her son.' Nonna stepped around me on the opposite side to Kendall and lifting the chain with her fingertips she managed to drop it beneath the round neck of my dress. 'Now, Pearl do you have the things I gave you earlier?' she questioned.

'Yes… hold on.' I turned my head to the side to watch Pearl retrieve whatever it was she was looking for, just as Kendall began to stand up and flicked down my skirt as she righted herself.

'I hope you'll accept these from me, Bee.' I looked up from Pearl's closed hand to her face. She was almost unrecognisable, wearing a smart cream suit, with the roots of her pink hair also having been recently done and some subtle make-up on her face.

'These are a few of the things that according to Greek tradition,' Pearl slightly nodded at Nonna, who I knew was once again stood behind me, 'are to be given by the bride's family to the bride on her wedding day and as we are as close as family, I hope you don't mind them coming from me?' I watched her dab at her eyes with the lace handkerchief she was holding in her other hand.

I could feel pressure building up behind the back of my eyes and not being able to speak momentarily at her emotion and my own, I shook my head at her and offered her a small smile. She stepped forward and I watched her tie a sugar cube into the inside of my bouquet.

'This sugar is given in the hope that you and Nico will have a sweet life together. This small piece of iron is given to ward off all evil spirits from entering your marriage.'

My eyes rested on her fingers as she deftly placed and tied the rust coloured iron once again inside my bouquet.

Evil spirits are one thing, but mafia is entirely different. I managed to stop myself from blowing air out forcibly through my closed lips at my thoughts.

Looking back up at the mirror I cast my eyes over myself fleetingly, unable to hold my own gaze for any length of time as the feeling of confusion hung heavily over me. Then I took in each of the three women stood in the large room with me. I had known only Pearl for any length of time and understood the love and commitment she had to making sure my wedding day was truly happy. But, Nonna, as I'd been instructed to call her from the moment we had met a few days ago and Kendall, as the wife of Nico's best friend, were as equally committed into making this a day we would both remember. The two women loved him, so surely that meant that he couldn't be all bad, could he?

I smiled at them all in turn, trying to wordlessly show them my thanks and gratitude. Then after watching Kendall check the time for the umpteenth time, I turned away from the mirror to face the door and my impending future.

'Okay, it's time to go… the chapel is only a short five-minute walk up the hill, but we're already late and we don't want to keep your husband-to-be waiting any longer than necessary, do we?' Kendall assertively put out into the room and made her way to the door.

I laughed nervously out loud in response and put my fingers to my lips to silence it.

'Can you both give us a couple of minutes please?' Nonna asked, looking between Kendall and Pearl.

'Sure,' Pearl answered and placing a hand on Kendall's arm they walked out of the door talking in excitement.

Please don't say I've cocked it up.

After hearing their shoes click down the wooden staircase, I turned back to face Nonna and prepared myself.

'I never thought this day would come, Barbara. You look so beautiful,' she started and then when she took another breath, I knew that there was more to come.

'Thank you,' I replied, having really hoped that was the end of her speech.

She was a petite lady, but inside her was a strength and force that would take some reckoning with. Everything about her was borne from her desire to provide for and protect her family. It was very evident that she'd had to fight for her family before and she wouldn't hesitate to do so again. Now that family only consisted of Nico and his brother Cade, they were all that mattered in her world. I had grown to admire her over the past few days and honestly believed that I could easily like her very much, I just hoped she felt the same about me.

'I don't know if Nico has already told you, but I was married to his grandfather, his namesake, for many years and after an unsteady first few months, they were genuinely the happiest of my life.'

I nodded at her nervously, unsure of what was coming next.

'But as the wife of one Morello to the soon-to-be wife of another, I feel I need to offer you some advice…'

Nonna stretched out her arm and touched her hand to my forearm as she continued.

'Barbara, I was once in your shoes, and I married to escape a life I wasn't happy with.'

'I...' I began to protest but was truly grateful when she lifted her hand to stop me before the lie fell out.

'They're not easy men to be married to, but when they love you, you become the centre of their entire world, the axis point from which they pivot... I can see that you are not in love with Nico, just as I wasn't with his grandfather when I married him.'

I took in a quick breath trying to stop the panic that had entered my body and to calm down the now very erratic beat of my heart as it stopped, stuttered and accelerated waiting for her next words.

'But that doesn't matter, because you see love can grow. The best and longest lasting marriages start as a seed of friendship. Then a kind word, some shared laughter, a thoughtful gesture and a loving touch are freely given and all of these things will enable that seed to shoot and flourish. In the past few days, I have seen Nico wholeheartedly give you all of those things and you have reciprocated. These gestures you are offering each other are all the things needed to make the seed of friendship you have, grow into a deep, long lasting love between you both. There will be ups and downs over your years together, of which I wish you many. But when you both accept and nurture these, a solid, loving foundation will be created. It becomes so strong and so much a part of you, that you will struggle to remember anything that came before it... So, Barbara, I just want to ask one thing of you.'

'Anything,' I replied, stunned with the woman's perceptiveness, acceptance and understanding.

'Often the men who are the hardest to love, need love the most.'

I let her words wash over me. I knew what she was asking. She wanted my promise that I'd try. That when things got difficult I'd try harder to love her brash boss of a grandson. She felt he was worth it, like her husband had been. But mainly she was checking my commitment to my impending marriage.

'I'll try,' I whispered back.

'Then you both have my blessing and my love, Bee.'

CHAPTER SIXTEEN

Nico

'THAT'S IT… I'VE HAD enough of watching you pace up and down and if you twist your arm around one more time to check that expensive bit of kit on your wrist, I'm telling you now that I'm likely to commit hara-kiri over there in the corner.'

Trip's voice brought me out of my thoughts. I stopped walking immediately and clocked him still attempting to sit comfortably on a chair I'd bought especially for the hallway and pointing to the corner by the door. It wasn't a chair that I'd ever thought anyone would try to sit on, as it was a designer piece more than a functional piece of furniture. If I hadn't been so wrapped up in my head, it would have been laughable to watch him. For the past twenty minutes or so as I'd paced, I'd seen him in my peripheral view twisting his tall frame into various shapes as he'd tried in vain to get comfortable while offering me the quiet companionship he obviously thought I needed.

The truth was I hadn't a clue what I needed.

I never thought I'd be in the position I found myself in today. I had made a vow as my mamma lay dead in my arms that I would never get married and although I knew that this was a marriage of convenience for us both, over the past few days I'd grown to like Bee more and more. She brought something into my life that as yet I couldn't decipher, it wasn't something I'd ever felt before and it had my perfectly ordered head in turmoil.

She had brought her life and soul into my very subjective and disreputable existence and I couldn't work out as yet if that was a good or bad thing. But it was unexpected, and I didn't do unexpected in my perfectly ordered world.

'Brucey, come on we're off,' Trip shouted out.

Bruce skidded into the highly polished, wooden hallway wearing navy blue smart pants and a white shirt that matched his dad's. Without saying another word to me Trip teasingly messed up his son's hair, then opened the large front door, bowing jokingly to me as he ushered me and Bruce outside. I took one last look up the stairs to where I knew Bee was getting ready and with an extra determination in my steps, I picked up my waistcoat, hooked my finger inside it and hoisted it over my shoulder.

The moment I stepped outside, I fleetingly closed my eyes and lifted my head to look up to the clear blue sky. The sun's rays embraced my face, like they had done for the millions of people who had come before me and I used that thought to ground me. Taking the few minutes I needed I inhaled deeply.

Just breathe.

In doing so, I effectively managed to shelve the unwelcome nerves and all the thoughts I'd been contemplating over, since I'd woken up in the early hours.

'You'll be needing these, Boss.' I shaded my eyes with my hand and looked down at what he was trying to give me. With a smile I took the very aptly named Aviators from his fingertips, put them on quickly, thankful for the shade and the very welcome facade they offered.

'Thanks... Once a pilot...'

'Yeah, always a pilot,' he added and laughed, 'and well it's the least I can do, best man duties and all that.' He grinned back at me after placing a matching pair over his own eyes and a child sized pair on Bruce.

We began the walk up the hill from my home to the nearest village, probably looking like we'd walked off the set of The Blues Brothers. Although we walked slowly and stopped occasionally to speak to a local who wanted to offer their congratulations and to shake my hand, we still arrived at the church far too early. I decided to take advantage of the free time to have a good look around while Trip played with Bruce in the small, paved area outside.

The church had been built when Crete was part of the Byzantine empire and loving history as I did, it was a great place to try to waste time before I had to take my place in front of the alter. It was an amazing structure and I made a mental note to bring Bee back up here on another day so she could photograph it. I could already picture the happiness on her face as she spent the time trying to capture the way the sun hit the building with her new camera.

What the hell?

I pushed my Aviators back up to the bridge of my nose hoping the action would dislodge the strange compulsions in my head and looked up. I ran my eyes over the church's terracotta roof tiles that protected the one storey building and then down to its thick, sand coloured walls on the outside and the sign that advertised the World Heritage protected frescos on the inside.

Finally, having nothing else to look at outside, I took off my sunglasses and made my way in. In a bid to offer some protection to the fading colours on the plaster, the small chapel that would only seat ten on a good day was lit by candles the way it had been for the many centuries before. I knew Trip had already gone inside and looking around quickly as my eyes slowly adjusted to the dim light, I saw that he had sat down in position with Bruce alongside him. I nodded at him when he caught my eye to check I was okay. Then I began to walk around trying to focus on the pictures that had been painted hundreds of years ago on the now damaged walls, hoping my interest in them would help me not to overthink what I was just about to do.

I could rarely remember feeling more uncomfortable in my own skin and the occasions that sprung to mind, all had a bad memory attached to them.

Let it go. You're in control of this one.

But was I?

I knew that this hurriedly thought up arrangement had the potential of going ass up. I wondered, and not for the first time since I'd kissed her back at the IHOP, if I'd thought all of this out as thoroughly as I did everything else in my life. I knew the answer, so refused to reply to my own thoughts.

I put one finger inside the collar of my fitted white shirt and moved it around in front of my throat. I tried without much success to create a pseudo feeling of release instead of the constricted feeling the tailormade shirt was giving me. Even though the inside of the church was cool compared to the outside temperature, I was thankful that I'd decided to skip the jacket to the light grey, three-piece suit I'd bought especially for the wedding ceremony. I now understood that it would have only added to the feeling of restriction that was beginning to grow inside of me.

'Sit down… here have a drink' As he spoke Trip smacked one of his hands down on the empty wooden chair next to him and the sound reverberated around the quiet space. I looked over at him as he shook a bottle of water at me trying to tempt me.

'What, are you the boss of me now?' I asked half annoyed and half entertained that he could see right through me and crossed my arms over my chest in defence. I knew I was being an asshat, but I seriously couldn't have cared any less than I did right in that moment. I was way, way out of my comfort zone and I was determined I was going to drag his ass right down there with me.

'Calm yourself… as I've said before, it's my best man duties that's all.' His grin showed me just how much he was loving how uncomfortable I was beginning to feel. 'I can see your mouth is drying up and we need to be able to hear your dulcet tones as you say your vows, don't we?'

'I'm fine.' I said the words, but I hadn't even managed to convince myself they were true. I hadn't felt this ill at ease in a long time.

I wasn't sure what I was most uncomfortable with, the fact that I was ill at ease or that I was actually feeling.

The laughter that left Trip and Bruce after Trip nudged him and pointed his finger at me so his son could join in, amused me enough to half-heartedly join in with them.

'Nic, I've never seen you look more agitated.'

'I'm… well, I've never been married before. I'm not sure what I am.' I sat down as instructed, making sure I pulled my trouser legs up a bit so they wouldn't knee and resisted the temptation to run my hands through my perfectly held in place hair. Instead I took the bottle he had previously offered and after ripping off the top, I glugged down some of the cool, reviving liquid.

'You'll be fine once you see her… at least that's how I felt when I saw Kendall walking towards me… Although, I know this is different.' He said the last part slightly quieter.

'Yes, it's certainly different,' I replied, staring down at the worn floor that had seen thousands upon thousands of people as they had celebrated their new beginnings and I wondered if they'd all felt like I did now.

The clatter of heels on the flagstone floor behind me let me know it was nearly time. I passed the bottle back to Trip and stood up while I waited for Bee to enter.

The feeling of Kendall's hand on my shoulder made me turn my head towards where she had taken her place behind us.

'My…my, you three boys scrub up nicely, I might just have to marry one of you,' she teased.

'That'll be me, Perky. Don't you get any other ideas.' Trip grinned at her as he picked up the hand she'd placed on my shoulder and kissed it.

'This might just be your lucky day, Mr. Clynes,' she answered and as always when his parents flirted in front of him Bruce giggled at the two of them. 'And this is most definitely your lucky day, Nico. I can't wait for you to see her… She will take your breath away.'

'Thanks.' I smiled over my shoulder at the words she'd just bestowed on me and understood, as I swallowed deeply, that it wouldn't be the first time Bee had caused that reaction from me.

Watching her totally spellbound as she gazed at the dragonflies while they danced on top of the pool the other night and then again when I'd kissed her the other morning on the beach at sunrise.

Yeah, I totally knew the woman could take my breath away and truthfully it scared the fuck out of me.

Movement to the side of me caught my eye as Pearl took her place, then as my grandmother took the place next to her, I smiled my thanks over to her. Traditionally she should have been sat behind me, but not wanting Bee to feel like she only had Pearl, she had informed us that she would be sitting on her side of the church. I watched as she reciprocated my smile, then blew me a kiss and just on cue turned her gaze back to the front.

Trip elbowing me hard in my ribs as he wordlessly instructed me that Bee had arrived, made me turn to look back behind me at the stone archway. The moment she walked through the door and into the tiny church my breath was snatched away from me, just as I'd been warned it would. Nothing I could have rehearsed would have prepared me for the sight that met my eyes.

Stood by herself was the most beautiful woman I had ever had the unequivocal pleasure of laying my eyes on. Given the life I'd led up to a few weeks ago when she'd landed back into my life, I knew I'd looked at far more than my fair share. With the sunlight behind her, shining on her blonde hair, she reminded me of an angel in one of the many frescos I'd been studying so closely, while I'd waited for her to arrive. Her eyes were downcast as she looked into the flowers that she clutched tightly with both of her hands and for a split second I had to resist the urge to go to her. Instead I waited, with a fear that felt like a dagger twisting in my heart that we'd got this far and now she was about to change her mind and run.

Feeling like a fish out of water I shifted my stance and my shoes, which I'd had polished to within an inch of their lives, scuffed the stone floor. The sound travelled around the silent church and appeared to break her from her thoughts.

The moment she lifted her head and our eyes met, I knew that my life as I knew it so far, was well and truly over. I heard myself clear my throat out of habit and then sensed as the emotion that had been trapped inside of me dissipated.

Standing in that small place which was dedicated to a God my family believed in, I swore right then and there to him or her, to do better, to be better, in the hope he or she would allow me to have the one thing I hadn't even realised I truly wanted or needed.

Barbara Daniels.

The very beautiful Bee.

I offered her a smile and as if she had been waiting for some sort of acknowledgement from me, she started her slow procession down the aisle. Her slow walk gave me all the time I needed to take her in. Her dress was perfect, it was simple and understated which showed off her natural beauty. I knew her choice would have pleased my grandmother, but as it fitted her to absolute perfection and showed off her figure it also ticked all of my boxes. The bouquet my grandmother had picked from my exact instructions made her eyes pop even in the dim candlelight.

On instinct, and without giving it a second thought, I held out my hand to her as she took the final few steps to stand next to me. Without any hesitation she placed her hand in mine and I was sure that I was the happiest I'd ever been.

I led her towards me and lifted her hand up in mine to place a gentle kiss onto it. Still smiling at each other and giving a great rendition of a couple of lovesick fools we turned to face the priest.

Slowly, we walked out from behind the heavy oak door of the Greek Orthodox Church, to be greeted by clapping and the flurries of petals that were being thrown into the air by the local villagers. Looking at Bee stood next to me, absorbing the congratulations and excitement from the strangers outside of their local church, made me glad that I'd made it a priority to help the local people as soon as I'd made up my mind I wanted to live here.

She looked happy and I was pleased I'd played a small part in that.

In truth, I'd done what I knew worked, I'd greased the wheels in the local area the only way I knew how, with money. Not only did it make my planning application more straightforward for the house I wanted to build, but it had also meant that we'd been accepted into the local community when we'd helped to rejuvenate their local clinic.

For a few minutes, the air around us was full of the smell of the wildflowers they were throwing over us. Holding onto her hand and placing my arm behind myself I kept us still, just on the outside of the open-sided, oak beamed porchway. It was polite to wait to accept their congratulations and although it was now late in the afternoon the strength behind the sun's rays was still almost as blinding as it had been on our walk up here earlier. I knew our eyes would need time to adjust from the candlelit church we'd just come out of. But the overwhelming thought running through me, was to prolong the feeling of happiness that being stood there, holding Bee's hand and knowing that we'd just been married, gave me.

Again, what the hell?

As I waited for my pupils to become adjusted to the sudden bright light, I once again became aware of her small hand that I'd clasped tightly in mine. She turned her head to look up at me, unsure of just what was coming next.

'Time to go home, Mrs. Morello.'

The smile that lit up her face, I knew I'd remember for the rest of my life. The sense of panic that quickly followed, bolting through my body at the words I'd just used, I knew I'd remember even longer.

CHAPTER SEVENTEEN

Bee

'TIME TO GO HOME, Mrs. Morello.'

His words and the tone of voice he said them in thrilled me.

I looked up from staring at the gold wedding band he had gently pushed onto my finger to see a smile spreading over his devastatingly handsome face. I knew without a doubt my wedding band had cost far less than the diamond I had pushed onto the same finger a couple of weeks ago, but it meant so very much more. Although I knew that this whole scenario was a charade, I couldn't help the lump that formed in my throat with the constrained emotion inside of me and the happy skip of my heart.

All I could do was to smile back, and I knew without a doubt my guard had completely evaporated before his all-seeing eyes. I was happy, joyful and excited about our future together and it was completely wrong for the occasion.

For a split second his smile dropped and terror seemed to fill his dark eyes. Recognising he'd somehow slipped up in his own eyes, it was quickly replaced by a well-rehearsed smile he would probably bestow to the people he sat round a table with in a business meeting.

Trip's voice sounding, as he started to sing a line from what I knew from Kendall's explanation on the flight over had to be a **Beatles** song, came from close behind us. Totally out of the blue I heard, **'I wanna hold your hand.'**

Nico twisted his head to look over his shoulder and narrowed his eyes on Trip almost in warning and then burst out laughing.

Thanks to Trip, the tense, horrible moment between us was broken.

We walked back down the hill to Nico's home, occasionally stopping to have celebratory words spoken to us, and to have Nico's hand clasped and shaken over exuberantly as the older villagers offered their sincere congratulations on our marriage. Two of them had even pinned money onto my dress despite Nico explaining it wasn't necessary. But, after a gentle shake of Nonna's head in reprimand, we'd understood that we had to allow it to happen so as not to offend anyone. The walk in the sunshine, that should have taken ten minutes at the most, stretched to just under an hour, and although I knew our marriage was an arrangement, the longer he held my hand and gently guided me forward, occasionally holding my elbow to offer me support on the unmade road, the more it felt very real.

In truth, I had a rush of last-minute nerves as I'd entered the chapel. We were about to say vows in front of God and although I wasn't deeply religious, I also wasn't the sort of person who could make promises in such a holy place without feeling them deeply. But I remembered Nonna's words about how love could grow from a seed of friendship and when Nico had smiled and then lifted his hand to receive me, my feet travelled on impulse towards him. Apart from when he placed my gold wedding band on my finger his hand hadn't left mine and when we'd shared our first kiss together as man and wife, the touch of his lips on mine had drowned out everything and anyone else in the small chapel with us.

His kiss had felt like he was accepting me body and soul. With that gentle, chaste kiss of ownership my body had sprung awake feeling more receptive and positive than I could ever remember. When he called me Mrs. Morello in front of the small wedding party, I knew then and there that it was something I wanted to hear fall from his lips for much longer than just the year I knew he was allowing us.

I thought over the words of wisdom his grandmother had imparted to me before the wedding and wondered if I could make this small seed between us grow.

If I wrote down everything about us on paper, I was sure we wouldn't be compatible. Nico came from the sort of lifestyle you heard about in the media, watched in films and read about in historical literature. Whereas I came from what would be labelled as a regular Joe's way of life. We had been a young military family that had been posted abroad. Although that was where our regular life had ended. My brother and I had grown up quickly as we fought to survive our mom's neglect. We had been a family that was eventually driven apart by my mom's homesickness, subsequent addiction to painkillers and my dad's refusal to acknowledge that she needed help. I also knew what Nico was, where he came from and what families like his did to retain their success and standing. I understood that he had most definitely ordered things to be done that would terrify and sicken me. He himself had probably done things that I would find abhorrent, I mean the man himself had warned me against him and to not romanticise who he was.

I wasn't stupid. Sure, I had made some very poor decisions in my life, but no one could accuse me of being naive.

But, so far, all he had shown me was kindness. He appeared to think of others before himself. He truly was a mass of contradictions. A puzzle that I desperately wanted to learn the complexities of.

I knew I had to face facts. I knew what we were.

We were an arrangement born out of convenience.

But every single time he held my hand he made me feel like we were destined to be so much more. I wanted to be more than just a year in his life. I wanted to be more than the person he used to placate his beloved grandmother.

I watched our feet walk side by side over the uneven Crete road and recognised that I wanted to walk by his side always.

I wanted to be his forever.

For once my head and heart were in complete agreement, but having just started therapy for another addiction, I knew I needed to take a complete step back. I had to be sure I wasn't enabling the addictive personality my new therapist had diagnosed me with, by swapping one addiction with another.

'On behalf of my wife and I.' Nico looked down at me and tipped the top of his Champagne flute towards me as he spoke. The completely straight line of his mouth that he normally directed to the world changed when the corners lifted a little with the beginnings of a smile as I wholeheartedly smiled back up at him.

The twenty or so people who had been invited by Nonna, for a dinner on Nico's pergola and grapevine covered patio to celebrate our marriage, murmured and softly clapped.

'Well, my wife and I would like to thank you for coming to celebrate our wedding day with us.' He waited until the small gathering became silent again before he carried on. 'Bee and I want to especially thank my grandmother for arranging everything for us, for allowing us to have this day.'

Well ain't that just the truth.

I blinked away my thoughts and like everyone else who seemed to hold the matriarch in high esteem, I raised my glass to her.

'But I especially want to thank Bee, for marrying me. As I'm sure you will all agree she looks exquisite… alla mia bellissima moglie.'

Again, murmurs of agreement went around the small crowd and although I only knew a few of the faces I found looking at us, I smiled my thanks out to them all.

'You look beautiful, Bee... far too good for the likes of him,' Trip shouted out and laughter consumed our small audience.

Everyone knew Trip was joking, all apart from it seemed the man stood beside me. Nico shot him a look with his eyebrow rising so high it nearly touched his hairline and then he continued.

'Many thanks to my best man for his addition to my speech... I know I'm not an easy man to be with. You have to understand that I know she's far too good for the likes of me... So, I also want to thank Bee for bringing some light into the darkness I've been living in for years and to acknowledge her joy of life that she has so readily bestowed on me. It's been awe inspiring and appreciated in what has been a very discontented existence.'

For someone who I knew was only playacting, his choice of words were so heartfelt, and for a man who normally held all of his cards to his chest, so very painful. Agonising almost to the point that I could once again feel tears pricking at the back of my eyes.

The crowd in front of us seemed to still.

Suddenly feeling uncomfortable for my new husband, I went with my instinct and stood up quickly beside him. Nico's head dropped momentarily as he looked down at the floor. I knew he would recover quickly, because I knew what sort of man he was. I just needed to buy him a few minutes grace. As I'd hoped, all eyes now moved to me. I was as stunned into silence as our guests appeared to be, so I raised my glass up high.

'To my new husband,' I offered and smiled.

Glasses raised in the direction of us both and out of the corner of my eye I saw Nico lift his head once again as he cleared his throat. Despite having spent so little time together I already understood that it was something he did when he needed to draw a clear line under what had happened, in order to move on.

His hand lifted again as he offered up his glass to our guests, but the taut atmosphere still hung over the patio area where we were stood.

Moving quickly and wanting desperately to relieve the palpable tension, I scooped my fingers through the moist wedding cake on the plate in front of me. My hand moved fast, and without thinking over what I was about to do, I lifted it up quickly and wiped my fingers down his nose, covering him with the sponge, fruit and cream. Then as realisation washed over me at what I'd just done, my arm froze in mid-air and I withheld my next breath as I offered him a nervous smile.

Nico's head snapped around and his wide eyes met mine. The initial look on his face was one of anger and although strangely he didn't scare me, I knew in a bizarre way that I needed to be worried.

The room around us erupted with laughter.

I'd done exactly what I'd set out to do. I had lifted the fraught atmosphere. But what I hadn't taken into consideration was the way the man stood next to me would react.

I only inhaled my next breath when I saw the small crinkles appear at the corners of his eyes as he fought off a smile. I watched as he wiped a finger down the bridge of his nose slowly and as some of the cake fell into the blue rose he was wearing as a buttonhole. Still stunned into silence as I waited for his next move, I watched as his cake covered fingers pushed into his open mouth, a mouth that until now I hadn't noticed was shaped like cupids bow.

My core clenched as I watched his tongue flick out and start to lick his fingers clean. In front of our small party of gathered guests, I was embarrassed about the reaction I was having to such a seemingly normal action. The problem was the actions were being played out by the man who was stood next to me. He seemed to unknowingly have a hold over me, or maybe I was wrong. Perhaps he knew exactly what his actions were doing to me. Watching him again I knew he was being very deliberate, and he couldn't have given a damn who was looking at us.

Nico cleaned his fingers off slowly keeping his eyes fixed on me the whole time. My eyes however darted backwards and forwards from his fingers being sucked clean and the amusement I could now see in his dark brown orbs. Then as his expression changed and his left eye narrowed on me, I knew I was either in trouble or being thoroughly scrutinised or maybe even both.

'That's one amazing cake, Bee…I think you need to try some.' The gold threads that ran through Nico's dark eyes seemed to spark alight. I didn't think I'd ever seen him so lit up with life before and it was enthralling.

I smiled at him and shook my head. 'No, you wouldn't?'

'Wouldn't I?' he teased back.

I could already hear laughter beginning to ripple around the outside area.

'But my beautiful dress?' I watched him shrug his shoulders and then as I saw his hand begin to stretch out towards me, with a sudden primal instinct I was moving.

I darted to the side of the table and breathed a sigh of relief when I heard nothing crash to the floor, despite having pulled against the starched, white linen cloth as I'd brushed passed the table. Quickly, I steered myself in between the tables in front of me to the outer walled area of the patio and then I fled down the zig-zag walkway I knew led to the beach.

I was moving as fast as I could allowing for the fact that I'd already consumed three glasses of Champagne and was wearing the delicate, strappy heels we'd bought back in Vegas. I stopped momentarily, knowing they were slowing me down and pulled the shoes off my feet, dropping them unceremoniously on the landscaped rockery beside me. My heart was pounding in excitement as I looked back over my shoulder to see that Nico was stalking behind me, with the piece of cake still attached to his fingers and a broad smile on his face. I was running and he was only walking, but the strides he was taking meant he was ever so slowly catching me up.

I could hear the laughter coming from our wedding guests and a few of them including Trip and Kendall had come to the edge of the patio to lean on the wall to watch our descent.

Oh yes, I certainly knew how to detract from an uncomfortable situation.

I'd saved him.

Now, how was I going to save myself?

CHAPTER EIGHTEEN

Bee

AT LAST MY BARE feet hit the cool sand. Although the day had been hot, without a cloud in its blue skies, the sand below Nico's home had been in the shade of the cliffs around it for quite a while. Having been here for a few days already, I knew that sunset was nearly upon us and we would soon both be propelled into twilight and the limited light coming down from his house above us. Feeling the need to make better progress and even though I knew my dress wasn't long enough to really hold me back, I lifted up the full skirt and began to run.

Excitement and fear propelled my feet across the expanse of sand like I was completing the 100yard dash back in high school.

From above me, I heard Kendall's voice, 'Bee run, he's catching up... RUN!' she screamed and I recognised instantly that she was clearly excited by what she was watching unfold as her voice hit my ears.

I found myself at the large rocks that were dotted around at the bottom of the cliffs. Cursing under my breath as my bare feet left the soft sand and found the occasional chip of stone, I darted behind the nearest one hoping it would conceal me from him.

Desperate to escape him I held my breath trying to silence the gasps that were now leaving my mouth.

Silence enveloped me.

I clutched onto the rock in front of me and tentatively began to try to peer around it in a bid to find my pursuer. But as the light grew dimmer, I comprehended that I hadn't a clue where he was.

My heart leapt up into my mouth.

'Nico,' I called out nervously.

I strained my ears but could hear nothing over the soft ripple of the sea caressing the shoreline.

What's he playing at?

Slowly, I bent down lower, peered around the side of the rock I'd been hiding behind and looked back to where we'd both come from. But I still couldn't see him.

'Nico,' I called out again a little louder in case he hadn't heard me the first time.

'You can run, Bee…but you can't hide.' His voice sounded from behind me and I stood bolt upright in response. My body reacted to his voice and the bare skin on my arms broke out into goose bumps instantaneously.

I took a deep inhale, trying to give myself enough oxygen to fight down the growing sense of desire that was surging throughout my body.

Then I span around quickly to find him still looking as amazing as he had all day.

He was leaning on the rock not two feet away from where I had been hiding, with one hand pushed down deep into the pocket of his pants and the other still holding fingers full of our wedding cake. He turned his head to look up from the floor he'd been staring at and looked straight into my eyes.

In the early evening light of dusk, he looked every bit the dark and dangerous man I'd always thought he was, and a thrill of possession ran through me.

We're married. I've married him, were the two thoughts that ran on replay around my head

I let my eyes casually wander up and down his tall, broad physique. It appeared that he hadn't even broken a sweat chasing me and the two pieces of his grey suit that he'd worn for our wedding still looked immaculate.

'I don't believe you waited around long enough to taste our wedding cake, Bee,' he teased.

He looked amused as the words left his mouth.

'They can't see us anymore, you know. You don't need to carry on pretending, Nico,' I countered and lifted my head to look up at the cliffs above as if to demonstrate that we no longer had any spectators.

His beautiful mouth flexed as he briefly pretended to think over my words and then I saw a subtle shake of his head.

'Who's pretending?' he replied.

'You can't possibly mean to cover my face in cake… I only did it to you to help us both out.' I crossed my arms over my chest in defence and watched his eyes appraise my breasts. Then I looked at him defiantly waiting for an answer, and when his facial expression didn't even change, I carried on talking, 'You do understand that, don't you, Nico? It was just "playacting" with an audience and you appeared to like that before.'

He didn't even bother to answer me, but propelled himself forwards. I'd half managed to turn away from him to run again, when his arm came around my waist and I was pulled towards his hard body and unceremoniously lifted up and off my feet.

The squeal that left my mouth sounded so completely girly that I laughed out loud at the predicament I was in and at just who was sharing the moment with me.

'I like the sound of your laugh, Bee.' He buried his face into the side of my neck, and I shivered as I felt him inhale.

'The smell of you, Bee… you tempt and entice me.'

A flood of wetness hit the top of my thighs. Being trapped in his arms with the feel of his hard body behind me, I felt his every breath as it left and entered his body, playing out my fate on the over sensitive part of my neck and I melted into his embrace. It was all too much. In a sudden and complete panic, I recognised that the man behind me could very easily open the locked door to my heart and alarm swept through me.

What are you doing? Get a grip Barbara!

I pushed both of my hands down onto the forearm that was wrapped around me tightly, in a very poor and pathetic attempt to get him to release his hold on me.

'I think you need to let me go,' I pushed out breathlessly as I struggled again to show my commitment to getting out of his hold.

'No, that won't be happening.' I felt the shell of my ear burn with the warmth of his breath as it touched my sensitive skin and with the implied meaning I was imagining behind his words.

I could almost hear the final word *ever* as it floated in the sky around us and I wished hard to hear it fall from his lips. Then I let out a soft sigh of reprimand to myself that I was just being stupid. I had got carried away having drunk far too much Champagne for me, as I was nearly always a beer drinker.

I closed my eyes and then opened them suddenly when I felt his fingers cover my lips by circling my mouth with the cake he'd been carrying on his fingers. The moment a piece pushed up against one of my nostrils all of my thoughts once again evaporated and my fight returned.

'Stop,' I spat out.

As my mouth opened to talk his fingers pushed home and I received my first taste of the intense flavours that made up our wedding cake. For a few seconds, with his arm still wrapped tightly around me and with my feet at least a foot from the floor, I was just tasting the cake as Nico had insisted.

When that changed again, I couldn't quite pinpoint. But with him restraining me and with his fingers pushed into my mouth, my pulse accelerated fast and the air began to once again crackle around us.

I lifted my hand up to hold his and began to suck the two fingers he had happily used to attack my face with our wedding cake. My eyes opened wide as a groan left his mouth and the noise vibrated over my ear. Spurred on by the sound and still holding his hand in place, I began to run my tongue up and down the length of his fingers and then sucked on the tip.

'What are you doing?' he forced out into the night air. I could hear the danger lurking in his tone, as his Italian accent crept in.

I released his fingers with a pop and a small smile skirted over my mouth after taking in how much lust I could hear in his voice.

Touché.

'Taking what you offered,' I answered, smiling to myself.

Instinctively, I shifted as much as I could in his tight hold and arched my back into his erection that was now pushing hard into my backside.

Unceremoniously, his arm released its hold over me. My feet once again felt the chill of the sand underneath them. He abruptly grabbed either side of my waist and spun me around to face him. His arms wrapped around me and he pulled me tightly against him. With my forearms resting on his well-defined chest I slowly raised my hand to run my finger along the delicate edge of the blue rose he was still wearing. Then I lifted my face to meet his gaze.

'I'm a dangerous man, Bee.'

'I know… like you've said already, you own me. Only dangerous people own others.'

I watched his long lashes flick down over his eyes as he closed them to take in my words.

'You need to accept my help and friendship… and then keep the fuck away from me.'

'But…'

'But?' His head tipped back, his nostrils flared, and his voice grew in strength as he questioned the fact that I was daring to question him.

'But… what if I don't want to?'

His eyes slow blinked and his beautiful long eyelashes flickered at me again before he eventually narrowed his left eye to study me closely. I averted my eyes from his and back to the rose on his chest, the one I had unwittingly been caressing with my fingertip.

'I'm not the right man for you.'

'How the hell would you know?' My voice rose in volume at the annoyance he sparked inside me.

'I just know. You're a beautiful woman with a world of possibilities at her feet. You're kind and thoughtful to all that cross your path. I'm nowhere near good enough for you.'

The laughter that left me sounded hysterical.

'You forgot about the gambling addiction, my anxieties, oh and the fact that I'm in therapy *and* until you stepped in, I was up to my ears in debt with my life at risk.'

'I didn't forget those things. They don't define you… your goodness and your heart define you. Those things will one day just be a part of your past that you learnt and moved forward from. You need to understand that the reason I could save you from that world is because I'm part of it… a big fucking part of it.'

His hold over me hadn't relaxed at all and strangely, although I knew he was trying to push me away once again with his words, his hold over me and the way he looked at me was saying the exact opposite.

'Explain exactly why you felt the need to help me?'

'I was paying back a debt of honour to your brother.'

'A debt of honour? You do know we don't belong to your "family" don't you?'

'It was an unspoken debt that I wanted to repay.' I noticed how the previous threads of gold that had been evident in his eyes had disbursed.

'You stepped in before and helped me, surely that would have sufficed?'

I watched as Nico bit into his bottom lip and then rolled his head back as he stared up at the night sky. Exasperation was falling off him in waves. I could feel the fight he was having inside himself.

'The truth is, Bee, I think you're the most beautiful woman I've ever seen and I've wanted you for years...'

'And now you're taking the mickey out of me.' I sighed, upset by his words.

'Look at me!' Nico demanded as his eyes came back down to find mine. 'Do I look like the sort of man who would tell you anything that wasn't true?' Initially I didn't speak, but instead searched his soul with my own.

'No, you don't... But you've just said you've wanted me for years? I don't understand. Why wouldn't you have said something, or done something about it before?'

His head dipped further forward and he kissed the top of my head as he exhaled. I felt the warmth of his breath on my face and the heat of his arms wrapped around me. But as his words began to sink in, my body was beginning to shiver, and it wasn't the air temperature that was causing it.

'Because of the life I lead... I can't have you. Because I won't *allow* myself to have you... I refuse to destroy you like my father destroyed my mother.'

'You couldn't.'

'Yes, I could… and so very easily…' His words were forced out from between his teeth, showing me just how much he hated admitting the words to me.

I shook my head at him. There was no way I believed all of what he was saying. I'd heard stories about what a depraved, deranged asshole his father was from Pearl and many others. I truly didn't believe, as Nico held me tightly in his arms, that he was anything like the man who had sired him. Since he'd been in charge of his family's business I knew that most of it had been legalised. I had heard how he had been working hard at rectifying the many things his father had destroyed with his lust for destruction, death and bloodletting. His father, so the stories told, couldn't get enough of inflicting pain, violence and even death on others. It was as if within his obvious mania he thought he could cleanse himself by bloodletting, he was a truly evil character that even a movie wouldn't be able to do justice to.

'Bee, my heart is black, my soul already belongs to the devil one hundred times over and unlike you, I will never be able to look back at my past thinking it defined me and that I moved on, because I know I can never move on and walk away. I'm the exact image of my father at the same age and he recognised that within me from when I was a child. He created the monster that resides in me today as a way of punishing me for being younger and stronger. I can't step away from that, it will always be there just bubbling under the surface no matter how hard I try to disguise it.'

'I can make a guess at some of the things you've had to do, Nico. I live in Vegas for Christ's sake. But I refuse to accept that you're that man deep down inside… Do you understand me, Nico Morello? I point blank refuse.'

'Then, mio angelo, if you want me, despite what I've just told you… you need to possess me before I possess you.' The tone of his voice had changed again, with his Italian accent becoming more pronounced. The dark, deadly, arrogant man who resided in Vegas had returned to bait me, to put me off.

But although his words scared me a little, I wasn't put off at all. Maybe he'd been able to push everyone away before, but that wasn't happening with me.

The sky, for a more dramatic effect, chose that very moment to allow the sun to completely disappear and the beach around us was plunged into darkness. I took the one opportunity I thought I might ever have and lifted my arms up the small amount his tight hold on me allowed. I grabbed at either side of his face and feeling his stubble beneath my fingertips, I pulled his mouth down to mine. I wanted him to kiss me because he wanted to and not because we were acting out our roles in front of others.

His head came down and his full lips touched mine. He momentarily stilled as if he couldn't quite trust himself with what I was demanding of him. I drew back a couple of millimetres and then made our flesh connect again. I repeated this a couple of times still with my hands holding onto his face as I coerced and attempted to persuade this man into returning my embrace. It was a gentle kiss of acceptance from me because I now knew a little about how Nico saw himself, but I wasn't having any of it.

It was a strange feeling for me to feel like the stronger of the two in any relationship, but down here on the private beach, concealed by the night sky and after hearing him open up to me however briefly, I did. Knowing there was no way it would last for long because of the type of man he was, I held onto his face and with my lips on his I demanded he let me in.

Please kiss me back.

Running the tip of my tongue over his full, but still closed mouth, caused him to open his lips a miniscule amount to inhale and knowing I was affecting him I seized my opportunity. Standing up quickly onto my tiptoes, I simultaneously relaxed my hold on his jawline and pushed our mouths closer together. My tongue swept into his mouth and began to caress his.

I knew it wasn't audible, but I could have sworn I heard the moment he decided that he couldn't hold back any longer. His hold on me changed with one arm leaving my back. He placed his hand onto the back of my head and then threaded his fingers into my perfectly dressed hair. In the position of control that afforded him he pulled me further into his hard body and took over the kiss I had initially instigated.

He took control of me, like he controlled every aspect of his life. But I knew as his mouth consumed mine that this was also so very much more. Nico wasn't a man who let go of his perfectly ordered life easily, let alone allowed people inside the darkest part of his mind. He had given me access to something that could be undoubtedly used against him or the only two members of his family he had left. He had let me in, and I had absolutely no intention of leaving.

Our tongues teased and tangled around each other's in our bid to show each other how much we needed the connection. The kiss set light to the touch paper of our souls. I needed so very much more and feeling his erection pushing into my stomach as it demanded more, I knew he did too. Finally, my arms felt free enough to move and I lifted them up and flung them around his neck.

As our kiss continued, his hand released its hold over the back of my head and I felt some of my hair fall free from its earlier confines. Even the touch of my own hair on my feverish skin drove me further towards the edge of something I knew I no longer had any control over. His fingers trailed their way over the sensitive skin of my neck, onto my bare arm and then down the side of my body. The fine fabric of my wedding dress did nothing to lessen the heat I could feel resonating from his fingertips. The constant back and forth between us was coming to a head, I could feel it and I knew he could too. Where his fingers touched my skin, it was set alight with want and need for my new husband. He had one arm still wrapped around me tightly, but I still felt that I wasn't anywhere near close enough to him.

His mouth finally broke away from mine as he manoeuvred me sideways to place my back firmly against the large rock I had initially hid behind. With his dark eyes boring into mine, daring me to run and hide, Nico Morello the mob boss came out to play.

'It wasn't enough, mio angelo... not nearly enough... and now you've had your chance and failed... Now, I will possess you.' His teeth bit down into his bottom lip and almost at once he moved them backwards releasing the plump flesh and a groan at the same time.

His eyes stayed on mine, the connection between us effectively trapping us both to this moment in time. His dark orbs glistened in the moonlight as once again I witnessed the threads of gold appear in them, prompting me that he demanded all of my attention. Then once he knew I was there with him, he leant quickly to the side, his hand pulled up my wedding dress and his fingers hurriedly found the thin scrap of lace that was holding my off-white thong to my body. I heard the snap of the expensive fabric and then felt as it caressed my feet when it fell to the floor.

I gasped and momentarily his eyes left mine to focus on my mouth.

'This mouth is mine.'

With his hand under my dress, and with my pussy exposed by his actions, he moved my legs abruptly apart. His fingers swept roughly over my recently waxed and soaking wet lips with ease. I wasn't sure which of us heard me moan first, but the need the man was conjuring up inside me was all consuming. He was being rough, I knew it and so did he, but I didn't care. All I knew was that I wanted him. I looked down fleetingly and widened my stance knowing exactly what I was inviting him to do. I knew that if he didn't touch me where I needed him to and soon, that I was going to stand with my back against a rock on a beach in Crete and let him watch while I finished myself off.

'Look at me,' Nico demanded and with his free hand he took hold of my jaw, pushing his fingers into the skin around my mouth. Once again, our eyes connected and something powerful rushed through me, taking over me and holding me prisoner. But I wasn't a prisoner held against their will, oh no, I was right where I wanted to be. With this man, as his possession and ultimately his wife.

The second a couple of his large fingers pushed inside of me and he expertly hooked them forward to find the bundle of nerves he knew he would find there, feelings of pleasure erupted. I opened my eyes wider, staring purposefully into his and lifted my arms to clutch hold of his torso with one and his forearm with the other. As his fingers began to pump tenaciously in and out of me, he drove me further to the edge and I dug my fingers into the hard muscles I found beneath them.

'I want your come on my fingers, I want to feel your juices run over my hand… and then I can lick them, and you, clean.' Nico spoke and my body instantaneously reacted to his words.

With our eyes still staring at each other's in combat, I felt the walls of my core begin to pulse in reaction. I was unknowingly rising up on my toes and then coming back down to meet his fingers as he pumped them faster and faster in and out.

Finally, the night sky lit up behind my eyes as the fireworks inside my head exploded. I heard my cries of pleasure and saw the smile that captured his mouth as he watched me come as commanded over his hand.

Wave after wave of pleasure crashed over me. Nico gently removed his hand from me while the walls inside my core were still quivering and fell to his knees in front of me. My dress was unceremoniously lifted higher and as his tongue flicked out to taste me for the first time, I knew it would only be a matter of seconds before he took me to the edge of reason for a second time.

'And now, mio angelo, you are mine.'

His tongue pushed its way inside of me and as my hands took hold of his head to gently hold him where I wanted him to be, my head rolled back onto the rock behind me.

He was mine and come hell or high water I wasn't letting him go.

CHAPTER NINETEEN

NICO

AS HER CRIES OF pleasure travelled through my body for a second time, knowing she was totally spent, I pushed my tongue inside of her to taste and savour all of the sweetness her body had so willingly released. When I was convinced she was clean, still holding onto her hips, I reluctantly let her dress fall back down into place. Then I lifted my head away from her body and looked up.

Still kneeling on the floor in front of her, with the sand messing up an expensive pair of pants and honestly not giving a damn about it, I allowed my eyes to sweep up and over her quickly. I saw it as my one opportunity to take all of her in before she discovered me. This was one of those few all too short moments when I knew her eyes weren't on me, trying to work out my every move.

Vaffanculo. Fuck.

I closed my eyes briefly, trying to stifle my reaction to her. Terrifyingly, I understood that I'd never seen a more beautiful sight in my life than the creature stood in front of my eyes. Her beautifully dressed hair was now down over her shoulders in waves. I knew it had been loosened by my hands and the way she had turned her head from side to side when she was coming. My cock flexed suddenly against my smart pants and I bit down on my lip to stop a groan from leaving my mouth. Her cheeks were flushed, and her swollen lips were parted like she was inviting my cock to sink inside of her mouth to chase his own release.

Bee was leaning back where I'd placed her. Her hands were now either side of her body with her palms face down on the rock as she tried to gain some support from the solid structure. I was supporting her weight with my hands after recognising that she was effectively boneless, having had two orgasms burst through her in the space of about ten minutes.

For just those few short seconds and with the moon now lighting up the night sky, I let my eyes rush over her and understood I was ruined; she had ruined me. I could hear the sound of the waves as they gently washed the edge of the shore clean, and like the sand I knew they would take back into their depths with their movement, I felt my resolve and rules wash away with them.

I shook my head and sighed, then without releasing my hold over her I stood up and pressed a chaste kiss on her lips.

With equal amounts of reluctance and relief, I broke our kiss and swept her up into my arms. With her head resting against my collarbone and the frantically beating muscle of my heart, I moved my arms on her until one cradled her back and the other one was underneath her knees.

Without speaking or even daring to look down at her, I started taking the long strides I needed to get us both off the sand safely before the tide came in.

The moon had appeared again from behind a cloud and had once again offered the secluded beach a finite amount of light, but to me it felt like I was under a spotlight.

Everything I'd ever sworn not to do had just happened. I felt blissfully happy, but also so goddamned angry that I wanted to fall to my knees and purge myself.

My head was screaming at me to place her feet to the floor and to walk away. But my heart, my black incinerated heart was demanding that I held her in my arms and that I kept her there under my protection. Meanwhile, my eyes were now moving between making sure I walked a safe route back to the lit walkway and taking peeks at the woman I was holding in my arms, who was now my wife. Bee was tall and willowy in stature but curled up against me she felt small and so very vulnerable.

"You can't have anything nice to play with, Nico. Because you can't be trusted with her, you'll damage her beyond repair and destroy her."

My father's voice reverberated around my head. I closed my eyes rapidly and firmly to silence the bastard.

I'd worked hard over what was almost ten years to pull my grandfather's business out of the fucking cesspit my father had pulled it down into. In doing so, I'd pushed my family away to where I'd thought that they were safe until the tide could be turned again for us. I knew it was how it went with Mafia families like ours. You only had to research history to see that we could work side by side for a given length of time and then something would occur which meant the death and destruction of many. My father had been that catalyst and the bad blood and ultimately the power crazed fights that had followed his short reign had been like nothing ever witnessed before by the American people, even in New York.

Antonio Morello fit the bill as a violent, unhinged mafia boss, who cared for no one more than himself. He was a power hungry, sick, depraved asshole, who had taken many lives, including driving our mamma to her death. He had stolen money and grabbed hold of power in frenzied attacks that matched his psychotic disorder. He had abused his own children, making Cade and I take part in sexual acts with willing participants while he watched. The man got his rocks off controlling the lives of others and watching. The joke was he had delusions that made him think he carried himself well, he thought he wore clothes that concealed his evil heart and covered up the many sins he had committed against others and to us, his own family. He imagined that the expensive fabric of his suits showed everyone how powerful he was, but in reality, he had never looked good. He always had a look of sweaty mania about him. Our mamma had said that with his hunched over shoulders, his posture exposed to the world the weight of his sins. Her God, and supposedly his, had forced his tall frame into this position to carry those sins around on his back and no amount of expert tailoring nor expensive fabric could cover that up. Our father's face filled my head and I blinked him out before he took fucking root in there. We looked alike, my father and I, and it didn't matter how many times Nonna and Cade told me that was where the similarities ended, I didn't believe them. They hadn't witnessed what I'd had to do to ensure our survival in a primal world where only the strongest families survived and where the others were wiped out like the insignificant pieces of detritus they were.

I had killed with my bare hands to ensure their safety and it didn't matter how many homeless shelters and drug rehabilitation clinics I funded, I knew I would never be able to wipe the bright red arterial blood of my enemies off my hands, nor erase their eyes as they bulged out of their skulls before their oxygen supply stopped flowing to their brain.

She thought she knew me, but I'd made sure over the years that no one really knew me.

I wasn't sure I even knew myself anymore.

My father had created me, my mamma had borne and loved me. Then he had destroyed her and ultimately mine and Cade's world, when she had hung herself to escape him. Then thinking he was a God to be worshipped above all others, instead of the devil incarnate, he had set about remoulding Cade and I into his exact image. I had made sure that Cade got away from him as soon as I could, but I knew that even now, after he'd been dead for many years, I would never be able to escape his clutches.

He had told me himself as my index finger had squeezed the trigger to take him from this life straight to hell where he belonged, that I would never be free of him and truthfully, it was the one thing I'd ever heard him say that I agreed with.

Without saying anything to her I carried her back to our home. The walkway ascended, zig zagging the hundred meters and more that separated it from my own private beach. Not once did I consider putting her down, because that would mean she had left my arms and I didn't want to sever our connection before I had to.

Finally, we came up level with the outside patio where we had left our guests earlier and I stopped to readjust my hold on her. Glancing around the area I could see it had already been cleaned and emptied in the short time we'd been away. I looked around again quickly, nodding in acknowledgement as my eyes comprehended that the patio was devoid of people, apart from Franco.

The man was worth his weight in gold to me. He was always on hand, but knew just when to keep his distance and I knew without asking he wouldn't have followed us down to the beach. He would have placed security on any access to the beach other than from my property, without any order from me. I nodded my head in thanks to him and saw him speaking into his mouthpiece as he let the rest of my security team know we were back in the building.

I walked in through the open, bi-folding doors and heard my shoes hitting the tiled floor and the grains of sand grinding underneath them as I strode purposefully on. I crossed through room after room until I reached where I'd been heading to. Without giving the pro's and con's any more thought, I'd taken the stairs that led up to the master bedroom two at a time. I tapped the closed door with the toe of my shoe and once we were safely inside, I kicked back making it close swiftly behind us with a loud, resounding click.

Bee didn't even stir.

I took a deep breath and looked around the room we were going to be sharing from now on. Everything in it was familiar. The furniture, the smell of my cologne and the woman who had, I was certain, fallen asleep in my arms. I trod on the back of my Italian leather shoes, knowing I was effectively ruining them, and in my bare feet I walked over the wooden floor as quietly as I could and gently placed her down on the bed.

Once again, I fell down onto my knees and lifted my hands to tenderly brush the hair off her face. For minutes, I just stared at her and for no reason other than I could. In the moonlight that flooded into our room her hair shone like a precious metal. I pulled out all of the pearl pins I could see and placed them almost silently on the bedside cabinet next to me.

Walk away.

But like a love-struck kid I knew I couldn't, so I stood up and still standing next to her while she slept in our bed, I shrugged myself out of my vest and allowed it to drop behind me. After releasing the cufflinks on my shirt, I placed them down on the cabinet next to the pins and then I slowly flicked open every button on my shirt. I knew I was removing my clothes like her eyes were on me and that I was undressing especially for her, even though she wasn't watching. I abruptly pulled my shirt free of the waistband of my pants and stilled.

And just like that my little fantasy shrivelled.

The cold metal of my gun touched the small of my back and I was catapulted straight back into reality.

It was a reality that I knew I would spend the rest of my fucked-up life in, and there was no way in hell I was dragging anyone I could easily love into the depths of hell with me.

I leant over her with my loose shirt touching her beautiful skin and placed a kiss to her forehead. Then I pulled the dark green throw up from where it had been draped at the bottom of the bed and covered her up.

With one further look in her direction, I walked away.

CHAPTER TWENTY

Bee

THE SOUND OF RUNNING water woke me. A bright, sunny day hit my eyes and for a few seconds I closed them again to stop the sudden pain that the light had caused inside my head.

Why can I hear water?

I sat up in bed and ignoring the brightness of the new day, I looked around. Slowly, with sleep still clouding my mind, I took in the room, remembering just where I was and just who I was with. I quickly skimmed through my memories of yesterday and felt my face flush and my core tighten as I recollected the feel of his tongue on me and how hard I'd come after he'd sucked my clit into his mouth.

I looked down at myself quickly and saw I was still dressed in my wedding dress. Something didn't make sense. The last thing I could recall was being carried in his arms back home up the long walkway from the beach.

Well that's embarrassing. I'd got mine and had obviously passed out. I rolled my eyes up into my head and sighed out loud.

The water stopped suddenly and my heart began to beat frantically in my chest. Straining my ears for the slightest clue of what was happening in the room behind me, I heard the man in question as he vacated the ridiculously large walk in shower. Then the chrome towel rack rang out loudly as what I thought must have been one of Nico's rings contacted against it. I finally heard his feet pad across the marble floored bathroom.

My head turned on instinct and I watched him walking into the bedroom knowing that I couldn't have torn my eyes away from him even if I'd have tried. He was a vision. Still wet from the shower, I watched entranced as droplets of water ran down over his olive coloured skin, occasionally colliding with each other and conjoining to run even faster over and around his well-defined muscles. My mouth salivated with the need to trace their route with my tongue.

With a towel tied around his waist, he rubbed a smaller one over his wet hair which meant that his face was obscured from my view. Knowing he couldn't see me looking I stared at him even harder. When he suddenly stopped rubbing at his hair, I knew without a doubt he could feel my eyes boring into him. My eyes found his the moment he dropped the towel in his hand to the ground.

A smile that I wasn't expecting lit up his face.

'Buongiorno,' he offered.

'Morning…look I'm really sorry about last night.' I gesticulated around me and touched the skirt of my dress attempting to show him how mortified I was at having so obviously fallen asleep fully clothed.

Nico dropped the towel from his waist as he turned his back on me and as I took in the naked body of my husband for the first time, I felt my mouth fall slackly open. He was amazing, just beautiful to look at. He reminded me of a statue, the sort you could see at all historical places. Every single muscle on the man was taut and in perfect condition. But luckily, I already knew that there was where the similarities ended between him and the statues I'd giggled at as a child back in the U.K. His cock was far bigger than they depicted in the statues, I'd felt the size of it yesterday when he pressed it firmly into my body. I stared at him harder willing him to turn around.

'Don't be sorry, I enjoyed myself and you were undoubtedly tired,' he replied and thankfully broke me away from any further musings about his cock before my body spontaneously combusted.

I watched as he thrust both of his legs into some smart Chino shorts and then as he jumped slightly to pull them over his butt cheeks to fasten them. I made sure I closed my mouth before he turned back to face me.

'You need to be ready in one hour, can you do that, Bee?' He looked over his shoulder at me.

'What for?' I questioned, still feeling sleepy.

'I've made some arrangements this morning, there are places I want to show you around the island and although we can drive to them all in a day, it's better if we stay in a couple of the places as it'll be more relaxed for us all.'

Nico walked down the side of the large bed and picked up his wristwatch, which was on the low table in front of the couch that looked out of our large window and onto the balcony. For the first time, I understood that he had spent the night on the couch when I saw that the bed was neat beside me and that blankets were strewn on the floor next to the low table.

Slowly, he began to fasten his watch and then turned back to me when I didn't answer immediately.

'For us all?' I questioned.

'You, Trip, Kendall and me... they'll be here in an hour.'

'Did they not all stay here last night?'

'No...' He looked at me amused. 'It was our wedding night, remember?'

'Again, I'm sorry,' I offered, feeling sheepish and wondering if somehow he was punishing me for falling asleep with some sort of mind fuckery.

'Don't be. It was my grandmother who planned that they would all spend the night away from here, not me.'

Not him?

'Why would she do that and not you?' was all I managed to ask, when there was so much more going around my head that I needed an answer to.

'There was no need, was there?' For a few seconds the room fell uncomfortably silent as we looked at each other. 'I didn't see the point in making sure we had privacy, because I knew we wouldn't be needing it.' I could feel my face contorting into a puzzled expression at his words and pain began to unravel inside of me. The room was so full of things that needed to be aired it was almost stifling.

Why is he being so distant?

Very gingerly I held out my hand to him. I saw him look at it once or maybe even twice before his shutters came down and everything that had happened between us yesterday evening was pushed so far into the past it was unreachable.

'Why won't you touch me?' The words left my mouth and even I was stunned I'd had the balls to ask. I refused to drop my arm, even though it was beginning to ache.

His long eyelashes closed as he tried to erase the question. When he opened his eyes again, I was still in the same position offering him my hand.

'You just don't get it, do you?' He almost spat the words out and hearing the Italian accent back in his tone I readied myself for what was to come next.

I couldn't answer him, my throat was tight with the constriction of the emotion I was just about managing to keep a lid on.

'These hands.' He lifted his hands and stared down at his palms as if he could see something on them. 'They've taken lives… stopped hearts from beating. I *refuse* to taint your skin with them.'

Oh God!

'But, Nico… you don't understand… if I don't feel your touch on me, you inside of me… then my heart will stop beating and you will have effectively killed me too.'

Silent tears began to run down my cheeks.

I kept my eyes on his so he could experience my pain, but his feet remained fixed to the spot. I knew then that he one hundred percent believed the words he had just spoken, and I could see that nothing I could say or do in this brief moment in time would convince him otherwise. Once again Nico cleared his throat and I knew the moment was over. He started moving around the large space to break our connection. I wanted to hide under the blanket that was still draped over my legs, but I refused to let him off the hook that easily. I wanted him to feel the strength of my presence, and if possible to experience my pain.

He pulled on an emerald green, round necked T-shirt and although I could see by the small design on his chest that it was an expensive designer one, I knew I'd never seen him dressed so casually, it appeared he was totally prepared for his role. This was a man who was well practised at shelving his emotions and carrying on like nothing had happened.

'You need to pack enough for about four days and don't forget your camera, because while we're gone, I'm having you a dark room built.'

'Okay… You are?' I replied, feeling knocked off kilter. It seemed the man took away with one hand and gave with the other. Feeling completely discombobulated I bent my knees and holding them to me, I wrapped my wedding dress over the top of them. The cold metal of the dragonfly pin he had given me for our wedding day touched the warm skin of my leg and I wondered if all of yesterday had actually happened.

But of course it had, and now Nico was once again backing off.

'I forgot to say thank you for my wedding present.'

Without putting any product on his hair, I watched as he casually ran his hand through it a few times and left it standing on end in various places. He put on the Aviators I had seen hung on his vest yesterday when we'd married, then pushing them up the bridge of his nose he looked back at me.

'Sorry?'

'The dragonfly pin, it's beautiful and really thoughtful.'

'That was Nonna's idea.'

His façade was once again well and truly back in place.

'It was?... She said it came from you.'

He shrugged his shoulders at me, 'Anyway, I'll leave you to get ready.'

'Thanks, I think,' I quietly replied.

'I thought it would be fun spending a few days with Trip and Kendall. Bruce is staying with Nonna and Pearl and it'll just be the four of us,' he added, holding onto the door handle as he looked back at me.

'It sounds like you have it all planned out,' I accused.

'I do,' he answered, before he thought twice and crossed the floor to my side of the bed and placed a quick kiss to the top of my head.

He turned once again to walk towards the door, slowing to pick up his gun. Watching him, I could tell by the way he placed it into his waistband at the back of his shorts, and swung his holdall high over his shoulder, just how pleased he was with how his first business meeting of the morning had gone.

What he hadn't taken into consideration was although I felt tired and emotional right at this moment, I was now the wife of a Morello and a more formidable opponent than he realised.

CHAPTER TWENTY-ONE

Bee

I KNEW I HAD a strong ally in Trip the moment Nico stopped dead in his tracks and surveyed the vehicle we were going to be travelling in.

It was a jeep, a brand new and expensive looking jeep, but a jeep none the less.

Nico dropped his holdall onto the floor, shattering the quiet that had suddenly surrounded us as the metal studs on the base of the bag hit the unmade road. He took off his Aviators and without thinking through his show of hesitation, he began to walk around the silver coloured 4x4.

Trip found my eyes and waggled his eyebrows at me in amusement as we watched him. I knew then, that he and Kendall could also see straight through Nico. I grinned quickly at them both and then rolled my lips into my mouth and bit down on them with my teeth to stop the laughter that was building up from falling freely out of my mouth.

'You're joking?' Nico finally spoke from the other side of the vehicle as he wielded his sunglasses in the direction of the jeep.

'Look, Boss, you called me at five this morning...'

Did he now? That piece of information was interesting.

Trip carried on, 'You'd had an idea...' Trip gestured speech marks either side of his head as he quoted Nico, 'You wanted to show Bee a few of the places around the island and thought it would be fun if the four of us went together for a couple of days and nights away, and could I organise it all?'

Nico stared at Trip for a few seconds looking completely dumbstruck. It was so obvious to the three of us looking at him that he was way out of his comfort zone. Normally, he would organise everything, or others would do it to his exact specifications.

'Security?'

'Nic... I woke up Franco as soon as you put the call through to me. As always, you will be surrounded by security.'

'It's not me I'm worried about.' Nico looked at me from over the jeep, placed the glasses back over his eyes and tipped his head at me as he wordlessly answered Trip.

'Franco has it covered. You know damn well he won't let you down.'

'Best we get in then.' He nodded back at Trip.

I watched as Nico walked back around the jeep shaking his head from side to side. Slowly, we all saw the start of a smile beginning to make the corners of his mouth twitch. He picked up his bag, took mine from my hand and after dumping them in the back of the jeep he opened the small passenger door and waved his hand at me offering me to get in. I took hold of his hand and inhaled quickly as what can only be described as an electrical current travelled up the length of my arm. For the first time since yesterday our eyes really met each other's. I knew as soon as I noticed the gold threads appearing in his orbs and his eye narrowing on me, that he had felt the connection between us too. I jumped in quickly, fastened my seat belt and heard him clear his throat as he attempted to move on as always from what had just happened between us.

It had taken everything I had not to reach out and touch Nico, as he had very competently driven us along the main roads that had been cut through the mountainous area surrounding the place he had chosen to build his home. The inclination to connect with the man who was doing his utmost to maintain a friendly distance from me was powerful. In the small space in the front of the vehicle and with both of us only wearing summer clothes, occasionally our bare skin connected and I'd had to stop breathing momentarily to make sure I didn't gasp out loud. It seemed after our first and only real sexual contact, my need for the man had intensified instead of lessening.

I set about trying to relax into the comfortable wrap around seat and concentrated hard on the happy banter going around the jeep as Nico and Trip argued about whether we should be listening to Elvis or The Beatles. When they couldn't make up their minds, aiming a grin back in Kendall's direction, I'd taken control and switched the radio on low. We'd travelled onwards with Greek pop music playing faintly in the background. Then taking hold of the opportunity, I began to question Trip and Kendall, who were happily cosied up on the back seat, about the many places in the world they had visited.

Our first stop was about two hours away at Knossos, an ancient palace and settlement site near Heraklion. Nico explained it was thought to be the first city ever built in the whole of Europe, and I had truly never seen him look as captivated as he did wandering around the ancient city. The three of us trailed happily behind him, listening to everything he wanted to tell us about the magnificent site, and wanting him to have memories of this moment I snapped everything I could from every angle possible. Although, if I was truthful with myself, I knew it wasn't pictures of the ancient structures that were going to take up most of the space on my memory card, because in between snapping pictures of the site for him, I found myself taking pictures of the man I'd married for myself. Looking through the lens of the camera afforded me the cover to study Nico. Even after our fraught conversation this morning he was back within his comfort zone and was relaxing. Unfortunately, to me he was becoming even more beautiful and interesting the more he relaxed. I was a confused but very happy bystander, watching him unfold and slowly becoming the man who I believed he was always meant to be.

'In here is what was the original throne room and apparently, looking at the guidebook, an original stone throne still exists inside,' Nico informed us and we all took our place in the queue behind him waiting to enter the room he'd just spoken about.

It was damn hot, even for someone used to living in the dry heat of Vegas. The ancient ruins were reflecting the sun's rays straight onto the bare skin of my legs. I knew that after today it would not only be my face that looked healthy, but my limbs would also be tanned. With the intense heat on my legs, standing still on the spot while we waited to enter became uncomfortable. I stepped out of the line and moved about twenty feet away from the others, lifted my camera back up to my face and began to turn around to look at the various scenes for possible pictures. Through the lens, for the first time today, I caught sight of one of Nico's security team and a shiver ran down my spine.

Was he really worried about my safety?

I wanted to believe that it really was just a matter of security and something he'd got into the habit of having around him.

I turned myself and my camera around again and almost as if I was magnetised to the man, Nico suddenly filled all of my screen. Through the safety of the lens his eyes connected with mine when he looked up and found me watching him. I lowered the camera slowly, feeling the need to look at him properly and as soon as I did, he turned away. I watched as he spun around deliberately to show something to Trip on the 3D viewer we'd been given when we entered the palace.

'No way… So, this is the place that held the Minotaur?' I heard Trip answer Nico and then he took the 3d viewer from Nico to show Kendall.

Nico's eyes remained on the couple. I could feel the struggle he was having within himself not to look back over at me, and when he seemed to beat it so easily it hurt like hell.

Thank God we were with Trip and Kendall, they were the perfect couple to water down the tension between us. In a strange sort of companionable silence, we finally went in to see the throne he wanted to show us and then made our way back out to the jeep. At last we were back on the road and I had the chance to distance myself from him. I sat in the back seat with Kendall where I feigned tiredness and closed my eyes while I ran everything through my head again like a slideshow.

The way he normally held my hand and the way he had touched me on the beach last night were at the forefront of my mind. Then they were replaced with how he was now doing everything in his power to keep his distance not to.

I missed him.

But the longer the day had gone on, the more time I had to think over the facts that were presenting themselves. Being a card player, I knew all about feigning a hand and I was convinced that was exactly what he was now doing.

He hadn't touched me last night after I'd fallen asleep and I could understand why, but the fact that he'd not even slept next to me told me something had spooked him. Add that to the fact he had called Trip so early this morning to come up with a few days of travelling and it gave me enough evidence to give me what I hoped was an understanding of him. I'd heard his words this morning about not allowing himself to touch me, to taint my skin with his evil. I was now convinced that he was either trying to avoid us being around his grandmother or being by ourselves, or probably even both.

He was avoiding me, because he was scared he wanted me.

His words that he had spoken to me only yesterday swept through my mind.

"You can run, Bee… but you can't hide."

Well back at ya, Boss… Back at ya.

CHAPTER TWENTY-TWO

Nico

I HEARD THE GIRLS gasp on the back seat as Trip steered around yet another terrifying bend. We were crazily high up and on a single unmade track, which meant the back end of the jeep skidded ever so slightly on the loose gravel with every corner we took. For the first time today, I was glad Trip was in control of the jeep we were in. Because although I'd totally enjoyed driving the thing around for most of the day, it had to be said that with Trip being a fully trained pilot, he had better reaction skills when it came to taking in everything that came in our direction. He was still managing to keep up a good pace as we raced against the sun that was lowering in the sky. I knew, had we had more time, we might have reduced our speed a bit. But as the light was fading fast, we needed to make it through and out to the other side before the sunlight finally left us.

Christ knows why he was so adamant about being here tonight.

'Crap!' Kendall screeched out from behind us as we went around another corner.

'Calm yourself, Perky… I've got it all under control. Have I ever let you down yet?' Trip called out to her without taking his eyes off the track in front of us.

'This place better be worth this dangerous journey, else I'm coming for your ass, Carter and you too, Nico.'

I grinned listening to Kendall's words and knowing that for her to use Trip's proper name he really had the possibility of the silent treatment from his wife for a few days.

I checked the Sat Nav again before I jumped into the conversation.

'I haven't seen the beach, Kendall, but I'm told it's spectacular… we've got about three minutes left of this terrain and then it opens up and we descend down to Elafonissi.'

'You'd better be right, Nico,' Kendall replied.

'I usually am,' I offered laughing.

'Bit of luck I did my homework wouldn't you say, Nic? We definitely wouldn't have made this in a sportscar or whatever else it was you had in mind.'

'No… I know,' I answered him resolutely.

'Then tell me again how I was right and you were wrong.' I heard the girls giggle a little from behind us and I knew he was trying to distract them from the last bit of our journey. The track had narrowed again, with one false move from Trip we'd be off the edge.

I cleared my throat and started, 'For the hundredth time, you were right.'

Several times over he had made me admit to him in front of Kendall and Bee that he was right and I'd been wrong, after my gut reaction to the vehicle this morning. I'd had to agree it had been a fun and exhilarating way to travel and explore the island, even if it had at times put me closer to Bee than I would have preferred.

I knew by the silence that now suddenly engulfed the small jeep the four of us were contained in, that we were all praying for an end to the final part of our journey. Although I'd looked around my grandmother's birthplace before, I had only read about the beach and its island we were travelling to now. But, I knew I wanted to show it to Bee, so she could take pictures and wander around the uninhabited space. Coming from Vegas where crowds of people were often to be seen everywhere you looked, I knew the space and tranquillity this place offered would give us time to breathe and think.

I wanted that for her.

Although right now, I knew space to think was the last thing I needed.

Our first day had been cram packed full of adventures and experiences. It had been a day that I knew I would never forget, because I had spent it with the majority of the people that meant anything to me.

At last we rounded one final corner and the track opened up in front of our eyes.

To say I was rendered speechless was severely underestimating how I felt.

The island and beach in front of us sparkled even in the limited light of the setting sun. The sand was almost pink in colour and seemed to be made of glitter rather than glass.

Trip slowed down the jeep as we descended into what looked like another time and place from the world we'd left far behind us. To the left of our view was the ancient lighthouse, which although it had additions to it over the years still stood tall and proud as it guarded the ancient peninsular. To the right was the small chapel I'd read about.

'Okay, so you two have exactly five minutes to grab your bags and jump out. Kendall and I are staying back here in the village and you two are walking over to the island where you're staying tonight.'

'Pardon?' I questioned, making sure Trip could hear my hesitancy.

I watched him jump out from the driver's seat and run around to help Bee down.

'You heard,' he shouted out laughing.

'I know it's not going to be a proper bed, Nico… and that you have certain standards. But what Nonna and Trip have organised here sounds like fun and something the two of you will never forget,' Kendall added.

Nonna and Trip? Of course.

'I bet,' I whispered as I reluctantly got out of the jeep and offered Kendall a smile.

Fleetingly, I looked at the woman who was holding on to Trip's right hand as she carefully lowered one beautifully shaped, long, bare leg out the confines of the jeep and I swallowed hard.

'There ya go, Mrs. Morello.' Trip grinned at her as he lifted her hand up to his lips to place a soft kiss on it.

Watching that simple act made my stomach turn over with jealousy.

Jealousy?

I had gone out of my way not to lay eyes on my wife whenever possible today and hadn't, apart from where necessary, touched her since

I'd kissed her head as she sat up in bed this morning. It had killed me to take in just how hurt she looked at my lack of response to her being there, when truthfully, I hadn't slept all night knowing she was close beside me. I had sat on the couch doing battle with all of my senses. Listening to her soft sighs, the way she whimpered and moaned in her sleep. Watching pictures in my head of just how compliant she had been, coming apart while I'd finger fucked her only a few hours before. Even worse was inhaling her light floral perfume which was floating on the air in our bedroom. Every time I breathed in, I inhaled more of her and truthfully, I knew I was struggling.

So this morning, like the bastard I was, I told her how I wouldn't be touching her, and I'd watched as the pain I'd caused her ran down her cheeks.

She didn't need a man like me in her life. I'd battled with that thought over and over again as I'd lain awake last night. But right now, it was essential for both of us that we carried on with our agreement. I'd promised myself as I tossed and turned in my bid to find some sort of peace, that I would work harder on keeping a distance from her and that was how I'd spent today, with that newly sworn promise to myself driving me forward. What I hadn't reckoned on was just how hard it was going to be.

I'd tasted her plump lips.

Caressed her tongue with my own.

Watched her eyes roll high up into her head as she'd come apart on my fingers.

And even now I could still taste the sweetness of the woman after she'd orgasmed on my tongue.

Her moans, movements and taste were my new addictions and I was struggling hard to deny myself.

Her addiction was being fought. Mine on the other hand was becoming more impossible to ignore by the minute. Wanting her was becoming all-consuming and so fucking strong that I could hardly think straight.

With the weight of her addictions being aired, the debt and threats off her shoulders, the woman was transforming before my eyes and becoming more beautiful by the day. The constant anxiety I'd watched her experience for the past few years had abated. It pleased me that I hadn't seen any sign of it since I'd propositioned her back in Vegas.

I had to keep reminding myself that I was helping her by having married her and by staying with her. Whatever hell I had to walk through while trying to keep my hands to myself I would gladly do to keep her happy. The one thing I absolutely knew, was that she definitely didn't need an attachment to a bastard like me, because when it was time to do so, I would most definitely be walking away.

But now Trip was touching her.

I inhaled deeply making my nostrils flare and then exhaled loudly. His eyes lifted over her head and I widened mine at him in silent question. When he laughed in response, I stared all the harder.

'Thank you, Trip,' Bee offered.

'Come on then, you two. The water is shallow enough now at low tide for you to walk over to the island. It's uninhabited, but you will find a luxury tent erected, food, water and everything you need for your twenty-four hours in paradise.' He turned his head to aim the next bit more predominantly at me. 'Because it's uninhabited once the tide comes in you will be cut off from the rest of civilisation, so although security will remain back here with us, it is of course guaranteed that you'll be safe…But, you do need to start making a move.' Trip moved nearer to me as he spoke. Then he spoke again out of the earshot of our wives. 'And this lifechanging moment is brought to you by **The Beatles - All You Need Is Love**.' He grinned his fait accompli at me and waggled his eyebrows.

'You're an asswipe of a friend, Trip.'

'No, I'm the best sort of friend…' He lifted his hand and smacked the top of my arm as if to drive his message home. 'And you know it. This, as I see it, is your chance at a real life, a chance to no longer be a sideliner who watches everyone else live and I'm the friend who's making you take it. This is only one night, but watching the two of you it's fairly evident that it could be more… We're helping you to understand that.' As his words hit home, I knew he meant him and my grandmother.

'We're not…' I was shaking my head at him, but couldn't find the words to describe what Bee and I weren't.

No fucking way was I accepting this.

I had never felt so confused in all my life.

'The water's still warm.' Bee's shrill voice, childlike in its exuberance, broke through my reluctance at being backed into a corner and the joy captured within it warmed my insides. I turned my head to look at her. She was holding her flip-flops in one hand and jumping in and out of the gentle waves that were washing over her feet as she waited for me to go with her to the island.

It was one night.

Surely, I could cope with one night.

I couldn't deny her that, could I?

'Wait up,' I called over to her and with a nod of my head in thanks to Kendall and Trip as they climbed back into the jeep, I left our bags on the sand and jogged over to my wife who was stood up to the middle of her shins in the calm water. I kicked off my sliders and entered the sea next to her.

As I appeared beside her, she turned her head to look at me and for the first time all day I permitted myself to look back at her properly. Her long blonde hair was blowing in the warm breeze that danced around us. I watched as a piece of her hair whipped into her mouth and lifted my hand to pull it free with my fingers. Then without thinking, I gently caressed her cheek with my thumb before I took my hand away. Her eyes sparkled, the blues and greens captured there welcomed and invited me in further.

I watched as she smiled at me and it totally blew me away.

As I absorbed her smile, in that nanosecond I knew all the promises and bargains I'd made with myself and the devil overnight had just flown out of the window.

Without any further thought I moved quickly, and needing to feel her against me I swung her high up into my arms. With no words of disapproval coming from her mouth at my lack of attention over the past few hours or with my actions now appearing like a complete U-turn on my part, I smiled down at her thankful of her acceptance.

I gave her a real smile, one I knew she would understand and then with my eyes refocussing on the journey in front of us, I began to wade carefully through the rising water.

'They're driving away now, you can stop pretending,' she whispered up to me and at the same time proffered a wave of her hand behind us.

I could hear the fragility in her voice as she gave me the information that she thought I wanted to hear.

'I'm not pretending, Bee. You're in my arms and it's right where I want you to be.' My own honesty floored me.

What the fuck was it about this woman?

'Look at me,' she demanded.

Slowly, after first checking our path was clear enough, I took in a deep breath and made my eyes look down to find hers.

'Thank you, that means a lot.'

'I have nothing to offer you,' I reminded her.

'We have tonight and for now it's enough.'

CHAPTER TWENTY-THREE

Bee

I UNFASTENED THE TOGGLES on the large circular structure that was apparently our tent for the night and apprehensively peered inside. The space was lit by one lamp hanging from the centre of the roof. A comfortable looking double sized bed dominated the space. This was obviously the "glamping" I had heard other people talk about. The tent was furnished with not only the bed but also a couple of rugs and what looked like an old-fashioned washstand to one side. The bed was already made up and the whole space was a far cry from the couple of nights I'd spent camping out before in the English countryside. In my head I could still smell the damp, musty smell of the sleeping bag I'd shared with Brody and the tantalising aroma of the sausages my dad had sat out in the rain under an umbrella cooking for us.

My heart pounded with the memories of once being young and unaffected by the hurt and disappointments of the world. But, once again, I appreciated that the memory had made me smile and that it was the second time that had happened to me since Nico had pulled me out of my downward spiral in Vegas. I made a mental note to mention it to my therapist, Mrs. Davison, next time I saw her. It would be wonderful to think I could look back on my childhood memories occasionally without the ugliness and hurt which normally accompanied them.

I let go of the canvas flap, let it fall back into place and turned around to watch Nico wading back through the rising water with one of our bags on each of his shoulders. Trip hadn't been wrong when he'd said that the tide was coming in fast. The bottom of Nico's shorts were getting soaked with every step forward. With my heart beating ever faster, I watched totally mesmerised as the material stuck to his toned upper thighs and remembered back to this morning when I'd seen his naked body as he'd dressed in front of me.

Shortly we would be cut off and only reachable by boat and it was a nice thought to know that no one's eyes would be on us and we would be truly alone for the twenty-four hours we were here. Hopefully that time would help us to unravel what was really happening between us.

With my eyes still watching Nico from my peripheral view, I bent down to adjust one of the large cushions that surrounded the already blazing fire pit which was situated in front of our tent. Near the fire pit were a couple of large cool boxes, which I was certain would contain the food we needed to cook this evening and tomorrow. Still trying to occupy myself I moved towards them and flicked open one of the catches to take a look inside.

'Bee, quick grab your camera,' Nico shouted out as he at last made it out of the water and ran across the last of the space in between us, before dumping our bags unceremoniously on the sand next to me.

Lifting my head to the sound of his voice I saw that the sun was just about to disappear behind the cliffs that surrounded us and understood immediately what he was talking about. Without answering him, I unzipped the compartment I needed and pulled out my camera. Looking around quickly, I worked out that standing on the water's edge would offer me the best opportunity to photograph the stunning place as the sun retracted its warmth for the final time today. Still putting the strap of the case around my neck I ran towards the sea. When at last my feet found the water, I turned and lifted my camera to take the shots I wanted of the stunning beach with its pink shimmering sand and of the man who was stood watching the sunset with a childlike awe and rapture showing on his face.

I heard my camera relay the shots I wanted and then I removed my finger as the sun disappeared and we were once again bathed in the semi darkness. It seemed to me then, as I allowed my eyes to find Nico who was stood staring back at me, that this, like sunrise, was our time of day.

It was these periods of the day when we really seemed to communicate.

The strange almost eerie time between day and night, and night and day. Totally out of our control, when one thing was ending and another beginning, was the interval when he would truly allow us to be ourselves. In the light of the fire pit and the large torches he had just lit, a shiver ran over my body as I watched him run his eyes up and down me. Every hair on my body stood up in awareness as he swept his gaze appraisingly over me.

I lifted up my camera and took a couple of candid shots of the man as he stood motionless, unshackled from everything he had carried over to the island. But, what was even more amazing was that he looked like he was also unshackled from the life he lived in.

'How they had managed to pull this off in the space of a few hours is beyond me.' With my mouth now feeling unmistakably dry I shouted over to him, needing to desperately break through the suddenly strange atmosphere that had surrounded us. It was something that I knew I'd never felt before and I didn't know whether to accept it or to push it away.

Without replying Nico finally blinked a couple of times and cleared his throat, effectively severing the connection between us. As he bent over to the cool boxes to look for food, with his eyes no longer on me I righted myself. Rolling back onto my heels I comprehended that the longer he had stared at me the more my body had unwittingly leant itself in his direction, until finally I'd been up on my toes and leaning all of my weight towards him.

The push and pull between us was painful.

Suddenly, feeling out of place and wringing my hands together with the unexpected anxiety that had abruptly rushed through me, I placed my shaking legs one in front of the other and made my way back to him.

Not now, hold it together. This was why I was so bad at cards, eventually even though I tried so desperately hard to hold it all together my emotions came spilling out for all to see. I was so damn angry with myself I could scream.

'I hope you eat seafood?' he queried.

His head appeared from behind the lid of the box he had been looking inside and one eyebrow lifted up to me in question. I saw the moment he grasped that I was really struggling with what was going on between us. The lid was unceremoniously dropped back into place with a loud bang, he vaulted the firepit and after covering the empty ground between he wrapped his arms around me tightly.

'I'm sorry, Bee.'

Tears began to roll down my face again.

'What for?' I questioned, all the time desperately hoping he wasn't about to walk away.

'All of this... I've never been in a relationship like this.'

'A relationship? Are we actually a relationship?' I questioned as I lifted my head to look up at him.

He sighed loudly as he thought what to say next. 'You and I know that no matter how hard I try to fight it, we are.' He looked down at me then like a young boy looking for acceptance. I watched him twist his head slightly over to one side and rub at the scruff on his chin as he tried hard to read what I was thinking.

I couldn't help him. The whole of me was in turmoil. I didn't know what I was thinking or even doing. The situation between us was a clusterfuck. I knew I wanted him and that I was willing to fight for him. Even with what he'd thrown at me this morning and knowing the man holding me to him had killed others, I *still* wanted him. He might believe he was evil incarnate, but I didn't. I was instead convinced that he would have only taken a life if it was necessary to protect someone he loved.

But, when all was said and done, he needed to meet me halfway.

'Go on,' I encouraged.

'Normally I take what I need from a woman, throw money at her and let her move on to someone else,' he continued.

'Mmmm… peachy,' I uttered sarcastically.

He reached out and took hold of my hand and gently caressed the back of it with his thumb. My heart was beating so fast at his words and actions, I was sure he could feel it through my T-shirt.

'What if they don't want to move on?' I lifted my other hand and placed it onto his hard chest. Grabbing hold of his T-shirt, I held on to it tightly and used it to pull my body closer to his. I pressed my forehead as close into him as I could possibly get and sniffed as I attempted to shelve my emotions once again.

'They have no choice, it's the only way I've ever functioned.' His tone of voice let me know what he was saying was the truth.

'Until now?' I questioned hopefully.

'I'd like to think so, but honestly, I have no idea… I'm sorry.'

'What do you have to be sorry for? You saved me, Nico… you rescued me when I needed it the most, but now you need to let me in enough to reciprocate.'

'You just don't get it, do you? I can't let you in, it's pitch fucking black in here…like me you'd never find your way out.' I watched as one of his hands came up and his index finger jabbed at his temple. 'I'm trapped in here. I'm trapped in a hell of his and my own creation and the only thing that can release me is a bullet.' His Italian accent had crept back into his voice and I'd already worked out that it only happened when he became emotional or angry.

'DON'T. SAY. THAT!' The tears that had only just dried up released themselves and sped rapidly down my cheeks, soaking into his T-shirt.

'Whatever I am, and believe me I'm a lot of things, I always speak the truth and that's the truth as I understand it.'

I lifted my head from his chest and stared up at him. 'I don't believe you. I see you, Nico, no matter how much you try to keep yourself at arm's length. Forgiving yourself and accepting love from others will help you to find the light and the way out of the hell you say you reside in.'

His head tipped back, and his laughter pierced the silence around us. 'I can't be saved or rescued; it's far too fucking late for me.'

'Then let me love you,' I whispered. 'It's never too late for love.'

His head tipped forward again. His chest expanded with the deep inhale he sucked in, his eyebrow lifted, and his eye narrowed on me. 'Do you really think you could? I mean love a deranged bastard like me?'

'I could love a *man* like you, Nico… I truly do believe that.'

For a few seconds, we just stood there wrapped up in each other's arms staring intently at each other.

Finally, he broke through the silence.

'Then God fucking help you, because I can't push you away any longer, mio angelo… I'm not denying myself the light you bring into my life anymore… but when the darkness consumes me again and I break your heart, please don't hate me… because I warned you all along it would happen.'

'I could never hate you.'

'Never is a long time… now give me those sweet lips of yours.'

With more gentleness than I thought a man like Nico could possess, his mouth found mine. My lips parted on demand and I welcomed all of him home. I welcomed the light, dark and everything in between. I offered him the love I believed he needed and hoped in time he would be able to love me back in return.

Once a gambling addict, always an addict. I knew it.

But so help me, I couldn't help myself. I knew I was gambling and although this time it felt more dangerous, I just couldn't stop. I felt that what we could possibly have was worth the risk and I had to try. Unlike before, I was now gambling with my heart and it meant far more to me than the empty life I had almost been willing myself to lose back in Vegas.

CHAPTER TWENTY-FOUR

Bee

'THAT WAS DELICIOUS.' I wiped around my lips with the paper serviette Nico had put on my plate along with the jumbo-sized prawns and white fish he'd cooked over the fire. 'You really are a very good cook.'

'Thanks… although I have to be truthful, the green salad was one of Nonna's.'

'I know, I recognised the dressing.' I smiled back at him and watched him run his hand over the two days' worth of scruff that had now grown on his face as he thought over his next words. Since our arrival three hours ago and my subsequent emotional breakdown, we had only kissed the once, but he had made me sit down close to him while he had cooked for me and had attended to everything I needed.

'Do you dance, Bee?'

'I do… although, I mean… I can't remember when I last did… but I can.' I looked at him properly and saw the amusement on his face as he took in my mumbling. I watched him stand up and after brushing the sand off his shorts he held out his hand to me.

I took hold of his hand and felt the by now familiar zing that sped around my body as soon as our bare skin connected.

'But there's no music.' I smiled at him as he began to lead us around the other side of the fire pit.

'Yes, there is… I saw a speaker earlier in the tent. Have a think, Trip and Nonna with possibly some of Kendall's help organised this… So, what music do you think Trip's arranged?'

His hand released me and he moved away to go back the few steps to our luxury tent. Immediately I felt bereft at the loss of his hand on mine and shivered in response.

'The Beatles,' I offered and laughed at the way he came to an abrupt stop, turned his head to look at me in disgust, raised his eyebrows and shook his head as he silently gesticulated that Trip better not have.

'Let's hope not,' he laughed from inside the tent.

Nico came back out clutching a compact speaker in one hand and jogged the few steps back to where I stood. I was unconsciously rubbing at my bare arms with both of my hands as I tried to replace the feeling of his touch. He turned the speaker on and was once again walking over to be at my side. The moment his hands reached out towards me the air around us changed.

'I don't think I got to claim our first dance as husband and wife, so I think you owe me one.'

'No, you were too busy eating cake.' I laughed a little, enjoying the change of atmosphere around us since the last baring of our souls.

Nico's face didn't change as he grabbed at my hand and pulled me so fast into him, it made our bodies collide with a thud.

'I still owe you for that.' He grinned down at me with amusement making the corners of his eyes crinkle.

'I think if you remember correctly, I've already had my comeuppance,' I responded, with a breathier tone than I would have liked. It seemed that a simple touch of any part of his body on mine sent me spiralling out of control.

'Oh no, mio angelo… those orgasms you so willingly gave me were purely for me and now we need to sort out the balance of power in this relationship.' With his hands wrapped around me tightly he hoisted me further up into his arms and started running down towards the water's edge.

'No, you wouldn't!' the young girl in me squealed out.

'You know I would, Bee, and the more you struggle against me the wetter you're gonna get… in more ways than one.'

The light of the fire pit and the torches were being left behind us the nearer we got to the water's edge and although we were face to face, I couldn't make out his expression, but I knew he was playing along and teasing me.

Well who knew?

'Can you swim, Bee?'

'No,' I lied.

The cool water was suddenly lapping at my feet as Nico had started to gradually lower me down the length of his hard body, the further he walked out into the sea.

'Then it's time you learnt, little one, he quickly replied.

I started to struggle the moment the water came up to my knees and instead of allowing him to have complete control over the situation, I began to attempt to climb him like a tree.

Our laughter filled up the night air as he held on and I struggled against him. All at once I had a better hold and with my arms wrapped tightly around his neck, I attempted to wrap my legs around his body. The moment my pelvic bone touched his rock-hard erection the two of us stilled.

A starting gun had been silently fired inside both of our heads. The laughter died away and our eyes met each other's in the moonlight. Nico's hands moved their hold on me and after placing them under my armpits he lifted me up high into the air, just so he could look at me it seemed. I held on to the top of his shoulders and watched the man I was falling so hard for, as the reverence he held within his dark brown orbs filtered into me. Then he began to lower me slowly, making sure I connected with him in every possible way.

I needed him to kiss me. I wanted him to kiss me. My body was screaming to his, demanding that he respond to my needs. Our faces were now merely inches away from each other's.

His head finally began its slow descent. With his lips still together, he placed a firm kiss onto mine. His kiss didn't initially change, his closed mouth was still on mine, as if he was trying to convey his thoughts and feelings to me without any sexual undertones. But it was too late. I lifted my hands to cup his face, knowing I could effectively hold him in this position with his lips on mine.

I needed more of him. I pushed the tip of my tongue through the tiny gap between my lips and touched his warm, soft flesh. All at once, with that small contact, he broke our lips apart and moved his head a few inches away from me. For a second, he studied me closely and then his face came alive. With my eyes now adjusted to the change in light, I could see the gold threads in his eyes, as they sparkled in the moonlight we were surrounded by.

Suddenly, his hold on me changed, with one arm now wrapped around me tightly holding the majority of my weight, his free hand came to the back of my head. He threaded his fingers into my hair, pushed his fingertips into my scalp to angle my head just as he wanted it and then his mouth came crashing back to mine.

With us still standing in the water my body sagged into his as he consumed my mouth. Everything he had held back until now I felt in that one kiss, a kiss I had been dreaming of for what felt like forever. We had no audience and no one to playact for. The only people involved in the connection were us two. He took everything he needed from me and I responded with everything I had. His talented tongue caressed mine and danced around so quickly inside my mouth that I struggled to keep up, creating sparks that set my blood on fire. Concentrating hard on this moment that I'd been so impatiently waiting for, I forgot to breathe properly. My head began to feel woozy from the lack of oxygen and it brought with it a transcendent feeling of detachment. Everything else in my head was forgotten in those few minutes. I felt nothing else, but him and us. Our teeth crashed together as he pulled my head further into his.

The man was simply unyielding as he showed me exactly how much he wanted me. Finally, he controlled his need and tenderly started to pull away, caressing my tongue with his as he got ready to separate us once again into two separate beings. Reluctant to let him go, I sucked his bottom lip into my mouth and nipped it with my teeth as I stared pointedly into his eyes. The whole of his body tensed, and he stopped breathing completely. His rock-hard erection found the underneath of my ass as he tried to find some relief. I heard myself groan knowing we were only separated by the thin fabric of my panties.

'I want you,' he released on a groan.

'Then take me,' I whispered back, lost in the moment that was us.

Still holding me up, he used one hand to push up my short Denim skirt. I gasped as I felt his hot fingers connect with my skin that had been cooled by the sea water. Once again, his fingers found my hip and he pushed them under the thin piece of lace. I didn't hear the rip as he tore the fabric from my body, but felt the very second the material gave way to his impatience. My pussy was now exposed to his touch and the myriad of sensations that whirled around us. His fingers swept through my lips just once as he checked I was wet enough to take him. Before he pulled his hand away completely, he pressed one finger firmly onto my clit. My body escalated up with the sparks of pleasure that it set free. Suddenly, I was balancing precariously on the edge of an orgasm.

With my elbows leaning on his chest and still cupping his face with my hands, I put my lips back on his, desperate to feel more of him as the rest of my body cried out in need. He responded with his own eagerness and moved me enough to pull down the zip on his shorts. He changed his stance by bending his knees and shifted me down his body as he prepared to impale me on his hard cock.

I broke our kiss and opened my eyes to put them back on his, I needed to watch him come apart as he had watched me before.

'This won't be gentle,' he warned. 'I need you too much.'

'I don't need gentle. I just need you to fuck me,' I whispered with a voice that sounded every bit as desperate as I felt.

With one swift movement, Nico had lifted me up and brought me back down onto his cock. He filled me up so quickly and suddenly that I heard a scream of pleasure leave my mouth and echo into the empty night air around us. His cock was hot and rock hard inside me, it felt like I imagined steel encased in velvet would feel. I knew the second he entered me that my body was only just able to accept all of him, but I couldn't have cared less. I wanted to feel him so much, that in the heat of intensity that surrounded us, I silently wished he would fuck me so hard it would leave me sore for days.

Although I had tried hard to keep my eyes on his, the sensation that tore through me at his sudden possession of my body caused me to throw my head backwards until I was looking up at the stars with wide eyes.

He stilled initially, waiting for me to come back down to earth. Gradually my head fell forwards again and our eyes connected once more. He changed his hold on me, supporting my back with his forearms and his large hands cupping the back of my head.

Then without another word between us we were moving. I met every thrust of his hips with equal abandonment as he lifted me up and down over and again. The heat of our bodies contrasted to the cool slap of the water on our bare skin. Knowing the level of commitment we were giving each other, set off a riot of sensations between us both. My core quickly tightened, and I began to quiver and shake as his movements drove me quickly higher and higher. I fought against it initially wanting our first time to last longer, but I knew I couldn't fight against the inevitable. His eyes were focussed so intently on me as he concentrated hard on wringing every single piece of pleasure from my body, that I quickly realised he was in total control and I had no choice but to let go. When he thrust inside me again and added a swivel of his hips, I knew it was game over.

'Nico…Oh God… NICO!' In complete abandonment I screamed out my pleasure and chanted his name over and over.

As my orgasm crashed through me like the waves on the shore behind us and all of my senses switched off, all I was left with was the way his hands held me, the way his eyes pierced into my soul and the feel of his cock inside me.

'I'm fucking burning for you… look at me… watch as you consume me.'

The words fell out of his mouth and I watched totally mesmerised as Nico relaxed into his own impending orgasm. Still holding us both up in the cool water, his body convulsed in my arms and he groaned. The sound he released vibrated through me as I felt his cum fill me up inside with long, warm, satisfying spurts.

At last his orgasm left him and he pulled me tightly to him as he fought to keep his balance in the water. Although I could tell he was totally spent he was somehow still managing to remain upright. My heart melted just a little bit more as I understood all he was concerned about now was getting me safely out of the water.

Slowly, but surely, he walked out of the sea still holding me in his arms. As soon as he was once again on the sand, he lowered my feet to the floor and rested his forehead on my shoulder while I wrapped my arms around his neck and held him to me.

'That was...' he started and as the words left him, he laughed lightly.

'It was,' I replied.

His head lifted up. I stood up on my tiptoes and pressed my lips quickly to his as I checked he was still real and happy to be in my arms.

A smile lit up his face and my heart opened up wide to silently embrace him.

'Now about that dance, Mr. Morello,' I whispered to him.

CHAPTER TWENTY-FIVE

Nico

'Now about that dance, Mr. Morello,' she whispered to me, with a smile on her lips that shattered the cast iron casing around my inky, black heart.

'I think I can manage that,' I offered.

Out of the water and with the solid ground back underneath our feet, I held Bee closely to me and began to move. Still holding onto her as we danced, was giving me time to sort out what the fuck was going on inside of me. In the sea, the feelings that had been unleashed between us had seemed as temporary as the tide turning direction. I had wanted to feel her tight, wet pussy wrapped around my cock, so I had. My head had been demanding me to feel her walls quiver as I drove myself selfishly in and out of her. The need to watch her come apart in my arms had been so fucking compelling back then. But here, back on terra firma, having shot my load into her not ten minutes ago, I needed... no... wanted to feel her all over again, and that was a strange and confusing compulsion that was rocking me to my core.

Our eyes were firmly fixed on each other's and I held her so close to me that nearly every part of our bodies were tightly entwined. She'd allowed me to possess her. In doing so, she had captured and enthralled me and I knew I wasn't going to be releasing her anytime soon.

She intrigued me and I wanted to know everything there was to know about her. Fleetingly that thought concerned me, but then I felt liberated. I'd spent what felt like nearly a lifetime, refusing to get close to anyone who could be used against my family and yet, here I was, I'd never felt higher on fucking life than I did at this moment.

Mio angelo.

My angel, without a doubt she was the soft candlelight that lit up the dark recesses of my desperate soul. Perhaps my mamma had sent her down especially for me, an angel from heaven. The more I dwelled on it, I could hear mamma's words telling me when I was younger, how I was going to be a man who needed the love of a good woman in my life. She'd said I would need the love and understanding that only a wife could offer me, and maybe she'd been right after all.

And now I have one, well fuck.

I moved us around gently to the sounds of the sea lapping the shore and the playlist coming from the small speaker, where we heard Elvis singing his heart out about love. I'd always loved his music, but now the words he was singing meant so very much more. When the compulsion took me, I had sung along making sure she heard and felt the meaning behind the words as deeply as I was feeling them. I pressed my face tightly against the side of her head and listened to her gasp each time my warm breath caressed over the shell of her ear.

When **"Let it be me"** by **Elvis** came through the small speaker I summoned all the courage I had and sung each word to her and meant every single one.

As a grown man I'd never been scared, my upbringing had conditioned me out of it. I had survived my precious mamma taking her own life and my repugnant father, despite his many attempts to break me and those I loved. I'd even endured having to kill others in order to keep my small family alive, but I wasn't sure how I would survive the woman in my arms when the devil inside me demanded that I had to let her go. But until then, I wanted to know everything there was to know about her. I needed to make enough memories in the short time I knew we'd have together, to last me a lifetime. I wanted her laughter. I wanted all of the smiles that lit up the exquisite features on her face to be for me. I wanted her pleasure, but most of all I wanted the love she was offering. She had let me take possession of her and I meant to have every single fragment of the woman.

Bee

Slow dancing with my new husband on a beautiful secluded beach could definitely be described as foreplay. The feel of his hard, muscular body against mine as he controlled our every movement and whispered sweet words into my ears meant that my body was climbing higher and higher with an animalistic need. Top that with the fresh smell of his cologne wafting up and into my nostrils on the heat of his body, meant that my core was once again throbbing and aching for him.

'Tell me something about you no one else knows, Bee?' he gently implored.

'I'm in love with Crete. I feel happier in the short time I've been here than any other place I've ever lived... and I think that's got a lot to do with sharing it with you.' That was an easy question to answer, but knowing I'd opened up a little about how he made me feel I prepared myself for him to pull away again.

When a surprisingly deep laugh left him, the warm vibrations travelled through me.

'What?' I asked as we continued to dance.

'I'm happy, what you've just said makes me happier than I can remember being in a long time.'

'You are?' Relief rushed through me. 'That's good... So, it's your turn... tell me something about you that no one else knows?'

I lifted my head away from his chest to look up at him when he suddenly stopped dancing and offered me no answer. Darkness had swept in and just when I thought our precious moment had been spoilt, I watched with relief as a smile lit up his face.

'There is something.'

'Yes?' I was desperate for any snippet on the man that could possibly allow us to get closer.

'I had that dragonfly pin made especially for you. I designed it with only you and our wedding in mind.'

'Oh,' I released on a soft sigh, as a feeling of warmth spread through me.

'I'm also eager…' he started.

Then suddenly we were falling.

His foot had hooked the back of my leg and we were going down to the sand. Initially, he cushioned my fall by letting me land on him, knowing he had taken me by surprise. Then he quickly rolled me over and began to run his fingers up and down my sides.

'… to know if you're ticklish,' he finished.

My spontaneous laughter at the position he had put us in took over and as he started his onslaught on my body, I began to try to push him away. Nico made it his goal to keep me just where he wanted me, lying down with my back pressed into the now rapidly cooling sand. He lifted his leg and threw it over the top of me. Now sitting on top of me and finding himself in a better position, he continued his onslaught.

'Stop…STOP, Nico.' I carried on laughing as his hands sustained their attack on my now aching sides. In between the tears running down my face I saw the look of complete pleasure on his face and cursed the fact I couldn't take a picture of the man.

'Stop, Nico… please stop, I'm going to wet myself.'

Having a big brother, I had always known what to say to get him to move away.

I heard him tut first, and although he did stop his attack on my very ticklish body so I could finally breathe properly, he still stayed in place. 'Mio angelo, that won't work with me.' He grinned down at me and gently swept my hair off my face.

I wiped the tears of laughter off my wet cheeks and returned his smile.

'What do you call me, Nico?'

He picked up my hand and pressed his warm lips against it which sent off a ricochet feeling of fireflies doing somersaults inside my stomach.

'It means, my angel,' he answered.

'Why?' I loved it, but needed to know more.

'When you stepped inside the church to marry me, in your beautiful dress with the sunlight surrounding you, you reminded me of an angel… my angel.'

'Oh…' His words, his commitment and the feeling behind them had temporarily rendered me speechless. I swallowed hard and carried on, giving him the words I wanted him to hear. 'I like that.'

Nico cleared his throat and rolled away from sitting on my body. He positioned himself to lie beside me, grabbing hold of my hand as he did so. The sudden awakening of the feelings between us was almost too much for me to take in. I also knew that was why he'd moved. Once again, he'd felt the need to sever the connection between us slightly while he regained his composure. I recognised it because it was how I felt too. The man I was lying next to, staring up at the night sky with, was beginning to take over my heart and soul. Ninety percent of me was rejoicing at the realisation that I had found my person and the other ten percent was running for the hills.

'It's so beautifully dark out here,' I whispered to him, trying to break through the sudden silence that had engulfed us.

'You should always be afraid of the dark, Bee.' I heard the warning in his tone and snapped my head around to face him.

The man was far beyond anything my head could have conjured up in my wildest dreams. Tall, dark and dangerous were the predominant descriptors for the man, but to me he was so very much more. With his dark hair and solid, now stubble-covered, square jaw, I was convinced he could turn any woman's head. Why he had chosen me to act out the role of his wife, when he could have had anyone, I was still unsure of. But I was so pleased he had. I could feel that, even with his warnings, he was opening up his heart and letting me in inch by inch.

'With you by my side… never.' I spoke the words and watched his head turn slowly towards me.

Although he shook his head slightly at me, his eyes found mine and the threads of gold I found inside them sparked a catalyst of hope throughout me.

'If we didn't all contain a dark canvas, how would anybody be able to see just how brightly the stars inside us all shine?'

Initially he screwed his eyes shut and exhaled suddenly through his nostrils in disbelief at my words. Then almost as if he could still feel me staring at him, wordlessly telling him that I meant every word of what I'd just said, his eyes opened again.

'You can see all of that in me?' I watched his eyebrow lift up in disbelief. 'My darkness and some shards of light?' he questioned.

'You're not just a shard of light, Nico. You're the brightest star in my sky.'

I saw the tears gather in his eyes as he digested the words I'd just spoken. Nico rolled over, pushed himself up on his elbow and placed the heel of his hand to his temple to lean his head on. I felt the fingertips of his other hand gently brush against my chin as he tipped my head back in readiness for his lips.

His head came down to mine slowly, but so very surely in its every movement. Eventually his lips brushed against mine. The connection between us was complete. His tongue came out to taste me like it was the very first time we had ever kissed and perhaps it was. It gently caressed my needy mouth until, satisfied he'd found what he was looking for, his mouth descended quickly to mine. The dance between us was slow, as we tasted and loved each other. The simple truths we were allowing each other were laid bare under the light of the stars on a secluded beach in Crete, and my life had never felt more perfect than it did at that moment. He lifted his head away from mine and for a few short seconds stared at me like I meant the world to him. My heart fluttered against my chest as I lifted my fingers and ran them gently over his still wet lips. In return he grabbed hold of my hand and kissed my fingers gently.

Grinning at me and without taking his eyes off mine, Nico jumped up suddenly and still holding onto my hand he pulled me abruptly up to my feet. Then unceremoniously he swept me up into his arms and strode purposefully to our tent. 'And now, angel of mine, it's time to make you mine forever.'

CHAPTER TWENTY-SIX

NICO

MY BLOOD WAS ON fire for the woman in my arms. But for now, I knew I needed to rein in my compulsions.

"You can't have anything nice to play with." My father's voice echoed around my head and I cleared my throat to free myself from him.

He'd trained Cade and I to be dominants, to recognise a woman's every want and need. Then he'd watched as, under his so called guidance, we'd trained several women to be submissive to us. It wasn't the sort of sexual experience any adolescent should have, but he didn't care about us. He had only cared about satisfying his own sexual needs.

Playing a dominant role still had its place in my life, but not now, not here with my new wife. For now, I knew I needed to shelve those urges.

She deserved to be treated tenderly. She needed to be made love to all night long softy and gently. Contrary to how I'd been trained and subsequently against what were now my own sexual preferences that was exactly what I was going to do.

I lowered her onto the comfortable looking bedding and stood back to look down at her. Not moving a muscle from where I'd left her, Bee in turn looked back at me expectantly with her expressive, teal coloured eyes. I watched as her pupils dilated and then when something else caught my eye, I allowed my eyes to wander down.

Her lips parted slowly as she tried to draw in more oxygen to fuel the adrenalin I knew was already coursing through her body. The tells of which I recognised from the blush pink colour on her chest and the heightened colour I could see in her cheeks. My cock grew quickly, until it was pushing uncomfortably behind the zip in my shorts. My balls were aching to be emptied inside of her again. I stored the feelings, knowing they would serve me well later and turned my attentions back to the woman who was offering me all she was and I attempted, for the first time in my life, to connect with someone else as Nico Morello and not their Don, or boss.

'Eyes on me, angel.'

Slowly, with her eyes focussing on me I began to strip out of the few clothes I was wearing. I'd felt her eyes on my back this morning as I'd dressed, and I wanted to give her what I knew she had wordlessly asked for earlier. She wanted to see me, to touch and to be fucked by me and who the hell was I to deny her. With her eyes appraising what she was looking at, I was so goddamned pleased for every single visit I'd ever made to my gym and every run I'd pushed my protesting body through.

'This is for you, Bee… all for you.'

With one hand at the back of my neck I pulled my T-shirt up slowly. I knew the minute my abs had been exposed to her as I heard a sigh leave her beautiful lips. Now concealed inside my T-shirt, I smiled to myself as I continued to slowly expose my body to her. The material skimmed up my own needy flesh and I imagined it was her fingertips casually brushing over my skin. The picture in my head was so fucking sharp I had to take in a deep breath.

Still I continued, slowly and tantalisingly I exposed my body to her. I knew I looked good naked, several women had informed me of just that and I could see the lustful looks I got from nearly every woman I'd ever come into contact with. But even if I gave them what they thought they wanted from me; I never gave them everything I was. But for this woman, this woman who was reclined out expectantly in front of me, my wife. Well, I wanted her to have me in my entirety. I wanted her to look at me as every fucking wet dream she'd ever had and to never look at another man again.

Finally, I pulled the T-shirt off my head and threw it to the floor behind me. Before our eyes met again, I took in the sight of her hand holding on to the edge of the bed and her fingernails as they dug deeply into the soft bedding.

I let one of my hands travel down slowly over the length of my abdomen making sure the movement caught her attention and that she watched my fingers travel over every undulation.

Then I released the button on my shorts and lowered the zip. By only lowering it an inch I knew my shorts would fall until they met my hips and revealed V shaped muscles that pointed to the nirvana I now knew she was salivating for.

I knew how visual stimulation turned women on. If you could control and feed their imagination, then you were halfway to satisfying them. But right now, this performance I was putting on especially for her, was driving me forward much quicker than I wanted.

Clasping my hands together, I put them on top of my head and inhaled deeply before I allowed my eyes to sweep up and down her body, not trusting myself to keep my hands to myself.

'Tell me what you want, angel?'

'I… I want you, your touch, your tongue and your cock inside me.' Her face looked shocked at what I'd got her to admit.

I felt a broad smile spread over my face at her admission.

Her toenails were still the pearlized colour she'd had for our wedding and that was where I was convinced her fucking innocence ended. I had no idea how many men she had slept with before and I wasn't interested either. I knew that she could have been a God forbid fucking virgin until she'd met me and she would still have instinctively known just how to please me, and she most definitely was fucking pleasing me.

Her long legs were bronzed from the Mediterranean sun and bare apart from the silver ankle chain she wore.

My eyes lifted higher to her short denim skirt, which was riding higher, and having ripped off her panties in the sea earlier I knew she was bare underneath. In the twisted position I'd laid her down in with her legs askew, I could see the swell of her ass and the very top of the apex of her thighs. The lemon, button-up lace top she had on didn't meet the waistband of the skirt. The tiny reveal of her toned stomach was so fucking provocative that I had to push my tongue into the side of my mouth as I fought against ripping the rest of her clothes off and sampling each and every square inch of her bare skin with my tongue and teeth.

At last my eyes found her face, and everything I found written there told me she was as fucking desperate as me.

Blood was pumping so fast around my system I could almost taste the salt in it and that's when I understood that I'd bitten down onto the soft flesh of the inside of my cheek as I tried to control my own compulsions.

I wanted to rip away her clothing, fall to my knees and devour each and every single inch of her. I knew that I was beginning to lose the fight against my desire to be tender with her.

I was quickly losing my mind.

I was burning with need.

I needed my hands on her, my cock in her mouth and my hands in her hair as I fucking controlled her movements.

Her tongue flicking out as she swept it across her dry lips pulled my eyes quickly back to hers.

'I want to take my time with you, Bee… but I also want to fuck you so damn hard that just thinking about it tomorrow will make you wet…' I told her everything she needed to know and leant my head over to one side as I waited for her answer.

'I want you, Nico. I want all of you… every single side of you.' Slowly, her hands moved and her fingers trailed over the frayed hem of her skirt. All too fucking slowly she lifted up the bottom and exposed her weeping pussy to me. The smell of her hit my nostrils and tipped me over the edge of the precipice I'd been balancing on. My restraint that had been coiled tightly up inside of me like a reel of steel wire sheared abruptly.

I couldn't think or control anymore.

Now, I just wanted to feel, and I needed it to be her under my fingers, in my mouth and wrapped around my cock.

I watched her mouth fall open as I silently answered her with my actions. Leaning over her, I put my hands on either side of the button that held her skirt to her and pulled my hands apart suddenly, making the button ping off somewhere inside the tent and then I swiftly pulled it down her legs.

Doggedly, I released her and walked to the bottom of the bed. In one movement I fell to my knees, removed her skirt and, grabbing hold of her ankles, I parted her legs. Then hearing a whimper leave her mouth as she envisaged just what was coming, I pulled her down the bed until her pussy was in my mouth.

At just the taste of her, my inner turmoil was calmed.

'Nico…Oh God, yes…'

I ran my tongue up and down her slit over and over again, licking up her juices as soon as they appeared, like a man desperate for his next fucking fix. With my hands pushing against her inner thighs I opened her up as wide as she could comfortably go and rammed my tongue inside of her, rubbing it against the quivering walls of her pussy. I held onto her firmly as she began to writhe in my hold, and I knew she was beginning to unravel. Removing my tongue, I replaced it with two of my fingers, savouring the sensation of just how soaking she was on my hand. Then I pressed my tongue firmly down onto the hood of her clit and after gently lifting it with the tip of my tongue I sucked the exposed, engorged flesh into my mouth.

Bee exploded around me.

Her screams filled my senses and her gasps of pleasure expanded my shrivelled-up heart and I knew I'd never get enough of giving her pleasure.

Every limb of hers flexed, spasmed and relaxed time and time again. I licked and sucked with my mouth and coaxed with my fingers inside of her until at last, she lay spent and motionless on the bed.

Placing a kiss to her clit I watched, smiling to myself as her body reacted to my action and the after tremors ran through her making her core convulse. Then after pushing my shorts to the floor with one hand, I began to crawl slowly up her trembling, prone body.

'I want to taste every part of you…'

I placed a kiss, lick or soft bite to every piece of exposed flesh I found in front of me.

'I want your bare skin on mine.'

When I eventually came up against her cotton top and it stopped me in my tracks, I inhaled the light floral fragrance that I knew would always and forever remind me of her.

I lifted my head to find she'd lifted hers up from the pillow behind her. With heavy looking, hooded eyes she was watching my slow progression up her body. With my hands now on the final piece of material separating us, I stared into her eyes and recognised the minute she saw what was coming. With a smile of ownership on my face, I kept my eyes on hers as the tiny buttons down the front of her top were torn off the material. The yellow fabric fell away from her breasts and down to the sides of her body.

My eyes feasted on her exposed flesh, and her breasts, for the first time. If I hadn't wanted her with everything I had before, what I saw in front of my eyes now would have fuelled me on. Taking in the dark colour of her areola and the pronounced swell of her full breasts, I was in fucking heaven.

'Fucking gorgeous, Bee… You're exquisite, my angel.'

She was more beautiful than I could have imagined.

It was my turn to groan.

Swallowing down the moans that wanted to force themselves free of my mouth, I moved myself further up her body and took one of her taut nipples into my mouth, using my tongue to pull on it and lengthen the needy bud. I sucked on it so strongly that her breast began to lift away from her chest. But her gasps and writhing underneath me let me know that along with the slight amount of pain my administrations were causing her, she was also experiencing pleasure. Her bare skin brushed against mine every time she moved and as always when we connected, electrical currents were passing between us both. I could feel the immense pleasure being released inside her as it was now travelling around her body and also into mine.

'Oh, Jesus… Nic.' I heard her words as she threw her head backwards and down onto the pillow behind her.

'You're the most beautiful thing I've ever owned, Bee. I do own you, don't I?' I asked the question after releasing her nipple. I'd let it slip free of my wet mouth and then I'd watched mesmerised as her heavy breast fell back down into place.

'Yes... you possess me,' she whispered in answer, referring back to what I'd demanded of her only yesterday.

'Then touch me, Bee... mark me as yours...use those fucking nails of yours on me and let me know how much you want me.'

Her eyes sprung open at my words and her arms came around me as I'd commanded. Holding me tightly with her forearms she proceeded to run her hands over my back, connecting her nails in places with my skin and I curved upwards to meet the pain and pleasure she was now clawing down my back.

'Yes,' I forced out through gritted teeth in response to her actions and then my head fell forward again.

My mouth eventually found her other nipple, sucking it so quickly into my mouth that she let out a scream of pleasure. In response, I moved to rest down on my elbows and took her other nipple in between my fingers, twisting and pulling her needy flesh. I moved my mouth quickly across her chest making sure she felt my stubble graze over her skin and swapped my mouth for my fingers several times over.

Her hips were beginning to flex in response, lifting up into my stomach. I could feel my cock weeping bead after bead of pre-cum as I forced myself to concentrate on her.

'Please... I need to feel you inside of me... I want...'

'What do you want?' I demanded as I pinched the nipple I was rolling in my fingers.

'Ahhhhh... I want to feel your body all over me,' left her mouth in a soft demand.

I cracked her legs further open with one of my knees and climbed higher up her body. Then I settled my weight in between her legs and pushed my cock into the unyielding pressure of her pelvic bone. The heat from her skin seared into me and I felt my teeth bite down onto my lip.

'Fuck… you feel so fucking good,' I groaned to her.

Enough.

In one swift movement, I let my hand drift down the side of her body, feeling her skin react at the touch of my fingers, took hold of her leg and making her bend it at the knee I made sure she was open wide enough for me. Shifting my weight and rolling more onto one side I found her eyes with my own and grasping hold of my needy cock I swiped it all the way through her soaked lips and then pressed it firmly onto her clit.

Just as her eyes began to roll up into her head, high on the heady pleasure the contact between us had created, I pushed inside of her, making sure I didn't stop until my balls could feel the heat of her lips surrounding them.

Then I stilled, wanting to hear just how desperate she was to be fucked by me.

'You're so fucking wet for me… how much do you want me to move my cock inside of you, mio angelo?'

I knew I was smiling down at her. No matter how much my balls were flexing as they demanded their release, I wanted to hear her voice how impatient I made her feel.

'I need you, Nico, please fuck me.'

I began to rock in and out of her, knowing how much we both needed to feel each other. My body immediately ignited at the pleasure being unfurled inside of me, but with our eyes still firmly fixed on each other's it was the feeling of love that came from her eyes that overwhelmed me the most. I lowered my head to her breast and I lathed at her nipple as I helped her body begin to chase her orgasm.

'More…' she released on a wavering exhale. 'Please, I need more… I need you to move faster.'

'This needs to be slow, angel… I'm gonna watch you as you fall apart with my cock inside you.'

Almost painfully slowly, I continued with the same torturous pace waiting to see what I needed from her. Her hands grabbed onto my shoulders and her spine arched underneath me as she pushed herself as close to me as she could.

Then it started, tears began to collect in the corner of her eyes as she climbed up higher and reached the peak of her orgasm.

'NICO!' Bee calling my name filtered into my ears, along with the screams she was now letting go into the night air with every thrust of my cock inside her.

As she started to pulse around me, my control snapped and recognising what we both needed, I picked up speed, fucking her hard as she rode the wave of her release and I chased my own. The walls of her pussy contracted around me as she unconsciously tried to encourage every last drop of my cum to enter her, and who the fuck was I to deny this woman anything. Now completely lost in my own orgasm, I allowed my balls to erupt inside of her, over and over again with every flex of my hips into her. In my head, I imagined my cum covering every part of her soft pink, velvet lined pussy.

Just as the last of my release threatened, I pulled out my cock suddenly and taking it in my right hand, I pumped it hard. Groaning out loud, I watched the long strings of white as they left my body and coated the underneath of the beautiful globes of her breasts, effectively marking her as mine.

'Angel...'

I heard my voice shout out her name and then spent, I collapsed on top of her. Holding her hips in both of my hands, I rested my head down onto her stomach. There we stayed unmoving, with only the sound of our heavy breathing and the waves as they caressed the beach outside. I felt her begin to run her fingers through my hair and at her touch my body stirred and so did the voracious need I seemed to permanently have for this woman, my woman, mio angelo.

My cock began to stir and my mouth formed into a smile.

It was going to be a very long, pleasurable night and one that I was going to make certain she would feel for fucking days and remember for the rest of her life.

CHAPTER TWENTY-SEVEN

Bee

'BARBARA.' I HEARD NONNA calling out my name from the large vestibule.

'I'm in my dark room, I'll be out in a few minutes,' I shouted back as I wiped my hands on the rag beside me.

I hung up the last of the photographs I'd been developing, switched off the safelight and opened the blinds. Then I stood back to admire the pictures as they started to dry. Every picture I cast my eyes over had a memory attached to it and for someone who was still very much learning this new hobby, I was very proud of the skills that I had already acquired. This was an old-fashioned way of producing my pictures, but I loved the sense of purpose it gave me. So, for now, I saved some of my pictures on memory cards and others that I'd taken with the camera Nico had bought for me which used film, I developed in the dark room he'd had especially built for me.

Strangely it was these ones that really hit home. Whether it was because I was creating something from start to finish, I didn't know, but perhaps it was because the majority of them were of my husband and the dragonflies that seemed to frequent our pool in the early evening.

I was in total awe of them both.

I loved how naturally photogenic Nico was and how completely at ease my camera lens nearly always witnessed him. There, captured inside the photo I'd taken, was the man I knew my husband was deep down inside. The one that he hadn't been allowed to be. The one I was discovering, at the very same time he unravelled me here on a small island in the Mediterranean Sea. I loved staring at the many pictures I'd taken of him. In some of them he was completely oblivious to me and in others he was staring so pointedly down the lens at me that my heartbeat quickened and my core tightened. It was crazy how he could make me feel just standing in this small room, looking at him on the flat pieces of paper.

I ran my finger down the edge of one I'd developed a few days ago and traced the outline of his silhouette, smiling as I remembered coating his nose with some of our wedding cake. We had been married for nearly four months now and I had more happy memories with him than in the rest of my very sad life put together.

I missed him.

With everything I was, I missed him.

He'd been back in Vegas for four days and although this was now the regular pattern we had in our lives, one week here and one in Vegas, I missed everything about him when he was gone. I missed the sound of his voice when his tone deepened as he called me his angel, the smell of his cologne, the way he looked at me and most of all the way he held me tightly, wrapped up in his arms all night. Missing him wasn't something I'd even contemplated when I'd agreed to our arrangement, but I hadn't known then how completely he would take over my life.

For the first time in my life, I appeared to be a natural at not only one but two things, photography and marriage. With Nico's help and direction, I was definitely moving forward in the right direction, making changes to leave my old life in Vegas behind.

I looked back up at his face grinning down at me from the wall and smiled back at him. I knew he couldn't see me, but what the hell. Then I quickly glanced at the various scenes of Crete that surrounded him on the walls. Some had been taken in the sunshine, some at sunrise and others at sunset. A few of them were of the historical places we'd seen with Trip and Kendall on our road-trip around the island.

I loved them all.

'Kendall is on the phone. Shall I tell her you'll call her back?' Nonna asked from the other side of the door.

Talk of the devil herself. I grinned immediately looking forward to a girly chat.

'I'm just coming,' I replied and, unlocking the door, I opened it to find her standing there, talking into the phone she held in her hand.

'She's opened the door, Kendall…' she smiled at me, 'yes it was lovely talking to you and Brucey… I'm looking forward to seeing you all back here in a few days' time… yes, yes I will… passing you over now, bye.'

Nonna smiled at me as she passed me the phone and at the same time she pointed at my dark room, and with a mouthed "please" she asked me if she could go in to see the pictures I'd just developed.

I took the phone from her and nodded at her as I moved out of the way to let her through.

'Hi, Kendall.'

'Bee, how are you?' I heard in my ear.

'I'm good, really good... I'm getting a little bit nervous about going back to Vegas, but I can't wait to see Nico. So, with that and meeting up with Mrs. Davison, I'm sure it will all be worth it.'

'It will, I'm sure of it... I think she's right in encouraging you to go back there.'

'You do?' I questioned, as I nervously ran my finger around the wooden frame of the painting hanging next to where I stood.

'Yes... absolutely. You said she was pleased with your progress and I think it's right to push it a little bit further. Being married to Nic it's not like you can never set foot in the place again, is it?'

Isn't it? In all honesty I would have been happy never to set foot off Crete again.

'No, you're right. Thanks for saying it as it is.'

Although I was nervous, I truly appreciated having her honesty and friendship in my life, when for the years that followed my auntie's death, I'd only had Pearl. Pearl had been wonderful, and I didn't know how I would have survived without her. She was neither my mom nor my best friend, so she'd been able to give advice like a friend and tell me off like a parent. But, however strange our relationship, I knew that the wonderful pink-haired woman had kept me alive until I'd been given another chance at life. I missed her and Tiger, and I knew it would also be good to see them both.

I had been truthful with Kendall about my addiction one night a few weeks ago, as we'd sat on the patio sharing a bottle of wine together. We had been talking about our childhoods. Surprising myself, without any hesitation I'd opened up and told her how my mom's addiction to prescription pills had taken her life. She'd told me about how her mother had been an alcoholic for as far back as she could remember, then with a look of melancholy on her face she'd said how much she respected people who had an addiction and were willing to combat it. On cue I'd told her about myself and how Nico was helping me work through what had contributed towards my downward spiral into the gambling I'd used as a crutch in the first place.

She had nodded at me as I'd spoken, almost as though she was connecting the pieces of a jigsaw together inside of her head and I'd understood then that Trip was of course aware of the arrangement between Nico and myself.

For a few short minutes, I'd felt violated that he'd told someone else about our arrangement. I let the thoughts swirl around in my head that someone else knew my business before I was ready to tell them myself. But then my anger started to subside as I realised that if I'd had a best friend at the time, I would have confided in them, too. Trip, Kendall and Nonna were constantly working in the background to make sure that Nico and I were happy together. With that reminder my anger finally disbursed, because I knew it was superfluous and would serve no purpose. The three of them were our biggest cheerleaders.

Kendall's voice broke through my thoughts.

'Anyway, if you weren't coming back to Vegas, who would I have to go on a shopping spree with?'

My anxiety was immediately shelved as a smile stretched over my face at her words. 'Are there no shops in Boca?' I asked laughing.

'Yes... but they're not like the shops in Vegas... my husband has far too much money and as a dutiful wife I need to help him out with that situation.' Her light laughter travelled across the miles in between us.

I could almost see her face grinning as she winked at me.

'Does Trip know what you have planned?'

'Well, he's far too busy working at the minute... and what he doesn't know won't hurt him, will it?'

I was well aware that the situation between Nico and myself meant Trip was working far more hours than his "semi-retired" situation would have normally entailed.

'I'm sorry he's away so much from you and Bruce,' I offered, and grimaced lightly. At the same time, Nonna leaving my dark room caught my eye. Holding her hand over her chest as she mouthed "wow" at the pictures she'd found inside.

'Thank you,' I whispered to Nonna.

When she blew me a kiss, I grabbed at her fingers and briefly squeezed them before she walked away.

'Hey, don't you be sorry. For Nico, and now also for you, we're happy to continue this arrangement for as long as necessary... and without it, Bee, what excuse would I manage to come up with to shop in Vegas?'

'I can't tell you how much I appreciate it.'

'That's fine… I don't need you to tell me. But what I do need you to tell me is that you're all packed up and ready to go?'

'I am.' My heart accelerated at the thought of being able to touch Nico soon.

'Trip should have landed at the airport now,' she sighed into the phone.

Of course, she knew his every movement. Nico and I were separated by thousands of miles and the time difference, but I always had an idea of what he was doing at any given time of the day. It made me feel more connected to him as she was to Trip.

'Yes, he should,' I agreed, after looking down the hall at the large grandfather clock and checking the time.

My stomach turned over in excitement. My bag was already in the car and Raul, who Nico had promoted to my personal bodyguard, had already told me he was ready to drive to the airport as soon as I was.

'I'll see you both soon then… I'll be the one in the plane with the handsome pilot,' I teased.

'Tell him we love him,' she insisted.

'I will… but I'm convinced you'll be able to show him yourself later,' I teased her just a little bit more.

'You can be sure of it. See you soon.' I could hear the smile in her voice

'Ciao,' I instinctively replied as I terminated the call.

Then I sped down the stairs, amused at just how much living with Nico and his grandmother was beginning to affect me.

CHAPTER TWENTY-EIGHT

Nico

THIS DEFINITELY WASN'T IN my remit, standing waiting on the tarmac at arrivals.

I knew it wasn't in the same league as McCarran Airport, but today the airport where I housed my aircraft was typically the busiest I'd ever seen it. Even though Henderson was a private airport, the fact I'd arrived with my security team who were now stood around me suited and booted meant we'd been getting a lot of interest.

A lot of very unwanted interest.

Although no one came anywhere near us, I could feel their eyes. I was pleased I was wearing the Aviators that Trip had given me the day I'd married Bee. At least it meant my eyes, and the anger they were projecting at the many stares the four of us were receiving, were effectively filtered.

Fuck, I should have stayed away. I could only imagine how we looked.

Our expensive suits and stance screamed exactly what we were, mafia.

I crossed my arms over my chest and probably creased the fabric of the ten-thousand-dollar suit as I did so and shook my head at myself. I was so desperate to see Bee there was no way, under any given circumstance, that I was prepared to stay away from the airport. I knew she was nervous about being back in Vegas as I'd been speaking to her via Facetime until she'd fallen asleep last night, like I did every night she wasn't in my arms, and she'd shared how unnerved she felt by it.

Because of that, I wanted to be the first thing she saw as she walked off the plane, down the steps and back onto Vegas soil. I wanted her to know I was here and that I was going to support her for as long as she needed me. Inside, if I was honest with myself, I seriously hoped that would be for a very long time.

Suddenly, my private aircraft came into view as it began its descent to the runway. My heart started pounding in excitement and I cleared my throat loudly as I watched every movement Trip made with my precious cargo onboard. All too slowly the aircraft grew bigger against the background of the blue sky until finally its wheels were safely on the ground and I loudly exhaled the breath I hadn't even realised I'd been holding. I watched the aircraft as it slowed and then turned towards its place on the apron. Trying to relax my taut shoulder muscles I uncrossed my arms, released the one button that was done up on my suit jacket and pushed my hands down deep into my pants pockets.

The moment the door opened and the stairs were lowered to the tarmac, I had to physically force myself not to cross the short distance between us. As momentum tried to carry me forward, I rocked onto the balls of my feet and then immediately righted myself. There was no way in hell I could allow myself to walk over to the plane with the many eyes, and also probably phone cameras, focussed in my direction at this very minute.

At last Bee peered around the door of the plane. The corners of my mouth twitched as my face began to break out its welcome to her and then my nostrils flared as I took in just how little clothing she was wearing. I ran my eyes up and down her to find a pair of white shorts that only just about covered up her backside, a cherry red, off-the-shoulder top and a large floppy hat which she was holding to her head with one hand as the wind that blew down the runway threatened to blow it away.

I shouldn't have come. The unease that rushed through me was overwhelming. I was completely out of my comfort zone, struggling between wanting to sweep her up into my arms to hold her to me one second and the next balling my hands into fists inside my pockets as the urge came over me to smack her ass at the amount of flesh she was exposing to the world.

I swallowed hard, feeling my Adams apple move in my throat. *Who the fuck are you kidding? You're here because you couldn't keep away if you tried.*

I watched with jealousy uncurling itself in my gut as the co-pilot offered her his hand to walk down the steps to the ground and I waited for her to find me with her beautiful eyes. Unable to wait any longer, I wrenched a hand from out of my pocket, and pulled my Aviators off my face, feeling them contract and spring in my fingers. Then trying to act naturally in a situation that was fucking alien to me, I calmly tucked them inside the top pocket of my suit jacket.

At last her eyes found mine and, in that split second, I couldn't have cared if CNN had a hundred cameras pointed on us. I pulled my other hand out of my pocket and on instinct I held both of my arms out wide for her.

Nothing could have prepared me for her reaction to what I was offering.

Dropping her purse to the floor and no longer caring if her hat stayed on her head, she started running towards me, as fast as her red chucks would carry her. Knowing that I no longer had any control over my feelings when it came her, and also understanding that I would give anything to feel her in my arms, I gave in and started to walk forward to meet her.

Just before our bodies collided, at the very last second, she put her hands on my shoulders and jumped into my arms, wrapping her legs tightly around my hips and then folding her arms around my neck. I clasped her to me and stood motionless, reeling inside at the way I now felt complete with her back in my arms. With one of my hands cradling the back of her head and the other on the bare skin I found high up on one of her thighs, I absorbed everything about her and committed the moment to memory. Fleetingly, I ran my index finger over the round swell of her ass at the tattered edge of her shorts. Knowing just how much others could see of my beautiful wife made my nostrils flare in anger and I retracted the finger fast, but my jealousy dispersed the second her hands found either side of my face and she caressed the stubble she knew I sported especially for her. As she felt the stubble under her fingertips, she smiled a brief knowing smile at me before pulling at either side of my face to demand that my mouth found hers.

As our lips connected for the first time in days, I felt I could breathe easier and my whole body relaxed.

'Bee,' I whispered in the small fissure I'd created between us. Then I breathed in the smell of my wife as a sense of just how much she was beginning to mean to me travelled rapidly around my body.

I knew at that moment how much I wanted the session with her therapist in Vegas to work, because I couldn't play at this marriage anymore, I needed her by my side always.

With her mouth once again pressed chastely to mine, I caught the shit eating grin on Trip's face as he picked up Bruce into his arms and grabbed Kendall's hand as they started to walk away from the plane. I'd hated that my wife had been kept away from me for an extra few hours, while he'd stopped in Florida to pick them both up, but as I looked at my friend and his small family unit, I finally understood just how much they meant to him.

Maybe you're not dead inside after all.

Without saying a word to her or even thinking about what I was doing, I inhaled her again like a man on death row trying to store away the very scent of life itself and with my angel now in my arms where she belonged, I walked us as one back to the car.

Bee

'I must say, Barbara… the Mediterranean air suits you. You look so well,' Mrs. Davison commented.

I cast my eyes around the large office the three of us were confined in. The decoration was light in colour and the furniture was wooden, but a soft silver in colour. Subsequently, the atmosphere of the well thought out space was light and relaxing. However, with it being my first visit to her office, I was struggling. I knew just how much was riding on my therapy sessions with her working. In order for me to share Nico's life with him, I realised how much I needed to understand my own compulsions in order to control them.

Feeling my hands starting to wring together, I decided to curb my own fidgeting by crossing my right leg over my left as I tried hard to relax.

Nico placed his hand onto my lap and gently took hold of one of my hands in his own. I looked up from my lap and turned my head sideways to look at him.

'We've got this, angel,' he whispered to me and squeezed my hand at the same time. I stared deep into his eyes, absorbing the strength he was willing to offer me and managed to give him a small smile in return.

'Can I offer either of you a water?' Mrs. Davison interrupted our silence.

'Yes please.'

'Not for me thanks,' Nico replied.

A cold, purple glass was handed to me as she walked around the side of my chair and took her place in front of us both. Without picking anything up to refer to, she started speaking and I couldn't believe how brilliant either her memory was or how in tune she felt with her patients.

'How is Crete?'

'Wonderful,' I replied immediately feeling a smile stretch over my face.

'And I can see married life agrees with you both.'

'It does,' Nico put in, and raising my hand to his mouth he kissed the back of it.

'And the photography, Barbara?'

'I'm really enjoying it. I love taking the pictures and... well it sounds silly, but giving birth to those beautiful pictures in my dark room is compelling.'

'That's not at all silly.' She smiled over to me. 'It's wonderful to see you looking so well and talking about something with so much passion. You see, most addicts who want to recover, just need the situation they're in to change. Yours has definitely done that, Barbara and I am so very optimistic about your future.'

'Thank you.'

'Now that's the pleasantries over with ... Let's get down to the nitty gritty. How have you been feeling about coming back here today?'

'Nervous, anxious... you know.'

'I do, but I like to hear it in your words.' She smiled back at me.

'Well, here... this place... it's where I think the catalyst of all my troubles is situated,' I offered.

'I agree, Barbara, but it is also where you met your husband.' She held her hands out in front of her, with her palms facing upwards as she gesticulated the balance that life needed.

'Yes,' I agreed and although I didn't feel thirsty, I placed the glass to my lips to take a sip of the cool water inside.

'Coming back here today meant you were reunited earlier than normal, is that correct?'

'Yes.'

'And surely that was good?' I watched her ask the question and glance at our entwined hands at the same time.

'I was looking forward to that part.'

'Then that is a huge positive, because life is about balance,' she answered and smiling at us both she leant back further into her black, ergonomic leather seat.

'Okay, so far in our previous meetings we have covered how you have used gambling as a crutch.'

I nodded at her.

'The breakdown of your parents' marriage and the forced distance between you and Brody left you unsure of who you were… you were stumbling in life and feeling almost deserted by the decisions they made. Do you agree with me, Barbara?'

'Yes.'

'Then losing your mom when you felt like she chose her addictions over staying with you, left you feeling out of control.'

'Exactly that,' I muttered under my breath. 'Everyone made their choices, even my brother Brody when he refused to leave England and stayed with our dad. But as the youngest child, I was just bundled along with their decisions… I hated it… and for a time I hated all of them.'

'Go on,' she gently encouraged.

Tears were falling silently down my cheeks as I recalled hitting the back window of the car my mom drove us away in. I'd screamed and shouted at Brody to stop her and to save me. I could see him in my mind's eye standing there, holding my dad's hand as neither of them moved to stop the car. Of course, I understood now that as a small boy who wasn't much older than I was, he couldn't do anything to help, but we had pinkie sworn to always be together, and he had let me go. My dad had tried everything to get her to stay, but once she had started the engine, resigned to the inevitable, his feet had remained firmly fixed to the spot. He'd watched with his eyes focussed on me the whole time, as we had driven away from the house that we had all lived in. I'd watched in return from that small back window as pain overtook his features and saw the very second his heart had broken in two. The pain of loss inside me was so acute that I could still feel it nearly thirty years on, as if it had happened only yesterday. I continued by revealing that occasionally now, when I shared a memory with Nico, I would sometimes find myself smiling at a happy recollection instead of feeling only the pain connected to it.

'That's amazing... It's a great step forward.' She took a sharp inhale of breath and I knew she wanted to force me forward once again. 'Then after your mom passed you lived with your aunty?'

'Yes... I wanted to go back to my dad... but by then he had cancer and couldn't look after Brody as well as me.'

'So, once again you felt you had no control.'

'Mmm hmm,' I offered.

'Then your dad died.'

Unsure of why we were having to go over what we had already aired before, I nodded at her, unable to answer her with actual words at first. 'I didn't even get to see him before he passed... Once again, a decision that was made for me with my best interests in mind, obviously.' I couldn't help the air of sarcasm that laced through my tone.

'Barbara, you are so much stronger than you realise. You have lived through the loss of so much and yet here you are... living and taking control of your life.'

'Me?' I questioned.

'Yes... you.'

I could feel the stroke of Nico's thumb on the back of my hand, as he let me know he was right there with me.

'I can hear what you're telling me, Mrs. Davison, but I'm not sure how you've come to that conclusion... I chose addiction, even after what I'd seen with my mom... I chose to gamble.'

'You did. I believe originally when you started to gamble that it gave you the element of control in your life that you'd been searching for.'

I slumped back in the chair I was sitting on and began to think. The astute woman wasn't far from the truth. The cold calculated way I could, in the beginning, count on the roll of the dice and each turn of the cards in front of me, was calming. I had a mathematical brain and I loved the control I had over whatever table I sat down at. Initially, I had respect from the others there. I could walk away when it wasn't going well, or stay and gamble some more in a place where people respected and listened to the decisions I made. Until it started to go wrong and the compulsion to try to control it once again meant I could no longer trust my own decisions. Because the decisions I was making were borne from desperation and not from clear thinking. Then it dawned on me that my parents had been in the same position as me. Making decisions that they were forced to make and then struggling with the fall-out.

'What do you think?' she asked.

'I think I can understand what you're saying.'

'But?' she gently questioned, smiling over at me.

'So, how do I control it now?'

'You control it by trying to forgive the people in your life who hurt you and by understanding what compels you towards using it as your crutch. You control it by changing your situation, and you've most certainly done that.' She smiled at me and looked over at Nico.

'I've had rehab before, I'm not sure they used the same method as you, but...' I hesitated.

'I know, we've spoken about it previously... but this time is different. This time you *want* to have a different life. You are now in control of your own future and it's a future that has love in it and that is the very best sort of future.'

I looked down at my lap to watch Nico's thumb as it caressed my hand. Not once had he faltered in offering me the support I needed even when she'd mentioned the L word.

'Now, our time is up. I look forward to seeing you both in two weeks' time, and I think it should be back here in Vegas again. Because as much as I have loved visiting Crete this is where your ghosts are, and they need to be exorcised.'

'Okay,' I agreed.

'I want to leave you both with a couple of things if I may?'

I could see Nico nodding out of the corner of my eye and comprehended that she was actually in some way treating us both and not just my addictions.

'Firstly, at some point over the next couple of days, I want you to walk through one of Nico's casinos with your hand in his and out of ten measure the compulsion you think you still have to gamble, against how it used to completely dominate your life.' She looked over the top of her glasses at me and smiled as my mouth fell open in horror. 'And secondly, I want you both to understand and to recognise that we are in charge of our own lives. We are not our parents because although we may look like them, we are not created in their exact image. As children and with our dependency on the adults around us, we are made to believe certain things about who we are. But once we gain our independence, only then do we actually become who we were meant to be. There are other ways forward and we carve out those other paths by fighting for what we really want... Thank you both for coming. I look forward to seeing you in two weeks' time.'

CHAPTER TWENTY-NINE

Bee

THE LIMO WAS SILENT as we swept through the busy streets of Vegas. It was as though we were both caught up inside our own heads as we digested everything Mrs. Davison had just told us. But not once had our connection been severed. I looked down to the cream leather seat to see my small hand inside Nico's much larger one and even now his thumb was still gently caressing my hand as he offered me reassurance.

'Do you think I should get this over with and walk through the casino now?'

His head turned to face me. He lifted his other hand up and with his fingers now touching the side of my face to direct my eyes to his, he answered. 'I think that there's no time like the present to get things aired and then we can hopefully move on.'

'Move on?' I questioned.

I watched him blink slowly as if he was trying to clear something from his mind, but he couldn't voice what it was. So, helping him out once again, as I had on the day of our wedding when he'd struggled, I spoke.

'Yes, let's do it now and then as you say we can move on,' I agreed.

Almost on automatic pilot he listened to me, then reached over to the side of him and pressed one of the controls on the aluminium panel next to his seat. The privacy glass came down and the driver and Franco, who was also sitting up front, were revealed to us.

'Pull up at the front of the casino,' he directed.

I watched as Franco began to talk into the small microphone he always wore and then they both disappeared from view as the glass raised again.

Nico looked out of the window and then straight back at me.

'We'll be there in under a minute... are you sure about this?' he questioned.

I nodded back at him resolutely, 'Yes, it needs to be done.'

He pursed his lips and after taking in the expression on my face, he nodded back.

It suddenly felt like the car's air conditioning temperature was turned down way too low. As awareness and panic began to charge through me, my skin was suddenly covered in goose bumps. Involuntarily, I shivered and felt Nico strengthen his grip on my hand in reaction.

'If we can do this, Bee, together I believe we can conquer anything.'

'I'll never forget how you've taken every step with me, thank you,' I whispered over to him.

His other hand cupped my face and his lips came down gently onto mine. Every single stimuli in the whole of my body ignited at the kiss he offered me, but I recognised that the kiss we were sharing was about so much more than our sexual chemistry. In that brief possession of his flesh on mine, he was sharing everything he was with me and I returned it with equal fervour.

The car slowed and eventually came to a standstill. The door was opened by security, and Nico helped me to climb out of the car. Then without so much as a glance in my direction, he began to lead me into the bright lights of the casino. Swallowing down my fears and apprehension, I walked closer to him and held onto his forearm with my other hand as I leant further into him for reassurance and guidance.

Nico's main casino covered the whole of the ground floor of one of his family's hotels and I knew it would take us a while to walk from one side to the other. Initially, I looked down to the floor, unable to tear my eyes away from the wooden walkway to look at the various tables and machines we were passing, but feeling the strength surging through his body and into mine, I slowly began to lift up my head.

The place was bright, loud and filled as ever with people from all walks of life. I watched a croupier deal blackjack, and on another table, I saw the cubes of resin being thrown quickly to the other end. The sound of them hitting the side and falling to the baize ricocheted around my head. Handles on the slot machines were being pulled everywhere around me. For anyone not facing the demons I was, I'm sure they would be able to block out most of the sounds, but as someone battling the addiction of gambling, I heard every single one of them.

I could feel myself beginning to tremble the further we walked, and it seemed Nico could too. He changed his hold on me, releasing my hand he wrapped his arm around me and pulled me in tightly to his side. I inhaled his fresh ocean smelling cologne and allowed my mind to wander back to Crete, to the sound of the waves and the click of the shutters on my cameras. Suddenly, I comprehended that we were still making our way through his casino, but I could no longer hear the sounds of the gambling around me.

After about ten minutes, we reached the centre and at the juncture where several paths crossed Nico stopped, turned around to face me and pulled me tightly into his arms. He stared down at me with eyes so full of mixed emotions, for a second my heart stopped beating as I waited for him to find the words he wanted to say.

'Angel,' he released on a deep, breathy exhale. 'Have I told you how proud I am to be your husband?'

I could feel dozens of people staring at us and understood what a sight we must have looked. Nico in his suit, me looking like I'd just stepped away from a swimming pool and both of us surrounded by several good-looking men in suits.

I shook my head at him in answer.

'Well, I am,' he replied.

'Thank you.' I peered up at him through my fringe, feeling just a little bit shy at his show of affection in public, but loving it at the same time.

'Can you accept that this…' he let go of me with one hand and waved it around us both as he gesticulated the casino we were stood in, 'this will always be part of me?' he finished.

'We're doing this together aren't we, Nico?' He nodded back at me. 'So, yes, I can,' I replied.

'Buona.' His Italian accent had crept back in with his choice of words. 'Then you accept me for what I am?'

'I do. I mean, have you taken a good look at yourself recently?... It's hardly a hardship,' I joked with him, trying to lift the fraught moment.

The look on his face was so serious, I didn't think I'd ever seen his jaw set so square and ridged. When he made no reply, I tried again.

'Nico, I accept you, warts and all, like you've accepted me.' I tried again to convince him.

His hold on me strengthened and for a minute his eyes left mine as he tipped his head back and stared at the ornate ceiling above us. I could feel he was bracing himself, but for what I had no idea.

'Nico, you're beginning to scare me.'

His head angled forward and his eyes found mine. 'Unfortunately, my angel, I need to...'

'You need to... you need to what?' I was shaking my head at him.

'When my mamma died, Cade and I promised each other...' He inhaled deeply in order to carry on. Staring up and into his eyes I saw the pain beginning to fill them and prepared myself. I had no idea what was coming next, but knew deep inside that I would accept anything, as long as he wasn't leaving me. 'We promised that there would be no more secrets in our family... you have to understand, secrets are dangerous things especially in an una famiglia, like mine.'

I could feel a puzzled expression on my face and the swirl of anxiety as it forced its way into my bloodstream. I grabbed hold of the lapel of his suit jacket with both hands, knowing I was effectively hanging onto him for dear life. I wanted him and I wanted to be with him always.

Goodbye wasn't an option.

Suddenly, I felt like the stronger of the two of us.

I knew we were surrounded by people and I knew the noise of people gambling was still to be heard somewhere in the space around us. But I could find none of it, all I could focus on was his eyes on mine and the bleak pain to be found within the depths of them.

Blinking slowly, he broke eye contact with me and dipped his head down to the side of mine, so his mouth was as close as he could get to my ear without him physically touching it.

'This darkness that has me trapped inside of it... I want to tell you about it.'

'Here?' I questioned as my eyes flicked around the area we were stood in and the anxiety I had previously been feeling was pushed away as adrenalin flooded my system.

'Right here,' he replied. 'You're facing your demons and I need to face mine.'

I changed my hold on him, needing to feel the warmth of his body in my arms and not the expensive black fabric I had hold of at the moment. I pushed my hands underneath his suit jacket and wrapped my arms around his waist. I sighed out loud as I felt the warmth of his body escaping the soft, cotton of his shirt and I tried to absorb it to calm the panic building inside of me.

Am I strong enough? I had no answer, but I hoped I could give him what he had so far given me. This was truly going to be a test of who I was inside. I knew how I made decisions for myself for the rest of my life, hung on this very pivotal moment.

'I killed my father,' he whispered into my ear. 'I did it… It wasn't an order I had carried out for me. I killed him… I squeezed the trigger that ended his existence on earth.'

There was no emotion attached to his words, it was as though he was reading aloud from a badly written script. For a few seconds, I let his words travel around my head as I tried to come to terms with what he'd just said.

Maybe another woman would have dropped her arms and let them fall away from his body, as she felt repugnance travel through her. Then, unable to bear the touch of his hands on her skin, she would then break free from his hold and scream at him that he was never to touch or speak to her ever again.

But I felt nothing like that.

I pushed myself away from him slightly, to encourage him to look back at me. When he felt me move, I sensed him stiffen in response. I presumed that he thought I was going to break out of his hold at any moment, but when that didn't happen, he slowly lifted his head and turned back to look at me.

I hadn't a clue what I was expecting to find written on his face when he looked at me, but what I found there when his gaze found mine, was a childhood filled with pain and a look of absolute honesty in his eyes.

'Why?' I questioned.

'To protect those I love… he had taken our mamma away from us and there was no way in hell I was going to let him have Cade or Nonna.'

I lifted my arms up from his waist and placed my hands on either side of his face.

'Or you,' I added as I stared up at him.

'I don't give a fuck about me…'

'Well I do… I admire your honesty…'

'Bee?' He pleaded with me to put him out of his misery.

'I appreciate you telling me the truth…'

'I told you, I always tell the truth,' he interrupted.

'I accept you for who you are and for what you had to do, because I love you, Nico Morello, with everything I am.'

One solitary tear came rolling down his face and I brushed it quickly away with my finger. Nico nodded once and bit down onto his bottom lip before moving quickly and hoisting me up into his arms. As my body collided against his, on instinct I wrapped my arms around his neck and placed my head against his frantically beating heart, and only then did I understand the anguish my brash boss of a husband had gone through in a bid to tell me his worst nightmares.

'Where are we going?' I asked.

'You have possessed me, angel, and now I mean to possess you.'

CHAPTER THIRTY

Bee

'Happy four-month anniversary, mio angelo.' I felt the warmth of Nico's breath as it caressed my ear. 'Now, I wonder what my wife would like me to give her as a gift?'

I could hear the tease and ultimately the intention in his voice.

I stopped running my hands over my body and momentarily froze as I tried to absorb everything about the man who was now stood behind me in the large walk-in shower. I opened my eyes and looking downwards I watched as his hands came slowly around my sides, flexing his fingers as he did so. He found my hips first and then as his hands slid over the wet soapy skin on my stomach I gasped at the contact. Finally, he wrapped his arms tightly around me and pulled me into him, jerking my back into his naked front.

'I didn't hear you come in,' I replied in a voice that was already shaking with need for the man.

'You weren't meant to...' he answered, before he placed his mouth down several times onto the bare skin of my shoulders and exposed neck and ground his rock-hard cock into the small of my back. My legs began to turn to jelly as his attention on my neck and shoulders continued.

'I thought you were by the pool with our guests?' I questioned with a slightly reprimanding tone to my voice. 'What's wrong, was the water no longer inviting?' I grinned to myself as I teased him.

I could see him in my mind swimming the fifty lengths of the pool as he always did each and every morning before breakfast. Most mornings I took myself out onto our large balcony to sip at my coffee and to secretly watch as his well-defined muscles broke through the surface of the water. His strong, lithe body, as it completed lap after lap of the pool, would forever be imprinted inside my head. He commanded the water like he commanded everything else in his life and witnessing it, while knowing he was mine alone, was the biggest aphrodisiac ever. He was the perfect balance to me, so damned good looking in his well-fitting suits, that he turned the heads of women of all ages, but with an air of condescending arrogance that swirled tightly around him. He was the ultimate package. He was caring to those he loved, but he also exuded blatant danger. This made him sexy as hell, to the point that he turned women on and scared the hell out of them all at the same time.

And he was mine, I couldn't believe my luck.

His mouth broke away from kissing across the top of my shoulder and I cursed myself for stupidly asking him a question.

'They're more like family.' His mouth contacted with my shoulder again and his teeth nipped at my needy flesh, drawing a long audible inhale from my lips. 'They can entertain themselves. I have better things to do.'

'Like what?' I asked as his tongue connected with my spine and he ran it slowly up to my hairline, making my back arch in response.

'You,' he replied.

'And what if I don't want "doing"?' I grinned to myself, knowing I was effectively inciting the devil himself.

'There's no escaping me now, Bee.' I could hear the smile in his voice, even though his tone of voice had deepened.

'I'm all yours then.'

'Too. Fucking. Right. You. Are.' In between each word he bit his way across the top of my shoulders. The pain instantly abated and turned into pleasure. 'You. Are. My. Wife. My. Love. Mio Angelo.'

With a mixture of relief and pleasure I dipped my head forward, feeling the strong spray of the shower hit my head and the hair that earlier I'd haphazardly piled on top of my head to stop it getting wet. Now it felt like the water was in league with my husband as the strong streams massaged my scalp. Eased by the shower cream that covered my skin, Nico began to move his hands over my body and the pleasure coursing around my system at his touch ramped up several notches.

'How badly do you want to come, Bee?'

As he asked the question, his hands cupped my heavy feeling breasts and he rolled my nipples between his thumbs and forefingers.

'Ahhhhh.' The sound of pleasure leaving my mouth filled the large walk-in shower.

'Tell me,' he demanded as he pinched my nipples again.

'Badly… very badly,' I managed to force out.

'Your breasts, angel… they're beautiful and so very fucking heavy with your need.' I had to agree with him, my contented life with him had seen me put on all the weight I'd lost in the last year, plus a bit extra. Pleasingly to my new husband, my breasts were now more than adequate to fill his large hands and some.

'Please, I need you to touch me,' I gasped.

'Lean forward, hands on the tiles in front of you,' he demanded.

'I need you to…'

My voice stopped as his hand slid down over my stomach and over my bare mound, before two of his large fingers slipped in between my soaking wet, engorged lips and he pinched my clitoris between his two fingers.

'Ohhhh, Nic…'

'Shhhhh… now do as you're told.'

Sparks of pleasure ignited from that small area and reverberated rapidly throughout my body. Now a woman drunk on the pleasure I knew only he could offer me, I leant forward and felt out in front of me for the tiles he had demanded I should place my hands on. At last the cold reassurance was beneath my palms and I relaxed into whatever Nico was willing to give me.

'Spread your legs wide for me, angel.'

Feeling the coarse flooring, abrasive beneath my feet, I slowly began to open my legs and primed myself for whatever was coming next.

Nico moved quickly as his need for me took over.

With the fingers of one hand still holding my clitoris, his other left my body and without any warning he guided his cock along my soaking wet slit just once, before he pressed the heel of his hand onto my pubic bone and pushed himself fully inside me in one thrust.

A groan left his mouth at our initial contact. Hearing his carnal expression unleashed, a scream of absolute pleasure left my mouth and ricocheted off the green marble walls of the shower.

His hand lifted and after pushing his fingers into my hair he twisted his hand through it, and winding it around his fist he pulled my head up and turned it towards him. For the first time today, I laid eyes on my husband.

He was breath-taking, with his dark, wet hair framing his masculine face and deep, dark brown eyes. His need and love for me was sent wordlessly to me as our eyes connected.

'Do you want to fuck?' His eyebrows lifted and a smile twitched the corners of his mouth.

'You know I do,' I managed to reply.

The moment he knew he had me securely in his hold, he started to move in and out of me. At first it was painstakingly slow as if he wanted me to feel every single millimetre of where our flesh touched each other's. With a gleam in his eye he began all too slowly to rub one of his fingers over the engorged flesh of my clitoris and slowly he drove us on.

Upwards we climbed together, towards the pleasure we knew we would both find in our mutual release.

'Can you feel me loving you, mio angelo?'

His words of love fell effortlessly out of his mouth and I nodded at him unable to say a word.

'Now, I'm burning for you, Bee… I need to fuck you hard.'

'Then do it,' I forced out of my mouth. 'Fuck me and make me yours forever.'

The force he unleashed on us both was unyielding. I had no guarantees if the need we had for each other would always be this strong or demanding, but somewhere deep down inside of me I knew it would always be like this between us.

With our eyes fixed on each other's we rode wave after wave of pleasure until we arrived at the crest together and fell over the edge of our orgasms simultaneously.

Eventually, our heavy breathing and cries of pleasure subsided and after removing himself from me, he pulled me down onto his lap as he sat down on the floor of the shower.

All I could hear was the water as it cascaded from the overly large showerhead and all I could feel was the beat of our hearts as they spoke to each other with words of love.

In those few silent moments, as we held onto each other tightly, I understood that I had everything I hadn't even realised I was looking for and I hoped that fate would be kinder to me from now on.

CHAPTER THIRTY-ONE

NICO

I WATCHED FROM BEHIND my sunglasses as Bee finally emerged from the villa to come down and sit beside the pool.

'Look at me, Bee,' came a shout from Bruce who was using his water wings to good effect in the shallow end, going between Nonna and his mom. I watched Bee dip down and ruffle his dark head of hair after he'd splashed his way to the edge.

But looking at her through the darkened lenses wasn't nearly enough. I hooked my index finger into the top bar, dragged them down my nose and looked admiringly at her over the top of the glasses. At last I could see her properly and the sudden jolt inside my chest let me know just how far fucking gone I was for the woman. My cock stirred in my shorts, even though I'd only recently emptied everything I had inside of her. Casually I adjusted myself, making sure no one else would be able to see how much I wanted her. But it wasn't that part of my body that was causing me to worry, it was the fact that my heart skipped a few beats as I allowed myself to run my eyes up and down her.

'You are so fucked,' Trip uttered under his breath from the bed closest to mine.

I heard him, but not being able to tear my eyes away from my wife, I ignored his quip.

'And by not denying it, tells me you love the woman… this is the beginning and end of your life, Nic.' He laughed out loud at his own words. 'And this moment was brought to you by **The Beatles… Help!**' He didn't stop there but started singing the words at the top of his voice, which made his son and the three woman who were paying the small boy attention turn their heads and look at us both.

Bee looked over and smiled, before turning her gaze once again back to the pool. Her hair was once again coiled messily on top of her head, despite my fingers having pulled it down not an hour ago and her skin was sun kissed. But there was more, I narrowed my eyes to focus on her better and it clicked. Finally, she stood up to continue her walk around the edge of the water. I watched her walking with a confidence that I hadn't ever seen her own before and knew that it looked better on her than anything. Her eyes found mine again and she smiled shyly at me, but at the same time added an extra wiggle to her walk. With the yellow bikini hugging her curves and voluptuous breasts I was jealous as hell of the white chiffon wrap draped over her shoulders, as it blew on the gentle breeze and caressed her skin.

I heard myself clear my throat and I knew immediately, when her eyes darted to mine and she grinned, that I'd been caught admiring her.

There was no getting away from the fact I'd married the best goddamn looking woman I'd ever had the pleasure of laying eyes on.

The only thing that concerned me was the dark shadows under her eyes. She'd been tired since we'd got back from Vegas over a week ago and I had put it down to her struggling to adjust to the jet leg. I'd left her in bed this morning while I swam my normal lengths of the pool, but when she still hadn't surfaced afterwards my need to touch her had driven me to go and find her. Morning shower sex with my beautiful wife was now chalked up as one of my most favourite things to do.

I jumped up from the bed I'd been lounging on and reached out to take her hand in mine. The electric charge that travelled up my arm at the simple connection of her flesh on mine momentarily threw me, as it did every time we touched.

'Where do you want to sit?' I questioned, as I led her by the hand to come closer to me, like a starving man desperate for sustenance.

'I'm not sure,' she replied. 'I want to be out here with you all, but not in the direct sun… I think I had too much yesterday.'

'You're okay though?' I questioned.

'Yes,' she smiled back at me and placing a hand to my chest she carried on. 'I'm fine, as I say, I think I had too much sun. I might have lived in Vegas most of my life, but we're normally indoors avoiding it, aren't we?'

'We are.' Reluctantly I let go of her hand and pulled the bed I'd been sitting on under the shade of the large, canvas canopy next to me. 'Come and sit with me.'

I threw one leg over the other side of the bed, sat down and grabbing her hand again I guided her to sit down in between my legs and pulled her back into me. The warm skin of her back pressed into my chest. I wrapped my arms around her and held her, understanding quickly that I felt at peace with her there. The darkness that normally had its talons so far down into my skin that its spurs abraded my bones was nowhere to be found and I sighed out loud with the realisation.

No more secrets, Cade. As I spoke to my brother in my head, I tightened my hold on the woman leaning against me and kissed the top of her head.

It seemed that my mamma had always been right. I was a man who needed the love of a wife, but whether I deserved her or not remained to be seen. I only knew that I would do anything to protect my angel, even if it meant protecting her from me.

'Let's cross over to the shade.' I led Bee by the hand across the unmade track to walk in the shade the buildings were offering.

'Phew, that's better,' she spoke, and I turned towards her.

'The buildings in Crete were designed a long time ago to reflect a lot of heat, to keep the people inside cooler. So, once we get up to the church and inside the thick walls it'll be much more comfortable.'

She looked back up at me and smiled. 'Do you know, for a man whose reputation precedes him as a disagreeable, dominating, arrogant asshat, you make a pretty good husband.'

I shook my head at her, laughing as I mulled over her words. 'That's quite a list… but an arrogant asshat?'

'Yes,' she answered grinning back at me. With our hands conjoined she began to swing our arms and I fleetingly saw the young girl she once was.

'What else does my reputation say? Do I even want to know?' I questioned her laughing as we continued walking.

'Hmmm, now let me think.' I watched as she placed her fingers to her mouth, and I inhaled deeply as the urge to push her to the side of one of the small houses next to us to consume her mouth with my own tried to take over.

'So?' I probed.

'Uptight, overconfident, assertive, bold, cocky…'

'Woah! Stop…'

'I have more.'

'I'm sure you have… That lot didn't take you too long to come up with… and yet you still married me?'

'Yes, I did… Because you're also good-looking, fit and devastatingly handsome…' She cheekily offered me a wink.

'Thanks… but those things…'

'Did I also mention loving, caring and protective?' She interrupted me with words that literally blew me away.

'No, you didn't…'

I pulled on her hand to turn her to face me, put my fingers under her chin and lifted her gaze up to mine. 'I'm pleased you can see those things in me, angel.'

'Me too… now kiss me and then take me to see these frescos you think I should photograph.'

We continued up the short distance to the top of the hill hand in hand, and not for the first time I considered how much my life had changed for the better. I wasn't too sure who the hell I was when I was with her, but I liked him.

That was a fucking first for me.

'Oh, it's stunning, Nic.' Bee's hand let go of mine so she could lift her camera up to her face. Spurred on by the beauty the sand coloured, stone Byzantine building offered against the blue azure of the sea in the background, I heard the shutter quickly going off.

'Did you not take it in the day we got married?' I teased her a little with my words, knowing what answer I wanted to hear.

I saw her shrug her shoulders and remove the camera from her face before she answered me. 'I know ours wasn't a conventional marriage, but once my nerves had left me, I only had eyes for you.'

'Good answer, angel… good answer.'

The smile she offered me before going back to her photography lit up the deep recesses of my charred soul.

I heard myself clear my throat. 'Can I use your other camera?'

'Sure… I didn't think you were interested in photography?'

'If it interests you, I'm interested… I'll be the one waiting inside for you.'

'Inside? You're going to take my picture as I walk inside the church?' she questioned from behind her camera and then removed it to take a better look at me.

'Yes… I want to experience you coming through the archway again. I want to see the halo behind you, made up of the warm Crete sunlight. I want to witness you, my angel, walking towards me, saving me and I want to be able to look at that forever.'

'So, now we need to add romantic to your list,' she offered grinning at me.

I lifted my fingers to my mouth and blew her a kiss. Then turning I took the few steps that were needed and walked in through the arched doorway, immediately feeling the sudden drop in temperature that I'd promised her. As usual the simple place was lit with a few candles dotted all around. With every step I took towards the aisle the more at peace I felt, unlike the last time I'd been in here.

Finally, I heard her sandals connecting with the flagstones I knew were at the entrance to the church. I spun around quickly to see her, lifting the camera to my face as I did so.

Through the lens and with the dim light of the church surrounding me I began to snap my beautiful wife, as once again she froze in the arch of the doorway.

The bright yellows and oranges from the outside encircled her as my angel slowly made her way towards me. I could feel the huge smile on my face as I took in the breath-taking beauty of my wife and kept my finger on the shutter wanting to preserve every single second of her walking towards me.

'I can't come any further until you hold your hand out… remember?' she called over to me with happy laughter filling her voice.

'Of course, I remember,' I answered.

Semi reluctantly, I moved the camera away from my face and dropped it to hang on the strap around my neck. I held up my left hand and waited for my eyes to adjust to the light so I could see her better. Slowly her silhouette emerged from the brightness of the archway. I watched as she took the camera from around her neck and placed it on a nearby chair. Every step she took towards me shattered another small part of the casing I had built around my heart. Gradually, with my eyes adjusting to the light, she came into focus. I swept my eyes up and down her trying to absorb everything about this fleeting moment in time, that I knew going forward I would never forget.

The strappy leather sandals on her feet, to her expansive, tan legs. The short denim shorts and white, loose-flowing top she was wearing with the dragonfly pin I'd had made especially for her. The gold necklace around her neck. The coils of her blonde hair that were falling out of the messy up-do she had going on today, to rest over her shoulders. The colour of her eyes as the blues and greens within them appeared to dance around with her happiness and the slightly bee stung shape of her lips.

She was fucking stunning.

'It's funny, but earlier when we changed to walk up here, I put on a couple of things from the day we got married, thinking it was appropriate.'

'So, now who's the romantic?' I grinned at her, watching her take every step towards my open hand.

'I'm wearing my dragonfly pin.'

'I saw.' At last her hand touched mine and unable to wait any longer, I pulled her towards me and placed a quick kiss to her forehead, before I inhaled her light scent.

'And this… Nonna gave it to me the day we married and, as we were coming to church, I thought it was appropriate.'

I let my eyes drift down to her and watched as her fingers lightly picked up the rose-gold chain around her neck. She found the cross and lifted it to her lips to kiss it and I was rapidly transported back in time.

I was once again the young man struggling to lift up my mamma's body to loosen the noose from around her, attempting to calm the pain that my younger brother was releasing. I was back in another life and in another place, but it was the same. It was always the same, I came from scum and I was scum, no matter how hard I tried to claw my way out of the abyss.

Looking at the fine chain on her fingers, I could see the necklace all these years later entangled up with the coarse rope my mamma had chosen to end her life with.

Because of the life we led.

Because of another bastard who looked just like me.

Bile hit the back of my throat. I dropped her hand from my own and took one step away from her. I watched her face contort with surprise and then with the simple pain of rejection.

That simple chain around her neck reminding me of just why I would never have willingly taken a wife or would ever father children.

'I told you, you can't have anything nice to play with.' I could hear my father laughing manically in my ears. *'Pull the trigger… It doesn't matter if you kill me, because I will live on in you.'* Inside my head I could see him sneer at me as my grip on the gun in my hand started to tighten, to the point I could see the tip of my trigger finger discolouring under the pressure. *'It*

doesn't matter how hard you fight against it… you're the same as me and you know it, Nico.'

BANG.

I cleared my throat, as the sound of the bullet leaving the barrel reverberated around my head. Then standing taller I tried to shake away the hold he had over me.

The happiness I had only a few minutes before embraced was gone and I was left with nothing.

'Nico, what's wrong?' I could feel her eyes burning into me, but like the coward I was I couldn't return her gaze. Instead I looked to the doorway and lifted a hand to gesticulate to Franco that I needed him.

'There's a problem… I need to go, stay here and I'll get Raul to come and get you.'

'You do, I don't understand… why?'

My shutters had already come down. I heard the almost audible clunk as the steel casing sealed around me like a metal coffin that even the desperation in her voice couldn't penetrate.

She deserved more, so very much more.

But I didn't have it to give.

I moved to the side of her, effectively ignoring everything she was silently begging of me. Then, just at the last minute, I turned quickly and took both of her hands in mine. Lifting them up to my lips I closed my eyes and kissed her clasped together fingers.

'Ciao, mio angelo.'

CHAPTER THIRTY-TWO

Bee

THE VILLA WAS QUIET and felt empty, even though I knew there were others inside the beautiful building.

The sun had set and although I normally found that to be one of the most beautiful parts of the day, I hadn't been able to embrace it at all.

For probably the millionth time today, I was going over every part of the day, but once again I couldn't fathom out what on earth had happened. All I knew was that by the time Raul had picked me up and we had driven back to the villa, Nico had packed and gone. Normally we went through a bit of routine when he was going back to the States, but even that hadn't happened.

He was gone and try as I might to convince myself it was just like any other time when he flew back to Vegas, I knew it wasn't. Something had happened between us at the church and just like that he had upped and left me there. I'd even tried phoning him since his departure and although his cell had rung in my ear initially, it had then cut off. I'd tried to convince myself that the call had been interrupted because he was flying, but I knew deep down in the depths of my pain-filled heart that he had been the one to terminate the call.

In my head I could see him, sitting on a plane catching up with business. He would be back in a suit with his hair styled to perfection and his square jawline would be set stoically. I was convinced that by now he would also be clean shaven, after having removed the scruff he normally wore for me. I also hated that, like most of the others that I'd cared about, he could so easily remove himself from my life without a second glance.

I moved my bare legs around in the pool, making the water swish around my skin in circles, while I stared out into the bay looking for any answer I could find to my current situation.

Once again, I'd been left, and the pain was indescribable.

I knew our marriage had been an arrangement. But it was so very much more now, and up until the moment he had left the church we had been married in; I had felt like we might just be able to go the long haul.

Absentmindedly, I picked up Nico's mamma's chain that I was still wearing and caressed the metal cross with my fingers.

'Bee?' I could hear the silent questions in Nonna's voice as I heard her footsteps coming closer behind me.

Was I alright? No, I wasn't.

Was there anything she could do? Only getting your grandson to come back would be of any help at all.

At first, I attempted to turn my head, to look over my shoulder and to try to placate her with a smile. But I knew it wasn't in me and even if I managed it, I knew she would be able to see past it in a flash.

What was it with older people and their over the top sensory radars? Pearl was exactly the same.

'Can I come and sit with you?'

I glanced to my left to find her standing beside me. Her kind, understanding face was encapsulated in a gentle smile.

I nodded my head at her and then focussed back onto the pool while she sat down.

The bluey green of the dragonflies' wings hummed their way past my ears, and I inhaled deeply to stop the tears that threatened to fall down my cheeks.

Well isn't that just absolutely typical?

I had gone from being totally alone to sharing my solitude with Nico's grandmother and the dragonflies he and I had so often sat here watching. It was as if the world couldn't and wouldn't let me forget what we'd shared together. For a few minutes, we sat in silence with both of our eyes focussed in front of us.

'Did he tell you why?' I finally managed to force out from a throat that was so completely swollen and twisted with emotion that I was having trouble swallowing.

'No... I'm sorry, Bee, he didn't.'

Her hand reached out to grasp mine and I closed my eyes at the touch of her comforting hand on mine.

'I don't know what happened... he said he had to go and then he left. It was as though something inside of him just snapped. He shut down and took off.'

I continued to watch the dragonflies dancing their way around us both. Their sweeping motion was mesmerising, and it kept me from focussing too hard on the pain that was unfolding deep inside of me.

'Do you know what many myths and legends say about dragonflies?'

'Pardon?' I turned my head to properly look at Nonna for the first time since she'd sat down, wondering exactly just what she was on about.

'Legend has it that they were one of the first winged insects to evolve. In many cultures the dragonfly symbolizes the ability to change and to transform.'

'It does?' I couldn't believe I was even interested in what she wanted to tell me, but here we both sat surrounded by the still and dark night, watching the only things that were visible from the lighting spaced out around the pool.

'Yes,' she continued. 'But it's not the same sort of change you see in say, a caterpillar to butterfly... No, this is about understanding the deeper implications and maybe even the meaning of life itself. Dragonflies only live a short life as we can see them now, most of their lives are spent as immature nymphs and they fly for only a tiny fraction of their life. Yet here they are dancing and swooping in flight and living in the moment. When you live in the moment, it makes you more focussed on who you are and what you want and even what you are capable of. With that understanding comes the enlightening truth that anyone can in part control their own destiny.'

Her hand squeezed mine momentarily before she carried on.

'Their iridescent wings seem almost magical, don't they?' she asked.

I was focussing on the creatures she was talking about and only nodded to answer her.

'Their iridescence is the most magical part, I think. It's about discovering your own ability to change, finding your real self, exposing the person you were always meant to be and throwing aside the mantle you've surrounded yourself with. That means going beyond what you can see in front of you at first and embracing what you find beneath it.'

'This isn't about the dragonflies... It's about Nico and me, isn't it?'

She laughed a little and squeezed my hand again before relaxing her grip.

'Of course. I'm not going to lie, I watched the two of you on some of the many evenings you spent down here watching exactly what we are watching now and thought how very apt it was that the two of you found them so enchanting.'

'You did.'

'Uh huh. Call it an old woman's pleasure watching love grow between one of her beloved grandsons and a woman who I now consider like a granddaughter to me. One who I can tell has felt more than her own fair share of pain.'

Everything I had been forcing to stay deep inside me came spilling out on one breath.

'I'm in more pain than I ever thought possible, right at this minute. He's left me and I know he made it seem like it was because there is a problem back in Vegas, but I know it's not. One minute we were so together, then in the space of a split second he'd effectively tried to sever our connection. Then he walked away.'

The sobs I'd been holding in until right at that moment came brimming to the surface and overflowed. I couldn't hold them in any longer and I couldn't have cared who heard the anguish I was now feeling. My body shook uncontrollably, and my chest heaved as the pain he had left me with, escaped. I hadn't heard Kendall come down, but the second she put her warm arm across my cold shoulders, I knew it was her and I leant my head towards her to receive the embrace she was offering.

'Oh, Bee… what's he playing at?' she offered as she kissed the side of my head.

'I don't know,' I answered her in a voice filled with emotion.

'But I think I do, Bee.' Nonna spoke again. 'I want you to sit here with us and cry, and then I want you to get up and fight for him. Fight like you've never fought for anything before in your life… because you promised me you would do exactly that on your wedding day. Fight for him, but also fight for yourself. You are in control of this chapter of your life… do you hear me?'

'What if he just doesn't want to be with me?' I released the words out of my mouth, knowing they scared me more than anything I'd gone through before.

'That is so not true, he wants you but feels he doesn't deserve you…' She stopped speaking for a second, almost lost in thought. 'Bee, it's the dragonflies' eyes that I feel are the most significant to Nico,' Nonna continued. 'Between the two of you over the last few months you have helped each other to live in the moment and to control your own destiny. I even saw him throwing aside the disguise he has worn for many years and enjoying the person he found underneath it. But this is the one part of himself he still hasn't managed to embrace yet. You see, a dragonfly's eyes symbolize the ability to see beyond the way you see yourself to get past the self-created illusions. Unfortunately, Nico is convinced he's the same as his father.'

'That could be it,' I offered, looking down at the cross still between my fingers. 'Something happened when he saw his mamma's cross and chain on me. I'd worn it up to the church, along with the pin he'd had made for our wedding.'

'I think you could be right, Bee… You see, my son was a monster. An unfeeling, sadistic madman. He drove Nico and Cade's mamma into taking her life and abused them in ways they think I know nothing about…' Pain left her mouth on an exhaled breath. 'He's convinced he's the same, Bee. No matter how hard I've tried to convince him differently.'

'You think he left me because he was reminded of his mamma?'

'I think it's possible. I'm sorry, I should have thought about what giving you her necklace would mean to him. She was a beautiful and kind woman who thought only of her children. I wanted her there with us, to celebrate his marriage. She always said he was a man who would need the love only a wife could give, and I wanted her to know that he'd found her.'

'Do you really think he loves me?'

'I think you know the answer to that already, Bee,' Kendall added, and I whipped my head around to take in the fact she was nodding her head as she spoke.

For a few minutes we sat in silence, the two of them had effectively wrapped themselves around me to offer me their strength.

'The last of the legends of these beautiful creatures in front of us, the ones who are still dancing, swooping and embracing life, is that they represent happiness, new beginnings and change. But ultimately, they symbolise love and there is nothing greater than love, is there? Nico loves you with all that he is. Now all you have to do is to convince him that he is strong enough to throw away the hold his father put on him and convince him he's worthy of you.'

CHAPTER THIRTY-THREE

NICO

'MR. MORELLO, CAPTAIN CLYNES is here to see you.'

My secretary's voice filled my office and on instinct I looked away from the large windows I'd been staring out of for God knows how long and glanced back to the speaker on my desk. A long exhale left my mouth and I crossed my arms over my chest, feeling my leather shoulder holster pull tight across my back.

I knew it was only a matter of time before Trip arrived. In truth, I'd expected him sooner. How long had I been back in Vegas, was it three or four days now?

I hadn't a fucking clue.

I'd been holed up in my office ever since I'd arrived back in the states. Doing paperwork that I'd pretended needed doing and checking up on things I really didn't need to check up on. But it had helped to keep my mind focussed, by not allowing it to drift back to the woman I'd left in Crete. I hadn't been back out to Red Rock Canyon because... well, because I couldn't face it and the memories I knew it would, without a doubt hold.

Instead I'd been here, locked up in my fortress-like office. After having had clothes brought to me from the house, I'd been attempting to sleep on the couch and using the shower room that was connected to my office. I'd been using the space as my home, because I knew that for now and the foreseeable future it would be the only place I might get any peace.

'Mr. Morello?' Mrs. Busby questioned me, reminding me I still hadn't answered her.

I could refuse him entrance. I could, if necessary, have him removed from the building, but knowing Trip like I did I knew he would keep on trying until I finally spoke to him.

'Yes, thank you.' I swallowed, trying to keep some of the annoyance out of my voice as I answered her. 'Please send him in.'

I turned and walked towards the drinks' cabinet, unplugged the heavy crystal stopper from the Bourbon decanter and began to pour myself a couple of fingers.

The door clicked shut at the far end of the room.

'It's nine a.m.' Trip's voice chastised me.

'What can I do for you, Captain Clynes?' I stood myself up as tall as I could, expelled air from my flaring nostrils and asked him the question without turning to face him.

His laughter filled up the large office. 'And so it begins... first you pull away from Bee and now it's my turn.'

'I have another meeting in ten minutes, so can you say what you've come to say.'

'Okay, sure… let's get down to business. Firstly, I repeat, it's nine a.m. and you've got a pretty large drink in your hand and secondly, this shutting yourself down crap might work on everyone else including yourself, but not on me.'

'If you've come all this way to turn into my grandmother or to state the fucking obvious, then you can leave the same way you came in.' I lifted up the Bourbon I was holding to my lips. Then I flung it far back on my tongue and swallowed fast, closing my eyes momentarily as I relished the burn at the back of my throat. This meeting was already going to the fucking dogs. What was it with family and friends? Resigning myself, I placed the expensive glass gently down onto the silver topped cabinet as I resisted the urge to throw it overarm to the opposite wall and to watch as it shattered against the plaster and into a million pieces. I heard him walk across the floor and take a seat on the couch.

'Hello to you too,' he uttered sarcastically. 'I'd ask you how you are and if you're struggling, but by just looking at you I can see that the answer to both of those questions is fairly obvious. I know a good therapist, perhaps speaking to Dr. Lemmon might help you.'

'Good morning, I don't remember asking you to work. I'm not flying out anywhere… I don't need a fucking therapist, even yours… So, what can I do for you?' I asked, using a tone of voice that let him know I wasn't in the mood for a friend.

'Seriously, you need to get the fuck over yourself… Do I really have to put into words why I'm here? You're an intelligent man, Nic. At least I always thought you were, until three days ago when you ran away.'

'I had a problem and needed to come back here.'

The laughter that left him let me know that he wasn't taking any sort of bullshit today.

'Yeah, the understanding that you were allowing yourself to live and to love someone must have been a *huge* fucking problem. I've been there, remember?'

I turned around fast.

'Your life and my life are so very different you can't use yourself as an example… Just fucking go.'

'That's the first thing you've uttered that makes any fucking sense so far. In the few years we've known each other, our lives have been different, I'll give you that. Yet still we're friends. Understanding that, you need to know that I'm not leaving here until you tell me what made you leave her… What happened, Nic?'

'This happened,' I shouted back at him as I moved my hands up and down myself. 'Do you see this?' I waved my right arm around the huge space that was my office, with its bullet-proof glass. 'And this.' I pulled my Beretta 92x out of my shoulder holster and waved it in the air.

God love him, he didn't even flinch. His eyes went to the gun in my hand once and once only before they landed squarely back on my face.

'She knows who you are,' he offered as he leant forward to place his elbows onto his knees and clasp his hands together.

'She *knows* only what I've told her.'

'Then open up to her, tell her what hurts you, what scares you and let her make her own choice if she can live with it or not... She's stronger than you think. I think she'd choose you whatever.'

'I always meant to leave Barbara once she was in a better place, and now she is… So, it was time.'

'Barbara?... Do you really think that by flying thousands of miles away from her and using her proper name, you'll be able to separate yourself from her? Tell me you're not that fucking stupid, Nic.'

'I'm saving her from me, Trip… tell me you can at least understand that.' My voice had risen in volume and I watched as the gun in my hand gesticulated in front of him as I tried hard to make him understand just what I was doing.

'Saving her from you? Just who the hell do you think you are?'

'Now who's not using the brain they were born with? You know who I am. You know what sort of family I come from.'

'Yeah, I do. I know all of those things. But, why the fuck would you ever hurt her? You've moved hell and high water to change what your business is about. You've recompensed where you can, the pain your father caused others.'

I smacked my palm hard onto my chest.

'That's just semantics. Inside here I'm damaged, he impaired me to the point I'm charred and blackened inside…' My voice that had been gaining in volume dropped as I placed the gun next to the alcohol on the side and looking down to my feet, I pushed my hands into my pockets. 'She needs and deserves better than me.'

'Better than the man she married? Better than the man she loves? I never thought I'd say this to you, Nic, knowing what you've survived and lived through, but you need to grow a set of balls. You've taken the coward's way out instead of fighting for the life you want.'

Coward? The words he'd just spoken resonated around my head.

Still looking at the floor I saw his feet move as he made to stand up. I couldn't work out if he was getting up to leave or if he was coming closer to where I stood. Strangely I didn't want him to do either. I didn't want his comfort, so didn't want him any closer to where I was, but equally I knew I needed him to question me and the decision I'd made.

'You need to understand this… YOU are not your father.'

I lifted up my gaze and biting down strongly I clenched my teeth together.

'No, I'm not, but I AM my father's son.'

He sighed at my reply.

'No matter what actions I take, how many people I try to help to put right the pain he caused them… I will always be his son, his first born and the heir to this fucking throne of thorns.'

'Sell it all. Move on, move to Crete for fucks sake. Have babies and grow fat with the woman you so obviously love.'

The laughter that fell out of my mouth wasn't happy or light. It expressed the madness that I felt at his words. At what I would give to able to do just that.

'Trip, you've been a good friend over the years and for that you'll never know how grateful I am. But do you have any understanding of how "mafia" even works? I've let you in on parts of my life, but have you never seen the movies? They're not far wrong, yeah they're a little soft around the edges, but the basic concept of a decent mafia film is correct.'

'Explain.' I could see I was starting to get to him. Made more uncomfortable by my words than the gun I had waved about earlier in front of his face, he instinctively stood himself up as tall as his frame would allow, knowing he had an inch or two over me.

'You don't get to leave families like mine unless someone has your back or you're lucky enough to die.'

'It's a fucking business, sell it.'

Feeling more in control to gain the upper hand over the conversation, I walked past where he was standing in amongst the more comfortable seating and made my way over to the large desk that used to be my grandfather's. Turning, I placed my ass on the edge, sat down and crossed my feet at my ankles.

My eyes moved over the space between us.

'For sale. One mafia business…' I laughed at his suggestion.

'You told me that most of the business is now legal,' he shot back.

'And it is. Yes, I could sell it… but it wouldn't matter. I can't sell who I am, the family I come from and that by fucking default I'm the head of. Do you know how many families would love to boast that they wiped out all of the Morellos? Selling up here and going somewhere else makes us look weak and a prime target for any up and coming asshat.'

A sigh of understanding left his mouth.

'In order to protect my family, I have to stay right where I am and that's exactly what I'm doing. Maybe one day it'll be different…'

'So, you stay here and live this to protect those you love…' Our eyes found each other's, and he nodded at me in recognition. 'I take back the fact I called you a coward, Nic. I'm sorry for doing that, because I think I finally understand why this has to be your life.' His eyes looked around my large office.

A few seconds of painful realisation filled up the room.

At last Trip started walking towards me. I stood up and welcomed him into my hold. Silence filled the room as for a short while we embraced, then after a couple of slaps on the back we released each other. He took one step backwards from me and started speaking again.

'Nic, I still however believe that life is a balance. Bee knows where you come from, doesn't she?'

I couldn't answer, but nodded back at him in answer.

'She's stronger than you give her credit for. The two of you being together has made her strong. Can't you at least let her make up her own mind?'

'The things I've done… I'm too much like him, she doesn't deserve to wake up one day and find she's married to a man like my father.'

'A man has to fight to find peace,' he offered. 'And that's what you've been doing.'

'Does he have to kill, too?'

His head moved very slightly from side to side as he thought over my question.

'I think in some instances he does, yes. I know I would kill to protect Kendall and Bruce.'

Trip's body twisted and his feet finally began to move towards the door.

'Is she here, Trip?' I asked the one thing I'd wanted to know since he'd arrived. But even before he answered I knew she was, because I could feel her close by.

'She's here,' he replied with his back to me. 'I'm just the first wave of attack,' he added with a slight laugh. 'But then I'm sure Raul would have given you that information the minute we landed.'

He was right, the bodyguard I'd assigned to Bee had told me that they'd flown in a couple of days ago. But then I wasn't really asking that question, what I was asking in a roundabout way was whether he thought she would come to see me. I crossed my arms over my chest, not in a sulky, defensive way, but to try to trap in the feeling of excitement that she thought I was worthy of her.

I didn't want to stamp all over her already broken heart, but I also couldn't refuse her coming to see me. My heart rate had already accelerated and all because I knew that someday soon, I would lay eyes on her once again.

I heard the turn of the handle as Trip went to leave.

'One more thing... this life changing moment is brought to you by **Elvis and The Beatles.**'

'Elvis and The Beatles?' I questioned, amused and relieved that the fraught atmosphere had lifted between us.

'Yeah, both of them,' he reiterated. 'But it will be the one and only time... **Elvis and The Beatles - I forgot to remember.**'

He vacated my office without so much as a wave in my direction, leaving me with my head swimming with the lyrics of the song he'd just flung at me. He was right I couldn't forget her, and I knew without a doubt Bee would always be on my mind and making me remember.

CHAPTER THIRTY-FOUR

Bee

A CONTENTED 'PURRRR' HIT my ears. Followed closely by the rub of a furry face along my jawline. With my eyes still closed, I found his head with my fingertips and began to scratch behind the one fight-tattered ear that was available to me.

'I missed you too, Tiger,' I mumbled with a voice that still sounded like I was half asleep.

Right next to my face I could feel him turning around and around as he prepared himself to find the best possible spot to lie down in.

Suddenly, ginger fur was tickling the outside of my nostrils.

'Oh no… move away you hairy beast.' Quickly I moved my head back up on the pillow to separate the two of us. Then opening my eyes one by one, I took in the warm glow that filled my room as the sun began to set and settle behind the hills.

I miss you, Nic. With resignation I spoke inside my head the same words that were permanently on repeat. It was always the same, he was the first thing I thought of when I woke up and the last thing that floated around my head before my tired body eventually crashed into sleep. As always, the feelings inside of me made me feel sick with longing.

I quickly worked out by the lighting in my room that it was the time of day that Nico and I had always embraced.

No more… stop. With a sudden loud sniff, I effectively swallowed down my hurt and attempted to shelve the pain.

At the same time, I saw the moment the pink tufts of Pearl's hair poked around the edge of my bedroom door and I wiped underneath both of my eyes hurriedly with the backs of my hands as I attempted to conceal my pain from her.

'You're awake. I thought I heard you…' I watched as she came in the door and walked towards my bed, eyeing me with concern. 'Is he bothering you?' Her head tipped to where Tiger was already curled up and asleep.

'No, not at all. I think he missed me.'

'We both did. But I was happy because you were happy…' Her voice changed in tone and I felt the bed dip as she sat down on the edge of my bed. 'Can you tell me what went wrong?'

This had been a recurring theme, along with the fact she was worried I had made myself ill with the upset of it all. But finally, she'd asked the question outright.

I shook my head a little and exhaled, which disturbed Tiger's beautiful ginger coat.

'I'm truly not sure.'

Her eyes found mine as she appeared to mull over what she thought might have happened in her head. But obviously not coming up with what she felt was a good enough answer, she thought better of releasing the words into the world. Just as quickly as she'd sat down, she stood back up again.

'Well, the good thing is you look better after that sleep.'

Gently, so as not to disturb the cat, I stretched out my body, feeling the edge of the mattress with my toes and the headboard underneath my fingers.

'I do feel better. I'm not sure why I'm so rundown at the moment.' I looked up at her.

'Well I think I may have an answer for that... stay there.'

Pearl left my small bedroom. I heard her walking towards my kitchen and then her footsteps were on their way back. Once again, she appeared around my door, but this time she was holding a brown paper bag in her hand.

'This might help.' She nodded at me resolutely.

'This way, Mrs. Morello.'

'Thank you.'

I followed behind the impeccably dressed woman until we came to a door I was already familiar with. In truth, I wanted to stop for a few seconds to brace myself, but knowing he would already know I was out here, I held my head high and followed as assertively as I could. Luckily, I was holding a large, black, zipped folder in both of my hands, otherwise I knew I would be wringing them with my discomfort at the situation and that wasn't how I wanted this meeting to go at all.

'Mrs. Morello.' Franco tipped his head towards me.

'Good morning, Franco,' I offered him a half smile.

I watched as Franco placed his thumb on the scanner by the door and heard the click as the lock released itself on recognition.

'He's expecting you,' he offered me almost apologetically.

'Of course he is, because you wouldn't be doing your job very well if he wasn't,' I replied.

I reached out to touch one of his large arms as I tried to reassure him of the fact that I knew the whole of Nico's security team would be reporting back to him my every movement. It wasn't, as far as I was concerned, them taking sides against me, I knew they were just doing their jobs.

I looked on as Franco's large hand pushed open the door in front of me and after taking a deep breath I strode into Nico's office.

With every step I took I was thankful that I'd spent nearly the whole of yesterday shopping. As far as I was concerned this was going to be at the very least a business meeting. I had an agenda to run through and I wanted to look and feel the part. Having explained that I wanted to be wearing something powerful to the shop assistant yesterday, after already having had my hair and nails done, she'd pulled out several options in my size. My eyes had been immediately drawn to the bright red, fitted dress I was wearing now.

I had been in Nico's office a few times before today, but I had never felt more in control than I did at this moment and I knew it was the care I had taken with my appearance that made me feel that way.

'Bee.' His voice was deep and gravelly.

His voice came at me and my insides began to quake.

Don't you dare, Barbara… don't you dare.

I took hold of the back of the chair in front of me, but refused to dig my fingers into the expensive leather, knowing he would be able to read just how I felt by that simple action.

I took a few seconds to settle myself and then I turned my head and lifted my eyes to find him.

As my eyes took him in, I inhaled and held my breath. He was stood with his back to me. A black, button down shirt was stretched magnificently across his back and it was tucked into a pair of smart pants which fitted him like a glove. If I still hadn't been able to see every undulation and worked hard for muscle on his body in my head already, I knew the way his clothes fitted him would have given me a very good idea.

'Nico,' I managed to force out on an almost whisper.

Still holding onto the chair, I made myself stand taller on the four-inch heel, strappy, crystal-jewelled Louboutins, as I waited for him to turn around.

Finally, he did.

Our eyes met and our worlds as they now were collided. The power, the pain, hurt and silent recriminations swirled around the room so fast it was hard to draw in a meaningful breath.

I took him in for the first time in five days and although I knew we had been apart for longer periods before in our short marriage, I understood that I had never missed him like I did at this very minute. We were stood not twenty feet apart, but at this moment in time it felt like the distance of an ocean was between us.

I swept my eyes over him. His hair was impeccably styled, his jawline was clean shaven, and his thick framed glasses were covering his eyes.

My brash boss was back.

Just as I thought I couldn't go on with this so called business meeting that I'd conjured up in my head, and as the feeling of wanting to flee began to take hold of every sinew in my body, I watched his dark brown eyes as they ran over me and took all of me in. He pulled his glasses off his face and in the reflection of his eyes I could see everything he was trying to hide from me.

Hope replaced my need to flee.

'I have a business proposition for you.' I spoke and watched as his left eye narrowed in on me.

'You do?' he questioned as his head twisted slightly to one side when he tried to read the situation between us.

'Yes, because I need to make a living. I refuse to be a kept woman, especially one that her husband feels is a dead weight around his neck.'

'Bee… your choice of words,' he pushed in, interrupting me.

'Please do me the decency of hearing me out.'

Nico crossed his arms over his chest and nodded back at me. 'Please take a seat.'

'I prefer to stand, but I will need somewhere to spread these out.' I held up my zipped folder.

Nico waved one arm towards the meeting table next to him and summoning every ounce of strength I had in me, I let go of the chair which had been offering me the stability I needed and walked towards the table and closer to him.

His arms uncrossed, he pushed his hands deep into his trouser pockets and his loud exhale found me. I could feel his need for me being projected across the room. I revelled in it and used it to fuel what I knew I had to do. Clasping the folder in front of me with both hands I added an extra wiggle as I walked nearer to him.

Although I tried hard not to, my nostrils found his cologne floating on the air-conditioning of the large room. Like a woman fighting for her very existence, let alone her life, I breathed him in and let him fill up every single one of my senses.

Longing for him ran through me.

I opened my folder and trying to ignore how very close he had stepped up to the side of my body, I began to spread out the pictures I had especially chosen in front of me.

'I've brought these with me to give you examples of how I see my future.'

I stood back after speaking and let him close in further towards the table. One by one I watched as he picked up my work and began to examine them.

I could hear his breathing begin to quicken as he picked up one photograph after another. On the top I had deliberately placed the pictures of Crete, its heritage sites and its gorgeous beaches.

'A photography business? You know already that I think you have a good eye,' he offered as he took each one in.

Then I held my breath as he found the ones of him that I'd deliberately placed underneath. The ones in casual clothes. The photographs I'd taken of him when he wasn't aware and the ones when he'd been looking down the lens of my camera with such longing I'd almost disintegrated on the spot. As I heard him clear his throat, I knew that he'd found the one at the bottom of the pile. The one he'd taken of me as I'd walked into church not ten minutes before he'd walked out.

'Mio angelo,' he whispered.

My heart rate quickened at the words as they fell out of his mouth without so much as a thought. The same words I had mourned that I might never hear again. I knew then he hadn't left me because he didn't care, but because he cared too much.

The room around us fell into a painful silence and I held my breath before going into what I knew was going to be the biggest speech of my life.

'Tell me what you see, Nico.'

He picked up the photos one by one over and over again.

'Mainly, I see me.'

I knew he had turned his face towards me, but I refused to meet his questioning gaze.

'Do you? Do you really?'

'I don't understand.' He shook his head a little as if he was trying to arrange all the pieces of a jigsaw in his mind. 'Do you want me to back a business venture for your photography? Because I will without a moment's hesitation.'

'You didn't answer me… Do you really see *you* in those pictures? I mean *really* see you. I want the truth; you have told me several times that you always tell the truth.'

He looked down at the table again and I allowed my eyes to focus on the side of his face.

'That's the real you, Nico. You weren't playacting. You were being the man I truly believe you were always meant to be. Look at them! Understand who you are.'

'This is who I'm supposed to be.' He answered me but still kept his eyes on the mass of colour I'd placed on the table as he moved the smooth pieces of paper around with one finger.

'No,' I voiced louder than I'd intended. 'This is who your father told you to be and whether you want to believe it or not, by casting me and the life we have together aside you're allowing him to win… to win, Nic… please understand that.' I couldn't help the begging tone that entered my voice.

Suddenly, he moved and turning to face me he grabbed hold of my forearms and pulled me into him. All of the air expelled from my lungs. Slowly, I looked up into his face. The pain he was in was etched on every single part of the handsome features in front of me.

'I left to protect you.'

Gently, I shook my head at him and lifting a hand up towards him I let my forefinger stroke his cleft chin and watched as his jaw relaxed just a little under my touch.

'No, you left to protect yourself. You're scared of being alive and hurting. He still has such a hold over you that you still believe all the lies he fed you and you don't have the strength to push him away… You see,

Nico Morello, you can run from me, but you can't hide, because I see you, like you saw me.'

'You were wearing my mamma's necklace… in church that day.' He offered me the information so that I might understand. 'It was the same one I unravelled from the coarse rope she chose to end her life with.' A silent tear began to run down his face.

'I'm sorry, I didn't know,' I whispered up to him as he dipped his forehead to mine and let it rest there.

'I've never told anyone before, so you couldn't have known.'

I opened my hands and gripped onto his shirt, holding him tightly to me.

'Then let me in… let me all the way in and together we can put all the pieces of our shattered hearts back together.'

'I can't walk away from this life.'

'I know, and I'm not asking you to. I accept this is part of who you are, because I love you.'

'I wish you didn't, and this would be so much fucking easier.'

I summoned all the strength I had left in me.

'This is your chance to choose, Nico. Remember what Mrs. Davison told us both?' I questioned, and then I continued on not waiting for a reply. 'We are in charge of our own lives. We are not our parents even if we look like them, because we are not created in their exact image. The adults around us imprint on us growing up and we are made to believe certain things about who we are. Once we become independent, we can become who we were meant to be. There are other ways forward and we carve out those other paths by fighting for what we really want… Fight for me, Nico like I'm prepared to fight for you.'

I reluctantly pulled myself out of his arms and once again put my hand inside my folder. After finding what I was looking for I placed the small piece of white plastic, with the two blue lines that I'd been saving until last, down on top of the photographs. His eyes followed my every movement and he stiffened in response to what he found.

'This is both of ours chance to choose a different pathway. This isn't about you and Cade, or me and Brody anymore. This is about us. This is our child I'm carrying and I'm choosing to make their life different to ours. I'm choosing love, and happiness. I'm choosing a different ending. I choose you and our baby. I hope you can be strong enough to be the man I know you are to choose us... But if you don't, we'll be fine without you.' I managed to swallow down the sob that was creeping into my voice.

I turned on my heels and although I wanted to bolt towards the closed door, I made sure I walked calmly away. My face was wet with tears, but not able to give him any more of an insight into my feelings, I let them fall. Just as my hand touched the doorknob with my back towards him, I spoke again.

'Remember, you have to embrace your darkness to see your stars shine. Our baby is your star.'

I pulled open the door and walked through it, not knowing if I would ever see him again.

CHAPTER THIRTY-FIVE

Bee

'TRIP HAS REQUESTED OUR flight today with the powers that be. The crew we need are all available, and he's just let me know that we should fly sometime today. We're just waiting for an available slot and that's just about as much as I know, Kendall.'

I pressed my cell tightly to my ear with one hand and blocked out the sound of the airport with a finger from my other. I heard her repeating what I'd already said back to Nonna.

'Well, Nonna and I want to say that we both know you couldn't have done anymore. He knows where to find you. It's down to Nico now. We also want to say that we love you.'

A loud, unexpected sob left my mouth and I turned away from everyone else in the VIP lounge.

'Don't cry, Bee. I am convinced he will come to his senses. You know what men are like. You have to plant the seed and then let them think it was all their idea in the first place.'

Plant a seed.

I pressed a hand to my flat stomach. She wasn't far wrong.

'I have other news for you, but I'll save it until I arrive home.'

'Yes, Bee, you do that. This is and always will be your home.' Nonna's voice filled up my ear and I quickly worked out that her and Kendall had swapped places.

'BEE.' I heard Trip shout from the doorway of the lounge and snapped my head around to find him, as did several of the other ladies in the vast area with me.

Despite my melancholy over having to walk away from Nico, like many other females in the room, I could appreciate a handsome and charismatic man in a pilot's uniform. As I waved my hand to him, he took off his cap and walked quickly towards me.

'Trip's here, Nonna,' I explained to her as I removed the cell from my ear.

He finally arrived at where I was sitting.

'If we can board in forty-five minutes, they can give us a slot.' He tipped his forehead to me in question.

'I can.' I looked around me. I only had a small bag with me and had gone straight to the airport after leaving Nico, not even going back to Pearl's to pick up the rest of my stuff. I had made a phone call to her explaining what I was doing and my strong urge to get back to Crete as soon as possible and she'd said she understood completely, and she'd fly over as soon as she could.

'Is the plane ready?' I questioned.

Trip put his head to one side and although he didn't answer my question immediately his face gave me a "wadaya take me for" look.

'Refuelled, stocked and flight crew are getting ready to board as I'm stood here talking to you.'

I put my cell back to my ear. 'We should be leaving in about an hour,' I explained as I lifted my eyebrows to Trip for him to clarify my words.

He nodded his head and bent to pick up the small bag I had at my feet. Then after offering me the crook of his arm, we walked out of the lounge and through to security.

'Love you both.' I spoke once again into my cell as Trip shouted out to also be heard, 'Love ya, Perky… see ya soon.'

Then I disconnected the call and tried to settle myself. With every step I was taking I was walking away from the man I knew I would always love. I was walking away from Vegas, the one place I hated but always thought I would call home. To say I was upset was a complete understatement; I was gutted. I knew what I was doing was the right thing and for all the right reasons, but the finality of it all was breaking my heart. With my emotions threatening to get the better of me, I ran my free hand over my stomach again and used the strength of love I felt for the little being inside of me to drive my feet forward one after the other.

Trip produced our passports and my bag was checked. Then we each took a seat on the awaiting cart that would whisk us through the building to Nico's private plane. Almost as if Trip could feel my emotions falling off me, he picked up my hand and placed it through his arm and silently he offered me his strength by rubbing my hand with his own.

It was strange being the only one aboard apart from the crew. But in truth, I knew I needed the time to myself. I needed the chance to mourn what I had so briefly had and then I would pick myself up and be happy about the new life that was growing inside of me. I curled myself up like a child into one of the large, leather chairs and with tears pouring down my face, I watched through the small window to the side of me as Trip pulled the plane up high into the sky and circled it just the once over The Strip. I placed my index finger to the window and for a split second I touched the large hotel and casino that was Nico's, as in my head I said goodbye to him. Then I pulled the blanket one of the stewardesses had given me up and over my head as I feigned sleep.

I let the tears fall down my face, making no attempt to wipe them away. I could hear Trip going through the motions. This was the supreme commander speaking, we would be travelling at a height of such and such feet and it would be approximately so long until we touched down in Heathrow, London for our scheduled stop. I heard it all, somewhere in the background of my pain-filled brain, but registered none of it.

'Today's song isn't going to be sung by me, but by another member of today's crew… enjoy.'

The first line of the song sung to me by Nico as we'd danced together on the beach back in Crete entered my head, and initially I screwed my eyes tighter.

You've got to be joking? Why?

At that minute, I was trying to work out how life could be so damn cruel. Then to put the icing on the cake, it would stick a knife in just a little bit further before it twisted the blade deep in my gut.

Then as the second and third line of **"Let It Be Me"** by **Elvis Presley** filtered into my head, slowly I relaxed the white knuckled grip I had on the blanket over my head and let it drop down to my lap.

There, stood in front of the flight deck door, with his hands in his pockets was Nico.

He carried on singing the words and then after walking closer, he held out his hand to me. Without a single hesitation I lifted my hand and placed it into his, where he wrapped his fingers tightly around it.

'Dance with me, mio angelo.' His Italian accent had crept into his tone and I knew he was struggling to keep his emotions in check. 'Dance with me and I beg of you… let it be me.'

Using his hand, I stood up. His arms wrapped around me tightly as he pulled me into his body. I let the smell of his bodywash fill my senses and the black shirt he was still wearing from earlier soak up the tears that were now continuously falling from my eyes.

His voice filled with more and more emotion as he attempted to sing the rest of the song to me and at the same time, he swayed our bodies to the beat of the music that was only audible to the two of us.

When the words to the song came to an end, I removed my face from his chest and looked up and into his eyes. The face that stared back at me was so full of emotion that fresh tears sprang from my eyes and ran rapidly down my cheeks.

'I'm so sorry, Bee. This isn't and never has been playacting on my part, no matter how hard I tried to convince myself it was. I want this with you. I want to make our very own family with you. I'll never walk away again. I'll love you until the end of forever. This scares the fuck out of me, but it scares me even more to let you go, because I wasn't really living until you came into my world and I know I can't live without you in my future.'

I released a small cry of pain as Nico relaxed his hold on me, but my heart rejoiced once again as he fell to his knees and after taking both of my hips into his hands, he placed his mouth on my stomach and spoke again.

'You are very much wanted, little star... I don't know who ever thought I'd make a good daddy, but I will, I promise.'

I ran my fingers through his hair and slowly his gaze came back up to mine.

'Let it be me, Bee,' he begged with his dark brown eyes filling with tears.

'It's always been you, Nico... Even before I even knew you. It seems we were written to be together in the dark canopy of the night sky. Unknowingly, we each sent out a beacon looking for love and hope. Now, together we will hang our stars on that dark canvas, and they will shine forever.'

EPILOGUE

Bee

Two weeks later

LYING BESIDE THE POOL had to be one of my favourite places. The feel of the sun on my bare legs and the relaxing sound of the sea as it washed over the shore beneath us, relaxed me to the point of falling asleep. I knew I had at least another hour until Nico emerged from his office, so I placed my earbuds into my ears and set my music on shuffle.

Music blared out from the kitchen and I knew that Mom had turned it up again. I opened my eyes and looked at the houses on either side of us. Any minute now they would start to close some of their windows, as they always did when Mom played her music loudly.

I loved music, I loved that it made her happy, it meant Brody and I could be happy as well.

I didn't care that no one liked my mom, not really, anyway. She was my mom and I loved her, especially on days like today. When she was singing and dancing, it made me happy. I felt all warm inside and my heart skipped with happiness.

I heard a window slam, like I knew it would, and I closed one of my eyes to go back to my cloud watching. Copying my big brother, Brody, I put my curled fists together, one on top of the other, to make a telescope shape and I looked up again. Together with him we blanked out the shouts being aimed at our garden and went back into our make-believe world.

It was safe there.

'Look, Brody. That one there looks like a white, fluffy princess.' I used my small elbow to jab him in the ribs. He rubbed at his side and followed my pointing finger.

'It does, Sissy,' he agreed.

He turned his head to look at me and grinned. Feeling pleased with myself I smiled back at him. I poked my tongue through the small gap where I'd recently lost my baby tooth and worried with the hole it had left behind.

The tooth fairy hadn't come for me. I'd lost it at school after my tooth had come out in an apple I'd bitten into. But then I knew the tooth fairy never come for Brody either, although he said he didn't care. When the kids at school had laughed at me when I'd said I hadn't been left any money under my pillow, Brody had called them names and had got a bruise on his face where Harry had hit him. But Harry's eye had looked worse after he'd hit him back. Brody didn't know, but I was awake when he had placed a dime under my pillow that same night.

The adults at school didn't like my mom and most days the children there didn't like us either. Brody was big for his age, big enough to take care of us both and I knew he always would.

He had pinkie sworn that he would and I loved my protective big brother.

I watched him as he settled back further into the cushion of the long, uncut grass in our back yard and then he sighed as he bit into one of his favourite peanut butter and jelly sandwiches. He pushed the jelly that was running down his chin back into his mouth with one finger. Then as his finger left his mouth, he made it pop specially to make me laugh and I giggled at the noise.

Dad would be back sometime today, and we were both looking forward to seeing him. I'd said my prayers every day he'd been away. I knew it would be better this time. My worried tummy turned over, and I placed my hand over it, feeling it between the buttons of my school dress. The dress was too small, and it now only came down to the tops of my legs. Another thing that the kids in school made fun of, at least they used to, until Brody hit them and then they'd stopped.

I knew that when my dad came home, it was going to be much better.

The two of us had prayed every night that it was going to be different this time.

'Brody, come here and help me.' Mom's voice travelled over to the both of us and I instantly stopped daydreaming.

His head shot up from its soft, green pillow as he looked at my mom standing in the doorway. I watched as one of her feet suddenly stepped forward to stop herself from swaying and I wanted to be sick. I was scared, watching Mom. I reached out and grabbed hold of Brody's hand.

'I'm just coming, Mom.' He jumped up quick, ran over to her and I watched as he took hold of her arm. He helped her out onto the grass where we had been sitting and made her sit down. I watched as he ran back inside to bring out the last of our picnic and to turn down the music.

'Mom?' I questioned as she fell back onto the grass beside me.

'Fucking God!' Inside I heard Brody swear and frightened, I started to cry, not out loud because I didn't want anyone knowing how scared I was.

The prayers we'd both said since dad had been away seemed to have worked. Mom had been happier. Our clothes had been washed regularly and she'd cooked most nights. He was back today, and I knew from what had just happened my mom had taken her tablets. Praying was no use. No one was listening to us. I'd tried so hard to be good.

Couldn't God see how me and Brody were hurting?

There wasn't a God, just like there wasn't a tooth fairy.

Mom was lying down on the grass next to me, singing along with the song she had left playing on the radio.

'Mom, what do you want to eat?' Brody asked her as he dropped the food down on the grass.

She didn't answer him, the only words coming from her mouth were the words she was singing.

'Please, Mom. Please eat,' he begged as he lifted her head up off the grass.

Up and down our small road of military houses, we could hear doors slamming and excited voices.

'Brody,' I whispered. He looked at me just as I began to shiver, even though the sun was out in our yard.

We both knew what was coming next.

I heard our front door slam and scurried closer to Brody. He let go of our mom and cuddled me instead.

'I'm home,' came my dad's cheerful voice.

He didn't hurt us. Dad was a big man, but he wasn't violent. But him and my mom together, they shouted and screamed at each other, and she hit him until he held her arms behind her back.

When she had taken her tablets, it was always this way. We knew they loved us, but deep down inside they were hurting us. I had no friends at school, and I stuttered my words when I wasn't talking to Brody.

Living like this hurt so much and it never seemed to stop.

Sometimes, I had to go under my bed to drown out the sounds of them shouting and then of them kissing. We'd heard a neighbour down the road talking about our mom and dad and she'd said, "It's like they can't live with each other, but they can't live without each other." Brody had poked his tongue out at her, and we'd run off.

'There you all are.' His voice sounded happy, but I couldn't turn my head to look at him, instead I hung it down.

Mom had stopped singing and was now asleep in our yard.

Brody pulled me closer to him as he hugged me. Then he whispered, 'It's okay, we'll be okay. I'll look after you. Pinkie swear.' He wrapped his little finger around mine.

Together we looked at our linked hands and went back to our make-believe world.

'Hey.' I felt my left ear move as the earbud was pulled gently out of my ear.

I opened my eyes to see Nico's face descending to mine. The panic I was feeling inside began to dissipate as his lips came down to mine. The briefest of touches was all it took to make me feel steady again.

'What were you dreaming about this time?' he asked with concern etched across his face. It was becoming quite regular for me to be having bizarre dreams. We'd found out after some research that it was fairly normal when pregnant.

'Brody... well Brody and me when we were kids back in the U.K.'

'Sit up,' Nic commanded and pulling the other earbud out of my ear so my phone cable wouldn't pull my phone to the floor as I moved, I did as I was told.

I felt his near naked body, bar the swim shorts he was wearing, slide in behind me and then his hands held gently onto my upper arms as he pulled me back to lie on him.

'A bad dream?' he questioned.

'Well, yes and no.'

His arms wrapped around me tighter. 'Tell me.'

I lifted my hands up and held onto his forearms and told him.

'I was listening to music when I fell asleep. The last song I remember listening to was "Regret" by Default Distraction.' I then went on to tell him about the memory I had of that day and how I knew that the song which had been written by my brother was about the regrets he had in his life.

'You miss him, don't you?'

'I do, I always have… and now I have you, little star and our love… I miss him even more.'

'Then it's time.'

I turned around in Nico's arms, feeling his arms relax a little and then retighten when he was certain I was where I was wanted to be.

'It's time?' I questioned, as I traced a finger into the stubble filled cleft on his chin.

He used one arm to capture my hand and to place the finger I'd been using to draw on his skin onto his lips, where he placed a kiss to it. I watched as gold threads sparked to life in his eyes.

'This love I share with you it makes me want my family back together again. Cade and I have been concentrating on just that for a while now and I'm also working on a hotel project with Default Distraction. You've given me the strength to know that I can and will safely look after you all, so it's time. I want him back in my life properly and Brody back in yours… leave it with me.'

'I don't know what I'd do without you.' I snuggled down onto his chest.

'You'll never have to find out, because I'm never leaving you again.'

'I love you, Nico.'

'And mio angelo, ti amo anch'io.'

THE END

Want to keep up with all of the new releases in Vi Keeland and Penelope Ward's Cocky Hero Club world? Make sure you sign up for the official Cocky Hero Club newsletter for all the latest on our upcoming books:

https://www.subscribepage.com/CockyHeroClub

Check out other books in the Cocky Hero Club series:
http://www.cockyheroclub.com

Check out other books by the author A. S. Roberts:
http://asroberts-author.com/

Printed in Great Britain
by Amazon